A
Place
to Fall

CCL

A
Place
to Fall

Roger
Director

VILLARD • NEW YORK

Villard Books is a registered trademark of Random House, Inc.

Library of Congress Cataloging-in-Publication data is available.
ISBN 679-44787-3

Book design by Debbie Glasserman

Printed in the United States of America on
acid-free paper
9 8 7 6 5 4 3 2
First Edition

For Jan and Chloe

In memory of Tom Berman
(1947–1973)

"Base fortune, now I see, that in thy wheele
There is a point, to which when men
    aspire,
They tumble headlong down: that point
    I touched,
And seeing there was no place to mount
    up higher,
Why should I greeve at my declining fall?"

—Christopher Marlowe, *Edward II*

A
Place
to Fall

One

GETTING HANGED IN EFFIGY IS NOT FOR EVERYBODY. TAKE IT FROM ME.

You might muster contempt for the rabble-rousers. You might even feel haughty about whatever it is you did to churn up the public so. But in the end, try as you will to shrug and to laugh it off, watching people kill you is pretty unsettling.

For starters, the "thing"—the "you"—is a terrible likeness. The more on the mark the better, I'd always presumed, so everyone would know who the mob was referring to. You want everybody on the same page, so to speak. But you'll see at first glance that nobody bothered calling in Michelangelo. Take that as the merest hint at the low esteem in which you're held.

If that doesn't at least strike a telling blow to your vanity, you start off your mayfly-length mannequin life disfigured, too. I was given only one hand. Upon close inspection—

after viewing the tape dozens of times and freeze-framing the more spectacular moments—I saw that what they used to render the carefully manicured fingers I'd privately prided myself on as something straight off the Sistine Chapel was an oven mitt.

There you are, scarecrow ugly, your limbs contorted like some balloon animal. Now add to it that you are clad for all the world to see in the most revolting, mismatched duds possible. Stuffing splurts from your pants legs. Fiberfill flumes from your fly.

You might think this repellent dissimilarity would help you ignore things and repudiate your "twin." But you can't sniff, "That's too short and fat to be me" or "I suppose I've overimbibed on occasion and acted a little silly, but I wouldn't be caught dead in public wearing yellow pajamas and jiggling around on a stick, and everyone knows that," because you've got a lot of people there—in my case, the Cincinnati police estimated five thousand in Fountain Square, a number, it's safe to say, that constitutes a multitude —all jumping up and down and screaming and basically playacting hanging you and abusing your carcass with the sort of intense focus an Olivier couldn't match.

They convinced me. When I first saw my murder, I nearly began whimpering.

You might have been in that crowd. Or maybe in one of the dozens of others that had such frenzied sport with me. I was, after all, persona non grata from Guantánamo to Guam. But you know all that. Anybody who hasn't spent the last three years living off grubs and spores in the Amazon rain forest knows all that.

Back then, spearing the for-sale sign into my lawn, loading boxes into the U-Haul, all I wanted to do was forget about being one of America's all-time hated effigy figures and flee —Hollywood, Tony Paris, the ire of a nation. But so much spent ardor takes on a life of its own; it sort of tacks itself up against the leveling of time and claims the backward gaze, which lingers on this hallowed mound in the landscape of the past as if it were some prehistoric Indian dune. So I found myself viewing my effigy burning at odd moments and places during my personal diaspora, and there began to grow a gentle pride in the havoc I'd wreaked. Not the Samson-like satisfaction with which I'd wrung down chaos, but a more somber pleasure that, somewhere in a life whose prime punctuation nowadays is sharing saltines and jelly with my daughter of an afternoon, something so cataclysmic had ever happened.

Just now, by happenstance, I watched my fiery death all over again. The snow had been sifting out of a low sky since daybreak, covering the hillside below our farmhouse. I'd been out capering in the drifts almost since the moment I'd thrown the bed blankets off, thumping around in back with my wife, Dayna, and our daughter, Sophie, tramping across the slope, endlessly hauling our blue plastic Kmart-bought toboggan up the hill from the Common Road and skidding down in peals of hysterics until we came to a stop half-buried in the snow. Then Sophie, barely two, popped up on her knees in her red snowsuit, caked in white and clapping.

"Mun, Daddy," she pleaded in her husky little voice. "Mun!" This was her wonderful conflation of "more," "again," and "fun."

I ran into the house to get the camcorder. I had to record Sophie's first time ever sledding. I was clomping around in my snow boots here in the back room we use for storage, perspiring in my heavy coat, nose running, brow dripping. There was a blank cassette somewhere, or at least one that contained something I'd not mind taping over. I rummaged through the stacked-up boxes, searching through the dozens of tossed-about tapes from our glamorous Hollywood life before we'd moved here (the State Police have asked me not to give an exact address; let's just say I live in northern Vermont now).

I switched the recorder to the VCR function and squinted through the eyepiece. Boom!—there I was twirling around, my tissue-paper arms on fire in Cincinnati. And it was quite a jolt to see myself burning, being punted into the air and coming apart in showers of sparks and cloth, my head aflame and rolling down the gutter, as I stood, tiny icicles dripping from my hair, in the still air of this silent farmhouse room.

Don't think I've forgotten why you were so angry. I understand and remember completely, even at this distance, from my snowflake sanctuary. Let me digitize it for you:

758157.

You know that number. You know it the way you know your phone number or your Social Security number.

758157.

That was the automatic recording code for your VCR. If you had to go out, if you simply had to attend your mother's funeral, or your spouse was facedown in the rice pudding with a massive cardiac infarction and protested waiting an hour to get to the emergency room, you hit that code and taped my television show, *Father Joey,* because you would do anything not to miss it.

Wednesday at nine.

That was my time slot. And you set your life to that time slot as if it were some chronometer in Greenwich. That time slot kept you and the rest of America at peace by the hearth. That time slot became for a brief moment a cultural tent peg akin to election night or the Super Bowl. It was something you depended on, because people depend on television the way they depend on rain or erythromycin or the Bernoulli effect to lift the wings of the airplanes carrying them.

758157.

Wednesday at nine.

I owned it. I had a claim on all of America, had you in the palm of my hand. I stood among the highest peaks of all the glory-filled pinnacles America has to offer. Until I jumped off that mountainside and let everything smash to dust. And nobody could figure out why.

"SHE CAME UP TO ME LIKE OUT OF NOWHERE. I'M STANDING AT THE GAS PUMP watching the dial. I'm about to wipe the windshield. I look up from the pump. She's in my face. A real debutante. Cute. Blond. Great bozangas. She looks at me and says, 'You're Father Joey, aren't you?' I say, 'Yeah.' She says, 'Father, I want to unzip your fly right here and yank that big hard thing of yours out and go down on you.' Corner of Sunset and Fairfax, a million cars whizzing by. Then I said the best line I ever said in my life. I don't know where I got it from. Maybe this writer shit of yours is rubbing off. Anyway, I say the best thing. I just look at her. I don't blink an eye. I go— 'What's stopping you?' And so she smiles. And she just comes right up next to me. The pump is going. I'm bent over, fillin' 'er up . . . four gallons, five gallons . . . six. And she just leans up against my back and reaches her hand around and unzips me. Swear to God. Swear to fucking God. She unzips me and reaches in, no fucking shit. Hel-lo! Right there. I'm still leaned over pumping, right! She kind of gets to know it a bit. Pets it. Lemon Pledge time. Bites me on the ear, then pulls her hand out and walks off."

"Is that so?"

"Swear to effin' God."

Tony Paris smiled that playful little sideways smile of his —you know the one—and reached to sip his bourbon. We were in our hangout, Rose's, that night, and whenever I think about those days I steer my thoughts onto that barstool and that night, when we were at our best and me and Tony Paris were toasting each other five times an evening and together in the trenches fighting to keep ourselves alive.

People say it's that cockeyed smile that got him where he is. Doubtless it's a charmer in a close-up. But I've always thought it was his moody eyes. At least, that's what struck me when I first met him, when he was just breaking out of crappy action movies, the kind some buccaneer producer shoots in twelve days and sells to overseas markets because it's long on tae kwon do and short on nonessential bits like plot and English. But even in those cheapies, where the only character arc is how far someone flies through the air before kicking a villain through the window, Tony stood out. Those eyes bounce a lot of light back into the camera lens; they're so big, almost hyperthyroidal, a melancholy pale yellow tinge to them. I call them onion eyes. They flickered at me across the rim of his drink. Yellow moons setting into an amber bay. He tucked his chin down into his collar and spoke out of the side of his mouth.

"Tellin' ya, Billy, we gotta keep this show on the air. It's dynamite for my sex life."

"Sure, I'll call the network. Keep us on, Tony got a hand job."

He laughed. Cackled, actually. That's the Tony Paris laugh. We'd swung in from the studio to undo our collars and shrug off our braces. The joint was crowded as usual, crammed with locals, some industry people, most not. It was done up in a dark, Moorish decor, untouched since the '20s, with a tile floor and wooden booths. Painted on the plaster walls were autographed caricatures of the thirsty celebrity gods who'd presided here in the past: Betty Hutton, Joe E. Brown, Eddie Bracken. If we could just get a chance with our show, one day Tony Paris's name might be up there too.

But Tony didn't even rate a signed photo in a deli yet. We had finished only the fifth episode of our TV show.

Only two had aired. And nobody was taking seriously our series about the priest, Joseph O'Dell, who makes the dying requests of the terminally ill come true. Network Research detected no positive change in viewing habits, and they can detect the pressure of a fly landing on a remote channel changer in Chagrin Falls. That night we were just a couple guys laughing and scratching at a loud bar in Hollywood.

Me and Tony Paris.

My pal.

My bud.

My blood bro'.

Tony and I synched up in ways I'd never dreamed of with the other actors I'd written for. Dan Koslow and Stray Simmons, the stars of the previous show I'd worked on, *Under the Law,* had seen me as simply one more of their jailers, my script pages just the daily plate of gruel slid into their cells for their grumpy consumption. Not Tony. He saw my writing as his salvation.

Tony and I enjoyed the sort of creative and personal relationship I'd only imagined was possible. We butted heads, sure—occasionally hammering at each other on the set or in his trailer by the soundstage where we filmed—but it was always an avid, civil dialogue, always with an eye toward perfecting a moment, a gesture, a word, something to bump up the performance and better the film.

We were inseparable during what off-hours we got. Not just at Rose's. There were riotous dinners and late evenings spent club hopping; me and Dayna, Tony and his date, some D cup who'd get a little drunk and, following an obscenely small amount of coaxing, perform her high school cheers. There were ball games. The fights in Vegas. The track. Desert Hot Springs, the two of us side by side, mud up to our necks and yakking away.

But mainly there were just lunches—me and Tony around the set. Lots of amiable shooting-the-shit and the unguarded embracings and ready laughter of devoted buddies. Presents sailed back and forth almost as if in a regular trade route. Mountains of fruit. Cases of Dom Pérignon.

Tony Paris and I were alter egos.

"Well, what're you hearing from the suits?" Tony whispered. "What the fuck's up with those guys? When are they gonna pick up the show? They want to make me twist in the wind, they succeeded. I'm gonna puke I'm so dizzy already."

"The network is waiting for a sign," I said, parroting what I'd just been told on the phone that afternoon.

"I just gave you a damn good one, bro'."

"You coming isn't exactly a powerful presentation to advertisers."

"Hey, try me." He cackled.

I signaled the bartender for another round, raising my glass and nodding for him to replenish the others who joined us for these weekly outings. Our redoubtable line producer, avuncular Ralph White, with his sleepy, wide-apart eyes and his handy country boy's way of slowing things down so all could be adequately inspected, loaded, unloaded, and accounted. And Beans, a regular in our happy brood. He was a square-faced, beefy chum from Tony's knockabout days back in Chicago, who'd taken to driving Tony to and from the set and performing small chores for him when not standing outside the soundstage and combing his hair in the sideview mirror of the Mercedes he chauffeured Tony around in. A Ph.D. in hanger-on. Also, Dayna, who'd begun stopping in for these weekly soirees.

Dayna did some quick cheek pecking all around. She was a tall bird in a short blue dress. A tropical blue. Her brown hair fell over her wide forehead in bangs. In back she'd pulled it into a ponytail. Her brown eyes were shiny with excitement as she hopped onto a stool and let her bag fall.

"You're not going to believe this," she instantly burst out. "I was dropping off some slides at this commercial producer's on La Brea. And I'm standing by the receptionist's desk when some of the secretaries are going home. And know what they're doing tonight? They're having a potluck dinner together and watching the show. They call it a *Father Joey* party. And they combine it with some Bible study. This is their second one."

"They're studying the show *and* the Bible?"

"You and the Bible."

Tony looked at me with an eyebrow raised speculatively. I pursed my lips.

"Not bad."

"Not bad, Billy, that's all you can say?"

She shot a dissatisfied look at Tony.

"That's some primo linkage, man."

"Anecdotes are fine," I said. "But the network needs numbers. They need demographics. They need test results and advertisers and focus groups. Stuff like that. I've already told them my Aunt Matilda loves the show."

"But these women aren't Aunt Matilda. And they're all gooney about Tony. What a 'babe' you are. That's what they call you. 'A total babe.' So I said, 'Well, he is kind of sexy. I'll pass the word, I'm gonna see him tonight.' They went crazy. That I actually knew Tony Paris. They made me promise to get an autographed picture."

Tony nudged me. "I dunno-o-o, maybe somethin's happenin-n'," he singsonged in a sly melody.

I shrugged. I grasped the drink the bartender placed down. Dayna plucked up her glass and held it aloft, breezily saluting him before he could move away. "When Saint Peter sees him coming he will leave the gates ajar, for he knows he's had his hell on earth, has the man behind the bar."

The bartender and the rest of us grinned as she bolted back the whiskey, then gulped a hearty slug of beer and slammed the mug down on the bar top.

She motioned for seconds.

"What's your problem?" she said, responding with mock indignation to the amused expressions all around her.

"Where'd you pick that up?" I chuckled out of surprise. There was a properness to Dayna that made it funny when she trotted out her bar patter, and she knew it.

"I didn't know this was a Tupperware party. I thought I had exciting news."

She narrowed her eyes and looked us over and threw back half of a second shot.

"Yo, Billy, you got quite a señorita over here." Tony laughed. His mouth was half-puckered into a tiny opening, making a wry, delighted smile. "You're right, it is exciting news, Daynz—I'll take all the fans I can get."

"Yeah," I said. "Tony got simonized last night."

Tony hooted. He jackknifed forward, his head knocking on my shoulder. His feet quick-tapped on the footrest.

"We always gotta work together, man, you gotta promise," he said when he stopped laughing. "This show stays on the air ten years, we both get filthy rich, we buy places right on a golf course with palm trees somewhere. We're gonna shoot eighteen holes every day and watch reruns every night and get drunk on piña coladas. Whoops, sorry, Daynz, you can come too."

"Nifty. Watch you two geezers nod off? No thank you."

"Ten years on the air," Tony intoned. He downed his drink. "You gotta promise, Bill. Drink to it."

"Hey. I wish."

"Come on, man, you gotta believe. We're gonna hit. Daynz, what's with this guy?"

"You have to understand something about Billy," Dayna said, "he's a polite visitor from another planet. He calls his mother and gets the machine and says, 'Hello, Mom, this is Bill Ziff calling.' He hates being rude. He hopes he doesn't survive a plane crash so nobody will be able to say it was his fault. One night, back in New York, we were walking somewhere, the windchill was minus fifty. Some bum comes up to us on the street and says he lost his contact lens. So Billy jumps into a Dumpster with this homeless guy and scrounges around in the garbage for twenty minutes helping him look. I hope you don't mind being talked about like you weren't here."

"I love it, actually. Being talked about as if you weren't there is the only way to know you're alive."

Dayna and Tony laughed.

"Like I said—a polite visitor from another planet."

Tony suddenly unwound his finger from the shot glass and gesticulated.

"Mama mia."

He was motioning toward an overhead TV. The opening credits of our show were flashing on. Starring Tony Paris. Created by me. Line-produced by Ralph.

"Which one is this?" he wanted to know.

" 'Thin Ice,' " Ralph quickly answered without taking his eyes off the monitor. He wasn't really watching the show the way you do at home. He was looking to see there were no tears or pops in the broadcast print. To make sure the network hadn't brightened the picture to wash all the realism out of it, something they always try to get away with, thinking you viewers can't take anything too "down." And he was listening to make sure the sound levels matched from reel to reel across the commercial breaks so you don't have to readjust the volume. Adjusting sound requires pressing a button; you could just as easily change channels.

In case you spent the last few years living off husky meat in the wastes of the Arctic and couldn't get to a tube, this was the episode about the young Olympic ice skater dying of bone cancer who wanted to make one final trip to the victory stand.

The customers in Rose's were watching the show with a kind of dazed, lifeless grin on their faces, the sort people have when they are really enjoying something on TV.

Tony and I exchanged a glance, and then—I don't know what caused it—suddenly we were giggling. He tilted his head down on the bar, but he couldn't stop. Maybe neither of us could believe what was happening—two clowns halfway around the bend in their local, watching their stuff on the actual goddam TV—maybe it's just that we were working too hard against chances that were too slim.

Dayna drained her beer and shook her head. "You guys. You're a comedy act. How're you going to watch all those reruns?"

Tony managed to pitch a shoulder in my direction. "Ask him—" he gasped out.

I didn't have an answer. Not until much later. What do the French call it? *Esprit de l'escalier?* What you think to say after it's too late.

"Know something? This is all I want, this'll do just fine" is what I should have said to Dayna and Tony that night. "My show on the air. Something I wrote and created. Something of mine. I don't need anything more than this moment right here in our favorite bar. People watching my show on the box. Laughs with friends. Beer back."

But I didn't say that. When the show ended I slid some money down on the table and we prepared to call it a night. In episodic television the camera never stops rolling. Come morning our next hour would begin filming. It was the very last of the six we'd been asked to make. The next day I would be on the phone working the network executives again, plumping for our show to remain on the air.

Only two more weeks of shooting. And at that point, what? My mind was too clouded with the production concerns at hand to foresee anything else.

"Maybe we can try to start one of those write-in campaigns around the country," I said to no one in particular and in a voice that I instantly detected contained not a whit of the zeal necessary to dial even the first phone. And right then I realized I had run out of arguments to make. I didn't have the numbers and spreadsheets and printouts to bombard anybody with. The first show had claimed a 9.8 rating, which in Nielsen-ese tells the firing squad to finish breakfast and get ready for work. The network mind hadn't come around following that and wasn't going to. And at that moment, sliding off the barstool where we'd drunk to the future, the very sanest part of me began accepting that my show wouldn't be on the air for ten years. No, my show would be canceled the following week, leaving me out of work and, who knows, out of a career.

We hunted for jackets. And that was when Rose's owner, Cliff, hustled up to us, intercepting us before we passed the bar and got to the front door.

"I think you better come this way," Cliff said. There was a look of concern on his face. His eyes darted like a lizard's.

"Something the matter?" I asked.

"Not out there." He waved dismissively toward the front door. "This way'll be easier."

The rest of us exchanged puzzled looks as we filed behind Cliff. He led us down a corridor past the kitchen and bathrooms at the rear. He shouldered open a back door and waved us through to the parking lot.

"It's him!" I heard as soon as we hit fresh air. I couldn't really make out anything because lights were instantly flooding our eyes, blinding us. And suddenly people were swarming and pushing, jostling us, blocking our path, trying to get at Tony, trying to touch him. We were buffeted. There was hollering and tumult.

"Tony! It's Tony Paris!" they shrieked.

Nothing remotely like this had ever happened before. I was shocked. I don't know how many people were out there. There could have been fifteen. There could have been fifty or five hundred. How could they have known where Tony was? What led them here? Why? I clutched reflexively at Dayna. Because there was the sudden prick of fearfulness you get when you're caught in a tide that rips hard at your feet, so surprisingly hard it threatens to sweep you away and tumble you over and leave you fighting for breath.

But there was another wave—not a physical push, more like a giant pulse—that swept at the speed of those lights toward us, breaking over Tony, engulfing him, echoing his name. It wasn't material, it didn't knock us around, but all the same it left us dazed and momentarily panicked. It was something beamed like an X ray, something six feet of lead couldn't shield you from, because it was too powerful, too focused, too penetrating, as if it shot right through you, shearing the ionic bonds that held your molecules and tissues together. It flashed over us, transporting us in its surge to some destination we'd never been to before which lay beyond our capacity to resist.

The lights kept shining. The people kept pushing and yelling Tony's name and straining to touch him. We heaved ourselves toward our cars. We were helpless.

Call it adulation.

Better yet, call it limelight.

Three weeks after Tony Paris got that hand job in the gas station, we were the number-twelve show in the country and climbing.

Two

"WE COME NOW TO THE CATEGORY OF HIGHEST HUMANITARIAN ACHIEVE-ment in writing for one-hour television drama. Traditionally this is one of our most competitive prizes. And this year's fifteen-thousand-dollar Humana Prize is no exception."

Monsignor Lawrence Connolly pushed his black horn-rims back up his nose with his forefinger and gazed down from the podium across the vast, crowded ballroom he was addressing. His head was a big pink balloon bobbing above the floor, looking as if it had never been subjected to peril of any sort.

I'd been in Hollywood fewer than six months—but there I was sitting among the elect of the television industry. Some of the richest, most influential writers and producers in the world. In their Armani and Versace, they were a perfectly tended flower bed of blue-ribbon haberdashery. The re-mote-control car locks that chirped to open their expensive sedans fairly called to them from their breast pockets like the caged nightingales sported in the retinues of potentates.

"The most uplifting and inspirational aspects of the human spirit and potential were explored by all of this year's nominees," the Reverend Monsignor Connolly intoned. "And I wish to personally take the time to commend each of them for the insights into the human condition they shared with the rest of us and the planet."

Monsignor Connolly led a short round of appreciative applause.

"Well, let's get to it. For the fifteen-thousand-dollar first prize, the nominees are . . . *Under the Law,* executive producer Mark Werner, producers Peter Ostrow and Elliot Jarvis . . . the episode 'Another Mouth to Feed,' written by all three; . . . *Emergency Squad,* executive producer Barry Linder, the episode 'Crazy Like a Pox,' written by Mr. Linder; . . . *The Outer Banks,* executive producers Sharon Wolzacki and Chris Glover, the episode 'One Good Man,' written by Petra Schwartz. . . ."

My boss and "mentor," Peter Ostrow, tilted his chair back on its two rear legs and patted his belly as the rest of the nominees were read out. It was the gesture of a man both happily sated and ever hungry for more. He spent a good deal of time grandiosely patting his belly like that. He was stout, forty years of age, with a torso that was putty soft but nevertheless commanding. He had a rubbery face with piercing blueberry eyes and close-cropped red hair and, most memorably, the shoe-brush-thick bar of a bristling, vermilion mustache. He hunched forward, grounding his chair with a thud, and whispered: "Tax free, fellas! If you're lookin' for any investment opportunities, I got a welterweight—Iron Mikey Baron—fighting up at Reseda . . . six-rounder. Kid's a cinch. Now, whole fifteen large goes on him. We walk away like kings with our chests puffed out, we fly to Vegas, a little schvitz, a little sirloin, a little visit to this friend of mine, got a stable of select, thirteen-year-old whores who've undergone a sacred Burmese ceremony to remove their uvulas so they don't get in a man's way, if you get my drift, bing-bang-boom, we're back for Shabbas dinner with our wives."

He fixed on his partner and best friend, the spare, clumpy-haired Elliot Jarvis, who looked like a long weed that had just been yanked from the ground. "Whatdya say, you wrinkled old cunt?"

Jarvis stared blankly at his buddy, looking almost insulted by the frivolous itinerary just suggested.

"Or does it all get stuffed under the mattress?" Ostrow scoffed.

"How much do they go for a night?"

"What are you making, twenty thou a week?" our boss, Mark Werner, snorted. "You can afford it, Elliot. If you were tried for murder you'd ask for a public defender, wouldn't you? Rather than pay a top attorney. You'd suck cyanide rather than part with a thin fucking dime."

"Not true," Jarvis grumbled.

"Not true, my fuckin' ass."

"Prove it, you cheap cunt. How much'll you bet me I won't stand up right here and drop my trousers?"

"Fifty dollars," Jarvis grumbled.

"All right, get it out, you cheap cunt."

"Boys! Boys!" Werner admonished good-naturedly, "you're spoiling the swank in here. Behave yourselves."

I had no doubt that Ostrow was ready to bare his ass to the dais. He did it regularly at our studio offices, and didn't mind who saw. I'd never met anyone like him before joining the show. Flashing privates one moment, philosophy the next. A burlesque show of his own gaudy and chaotic self-loathing since abandoning a stellar political think tank and tenure-track career for tweedless Tinsel Town.

What magical company I kept then. At the very start of

things. Me, bottom-dwelling Billy Ziff from Massapequa Park, faceless tractland, USA.

I had lived the cliché of show business success. I'd been plucked from the dark, damp, urban grotto in which I'd toiled at a typewriter as a freelance writer, churning out squibs for a variety of trade magazines such as *Kitchen Counter Quarterly* and *Matte-Finish Tile Life,* working my way up to a job as a not entirely unamusing sports columnist for a New York weekly, snagging what bounties I could of life from those of my more successful friends who had enough of them to share. I had lived on so-and-so's expense account and at so-and-so's weekend house; my money had to be carefully counted before it made its way out of my pocket.

And then Ostrow's mother had walked into my father's midtown store to buy a fur coat. They talked as she fondled fox. Her son was buying this coat for her. Her son the rich Hollywood writer. His son the struggler whose shoulder could not dent the gates. Perhaps he could give her a very favorable deal on this coat. Perhaps she could ask her son to read something his had written. And so a spec script of mine reached Hollywood a few months later.

And then, Ostrow had called, with words I can still remember:

"I want you to come out here, kid. You got four-dimensional words, and I'm gonna make you a millionaire."

Thus had Ostrow, Jarvis, and Werner transported me to the wondrous ethers.

I had arrived in Nirvana. I sat there in the Ballroom of Glory with the producers and fellow writers of the best show on television.

Up on the podium, the Reverend Monsignor Connolly was tearing at an envelope with much the same seriousness he might have shown had he been ripping open a packet of powdered milk with which to feed a starving African child.

"And now for the winner. For the compassionate por-

trayal of an impoverished woman struggling to decide between motherhood and giving her child up for adoption, this
year's Humana Prize goes to the episode 'Another Mouth to
Feed'—the series: *Under the Law*. Executive producer Mark
Werner, producers Peter Ostrow and Elliot Jarvis, the episode written by all three."

Werner, Ostrow, and Jarvis stood.

The ballroom burst into applause. Werner kept his eyes
focused on the crowd, drinking all this in, and not in dainty
sips either, but he quickly bent toward me so I could feel his
breath on my ear. "In my office right after lunch, buddy-
boy. You and me are gonna have a talk. Between now and
then, you think up a good reason why I shouldn't fire you."

Werner adjusted his suit jacket and pushed at his tie knot.
And then, with Ostrow and Jarvis on either side of him, he
began his triumphant sashay up to the podium.

I DROVE BACK TO THE LOT FROM THE LUNCHEON AND IT TOOK ALL MY EFFORT NOT
to keep on driving past the studio and all the way to New
York. Because that was really the way things were for me
and my glorious Hollywood life at the very beginning.

I was cursed in Nirvana. Heaven had turned out to be
hell. The catchy jokes and phrase turns that had regularly
wrung plaudits from my editor at *Window Treatment* never
seemed to satisfy anybody at *Under the Law*.

Here I was, in a job any writer would have given up a
lifetime's use of a vowel for, and my employers made me feel
that I was incapable of writing a good scene, of making life
come off a page.

That morning must have been the last straw for Werner:
I'd put on his desk a couple short scenes between the stars of
our show, two cops named Caddigan and Blue. In case
you've been blindfolded and shunted around crawl spaces in
Beirut for the last five years—Caddigan was a corner-

cutting, gum-cracking, wiseacre cop, a swarthy, ends-justify-the-means man of the streets. Blue, his partner, was a blond, blue-eyed Ivy Leaguer with a doctorate in criminology, abiding faith in rules, and little savvy in the arts of the alley.

The story line for my scenes was simple and unimportant, a minor part of a script. Maybe you remember seeing it: Blue's vision hadn't been perfect lately, and Caddigan knew that his stubborn and vain partner needed glasses and wanted him to visit an eye doctor. Which Blue was refusing to do.

"What you'll do is, Caddigan's cagey enough . . . maybe he gives his partner a place to fall," Ostrow had declaimed earlier in the day, patting his belly and perfunctorily outlining what he needed from the doorway to my office before vanishing. "He gives Blue a way to retain his pride, his feelings of self-worth and manliness, while simultaneously submitting to the dictates of mortality and imperfection. It's the way we all live, Billy, rationalizing, the way we all get through life, draw the next breath, unknot the noose. The spectacles are a profound metaphor for the impenetrable abyss faced by humanity, a metaphor that will doubtless be appreciated by our twenty million or so devoted microcephalic viewers who will absorb your profound metaphor, then jerk off, piss into the sink, and go to sleep in the other end of their trailers if the raccoons don't make too much noise in the garbage cans."

"Got it," I'd said, eagerly swiveling toward the end table and picking up a yellow legal pad on which I composed my scripts.

Give someone a place to fall . . . a place to fall. I racked my brain all morning, but, as always, I couldn't control my own mind. Compose? Hah! My mind was spastic. I exerted no will over it or the characters in it, no ability to do what an author had to do: breathe existence into those imagined beings, get them up off the ground and move them about. Create. And what the hell did "a place to fall" mean anyway?

I'd thought I knew. I'd nodded as if I knew. But now, suddenly, I had no idea.

When I summoned the characters to center stage in my mind's eye, all I saw was the cartoonlike image of Caddigan, his legs unaccountably made of lumpy, gray stone, stomping like Frankenstein's monster up to Blue and bopping him over the head like one of the Three Stooges would do it. Whereupon Blue waddled like a duck. All of it set to kazoo music!

I'd done the best I could with the assignment, handed the scenes in to Mark, and gone off to the awards lunch. From which I drove back with a fibrillating heart. My armpits felt as if someone had just finished oral sex with them.

All around me, my fellow L.A. road warriors surged on toward their presumably less vile fates and happier appointments. Many of them held car phones plugged up against their ears, maintaining an unruffled, supervisory contact with the rest of the world I could only envy.

In Los Angeles, a city on wheels, car phones are a must. I welcomed them. Not because they helped you get business done while in traffic (I hated being "reachable" wherever I was). Not even for safety reasons, say, if you got lost, or found yourself in danger.

Car phones were invented to stop Angelenos from picking their noses while they drive. Before the proliferation of the car phone, every which way you looked on the freeway there was someone doing sixty on the accelerator and seventy-five up his schnozz with his free hand. Ten million people in high-speed proboscial excavation was a dirty little problem and, who knows, probably what spurred on the cellular revolution.

I found all that scant reason to appreciate my situation at that moment, though. I know I should have pinched myself for my good fortune at working in a real live Hollywood studio. I know I should have got down on my knees for the beautiful climate and the beautiful paycheck. But as Werner, Ostrow, and Jarvis had at me with each set of pages I turned in, uneasiness never deserted my side, and a rumbling pain in my gut accompanied my every move. As I drove past the guard gate, as I parked my car, as I trudged up the stairs to my office on the second floor.

There I had stowed a few mementos of my bygone life—a picture of myself standing before our New York brownstone apartment; a plate signed by every member of the New York Yankees; one of those miniature city skylines enclosed in water which, if turned upside down, would scatter snow-flakes on the Empire State Building. I was sitting, wistfully turning over and over my small, water-laden skyline of New York, watching the flakes descend, recalling an afternoon following such a snowfall and belly flopping down a hill behind the Belvedere Castle in Central Park on a fifty-cent sheet of plastic, when Werner's secretary Liz buzzed me and told me he wanted to see me.

Werner's office was a perfect blend of the CEO's top-floor power chamber and the frat boy's nookatorium. His digs were the largest and were set in the building's corner. Among the ten thousand dollars' worth of sofas and chairs, there were also a gum-ball machine and a tiny blue metal car lifted right off one of those amusement-park rides for kids.

A dozen baseball bats, numerous footballs and baseballs and mitts, were stacked in one corner. One bookshelf con-tained Werner's many Emmy statuettes. On the walls, Wer-ner had hung all his special citations, including one from the mayor of St. Louis, where our series was set, proclaiming it "Under the Law Day" by the Mississippi. There was a framed letter from the president of the United States telling Werner how much he liked the show and what a wonderful example it was to America's youth. There were also pictures of Werner with various celebrities and heads of state who had visited the set; and beside these a framed, candid shot of

Werner on all fours in his tux and throwing up by the side of the road outside his limousine after leaving the president's inauguration ball. It had been taken by his first wife, Lois.

Werner was now married to a slinky woman ten years his junior, Lanny, who was making a raging success of her own career in catering. She ran a haute cuisine diet service. If you were fat and rich and had lost nearly all self-discipline, you called Lanny's shop. She would cook and deliver and serve you all your meals on the finest china. The secret wasn't so much in stinting on the caloric content as in the quantity of food. The portions were nearly invisible to the naked eye. Basically, you paid Lanny two grand a week to drop by in her Rolls and bring you nothing.

As I entered, Mark was on the phone, but he quickly hung up and began twirling a football in the air.

"How's the award winner?" I said, trying to manufacture an offhand air.

"Couldn't be better," he said. "You wouldn't believe what a beyootiful dewey I made today. Laid out there like cable. Big, beautiful, thick, brown cable." He spread his hands in description of a long, arching span. "You?"

"Me? Fine."

My heart was a kettledrum as he leaned back in his seat and put his legs up on his desk. He picked up a printout of the scenes I had written earlier between Caddigan and Blue and the eye doctor.

"What the fuck is this?"

"What do you mean?" I said.

"I mean I read this," he said, waving the pages, "and it's shit. Worthless shit."

He tossed the pages onto his desktop.

"Where the fuck did you ever get the idea you could write?"

I made no response. I was frozen. He was spitting ropes of liquid nitrogen at me.

"I mean, pardon my French . . . but this is just . . . Is this crap what passes for writing where you come from? This is garbage. Totally unusable. I'm paying you good money, buddy. I have a right to know why the fuck I seem to be wasting it on you."

"I'm sorry you didn't like the pages," I said finally.

"Wrong—I didn't just not like 'em. I hated 'em."

He pushed my pages back toward my side of the desk.

"And where's this so-called solo script you begged me to let you write? I gave you permission three weeks ago, for Chrissake. And I haven't heard word one from you about it. Zilch. Not even a fuckin' story idea. I think I have a right to know just what the fuck you've been doing with my money."

"I've been thinking about the script," I said, which was true, although "think" evokes perhaps a stronger sense of organized neurological activity than I found myself bringing to bear on matters. Sensing my boss's displeasure, I'd prodded him to let me write one script solely by myself, without the usual collaboration of the other writers or of Ostrow and Jarvis, as something of a last-ditch effort at proving my worth.

"I was just about ready to pitch something to you," I lied. The thing I was truly nearest ready to do was to blow the back of my skull off with a shotgun.

He shook his head. "This doesn't cut it, my friend, not even close, I'm here to tell you. Something's got to change. Or I'll make a change. I want to hear a story for your script. And I want to hear it yesterday."

He nodded at the script pages which lay scattered on his desk, meaning for me to pick them up and for this to be the last he ever saw of them. And the tight-lipped look on his face meant for me to tuck them under my arm and get out of his office without saying anything more. Which I did.

I shuffled back to my own office, walking down the corridor past the other writers' warrens feeling as bleak and miserable as I'd ever felt in my life.

I made one stab at rethinking my pages after I'd flopped down on my couch. I conjured up Caddigan and Blue in my mind. Blue appeared on a golf course, wearing green-plaid plus fours and tam-o'-shanter, holding a putter. He looked up irritatedly at my interrupting him, then looked back down and drilled a ten-foot putt into the cup—plok!—and strode off to the next tee with Caddigan, the duo casting disdainful looks at me over their shoulders for bothering them while they were on the links. They were in open revolt.

This was interrupted by a chortle from the doorway. Ostrow grimaced and approached from the threshold dragging one leg behind him.

"I think I pulled a groin muscle," he moaned. One loose, baggy half of his scrotum protruded from his fly.

I couldn't laugh. Ostrow saw that. He stood over me and tucked his balls back in his pants.

"Looks like the boss worked you over pretty good," he said.

"Couple stitches," I managed to mumble.

"You know what you and me should do, kid? . . . We walk downstairs right now, three hours we're in Tijuana, we're makin' thousands at the jai alai fronton, I know this great place for carnitas up by the track . . . we're up to our eyeballs in señoritas . . ."

I pondered that. But this was nothing cerveza or señoritas were an answer for.

"I dunno . . . maybe I just can't do this stuff," I said abjectly.

"I gotta tell you, kid, I don't think Werner feels you can." He laughed hoarsely, as if that would make light of things. "You know, sometimes when you're this famischt you gotta take stock . . . decide what's the best thing for you to do. I know you do other kinds of writing real good. How about advertising? Or technical writing? I got a friend, runs some sort of real-estate computer bank up in Spokane, I could call him right now, get you a job with him writing ad copy. What're you—thirty-two . . . thirty-three maybe?— you could make a change easy. The air's clean up there."

"Clean air, huh?" I grunted. As if that was what I needed right now. What I needed fewer parts per million of going through my system wasn't carbon monoxide, I decided, it was Werner, Jarvis, and, particularly, Ostrow.

"Just say the word, you know I'll do anything for you. Y'okay?" He moved for the door.

"Yup," I said, and he left, bursting into a lusty version of "Bei Mir Bist Du Schön" as he trundled down the hall: "Bei mir bist du schön/Please let me explain/Bei mir bist du schön/Means you are grand. . . ."

I sat there trying to collect myself. Reassemble is probably a more apt word. So much for fishing for reassurance. I wasn't musing about my own failings to Ostrow because I wanted corroboration. There went my "mentor," with whom I'd palled around since he'd invited me and my four-dimensional words out to California, leaving me in greater torment than when he'd paid his cheering call. My champion, my nemesis.

My guts were a waterspout. Forget about Ostrow, I had to come up with an idea for Werner. Or else. I pounded my head with my fist. I banged my skull against my desktop. But no ideas came. Other than this: My office was opposite the stairway that led out of the building. I determined to make my only success of the day a dash across the hallway to an unobserved flight from the studio.

But I never made it. No sooner was I in the hallway than I saw Mark emerge from his suite and head my way, followed by two women and a young boy. He called Ostrow and Jarvis out of their offices.

"This is Timmy Squier," he said to us all. Timmy was a freckle-faced kid in jeans and a blue-striped polo shirt beneath a dull green windbreaker. He wore an *Under the Law* cap that Mark had obviously just given him. Mark introduced the two women with Timmy as being from the Answer a Prayer Foundation. I knew what that was: a charity that specialized in granting wishes to terminally ill youngsters. Timmy didn't have any hair under that hat.

"These people do wonderful work, priceless," Mark said, his tone having switched from that of hectoring Nazi death-camp commandant to unctuous uncle with candy bar. "Tim's here to meet everybody."

"You're a fan of our show?" Ostrow asked, bending over the kid, probably ending Timmy's remission.

"I watch it every week," Tim squeaked. "I love it. My favorite episode was the one where the guy cut everybody's hair off."

"I wrote that show," Ostrow said, chuckling like a grandee. "Won an Emmy for it."

"I was hoping to take Timmy down to the set," Mark said, "but I can't shake free right now."

"I'm jammed too," Ostrow said.

"Why don't you take Timmy down?" Mark said to me. "Introduce him to Stray and Dan. Timmy, I want you to do whatever you feel like doing while you're there."

Looking over Timmy's head at me, Mark rolled his eyes.

TIMMY, THE TWO WOMEN, AND I WALKED ACROSS THE LOT TO SOUNDSTAGE 10, where we were shooting. Each delighted chirp of Timmy's as he skipped across the studio boxed my ears, forcing me to summon up a pride in the show I'd been told I had no right having.

"Who writes all the episodes?"

"You already met Peter and Elliot and Mark. There are a bunch of other writers, including me. We divide up the scripts."

"What are Dan Koslow and Stray Simmons like?"

"Really nice guys."

"Yeah?"

Who'd think you could stuff one word with such boundless faith? The way he said it made a surpassing argument for not extinguishing the human race. But even that thought wasn't making me feel any better. Just the opposite—proximity to Timmy was turning out to be the equivalent of some medieval ritual wherein pure substances are applied to the site of something ill. I felt the poison being drawn to the surface. With each earnest exclamation of Tim's, I only felt more embroiled in my own surging woe.

"Did you win an Emmy like Mr. Ostrow?"

"No. Not yet. C'mon, right in here."

The inside of a working stage is a darkened maze with cables running all over the scuffed floor. Sawhorses. Long folding tables with snacks for the crew on them. Makeup tables with their mirrors. Walls and scenery from sets. Above, the latticework rigging for lights.

I warned our visitors to watch their steps and to be as quiet as possible. I led Tim back toward the set we mainly used, which was the interior of the police station where Caddigan and Blue worked. That was where we were shooting today.

Stepping across a stream of cables, we turned a corner and saw the squad room. The rickety, rusted cop desks where Caddigan and Blue were playing this scene were brilliantly lit. Ringing halfway around the room in the darkness were the canvas-backed director's chairs in which the crew sat—script supervisor, assistant directors, wardrobe and makeup personnel, stand-ins. The sound mixer sat beneath his headphones by his recorder. The boom operator waved his fish pole. The camera was mounted on its little rolling dolly, on which sat the camera operator and beside which stood the director.

The actors, ruddy-faced Dan Koslow and heartthrob Stray Simmons, were rehearsing a scene, so we stood back in the darkness and watched, Tim all wide-eyed. Suddenly I felt Tim's eyes on me in the dark.

"Are you feeling okay, Mister?"

I looked down at that bright face beneath the bill of his cap. How had he sensed anything? It was probably because of what I was giving off—I was rotting, and you can smell it in a person just as easily as in a cantaloupe.

"I'm fine, Tim, how about you?" I nearly gagged on my declaration. The words, bristling with static loathing, crinkled around my palate like just-unwrapped cellophane.

There were more important things calling for Tim's attention. The set. The magic. His heroes. But after a moment, he looked back up at me and whispered: "You know what we say at the doctors'? You have to keep the faith."

It was not just a statement, it was advice. The kid was taking time off from his dying wish to offer it. Because if there was one thing besides death he'd come to recognize in his brief life, it was despair—and he saw it in me. I had hit rock bottom. I wanted to cry. Suddenly, I heard Stray growl at the director: "Cut it, cut it!"

Stray mumbled a curse. Shading his eyes with his hand, he squinted past the lights toward me.

"You out there, Ziff? Weren't you working on this glasses story?" he directed my way in a combative tone.

This was a question to which I had to answer yes. First, because it was technically true. Second, because I was not going to stand there in front of the entire crew and the cast and Timmy and admit I had been totally rewritten by Peter Ostrow just that afternoon, which was what had happened.

He'd invented a minor character, Caddigan's obnoxious

brother Preston, who was a failing salesman reduced to ped-
dling goods from his basement. Caddigan asked Blue to do
him a big favor: If he would pick through the junk and drop
a few bucks, the brother might avoid bankruptcy and having
to move in with Caddigan. Turns out, Pres had some used
eyeglasses Blue could try on. Blue acceded. What the hell,
he was only helping his partner.

"Ziff!"

I took a step forward. Stray took a few toward me.

"I didn't hear you, did you write this shit?"

I barely nodded.

"I gotta tell you, this fuckin' story sucks. This white man
ain't wearin' no goddam glasses on the show."

A hundred eyes bored holes into me, and all my breath
escaped through them. Fortunately, one of the AD's took a
few steps forward and whispered something into Stray's ear,
and suddenly his face turned into a postcard of Hawaii.

"Hey, everybody, we got a very special visitor here today.
Name's Timmy. C'mon over here, Timmy."

And the AD quickly took hold of Tim's hand and led him
out into the lights, where he was swept up into Stray's arms
and held high. I couldn't tell what Timmy thought of Stray's
diatribe. I didn't stick around very long to see.

I SPENT THE NEXT FEW HOURS ABUSING MYSELF AS HEARTILY AS POSSIBLE AT THE
Ponytail Lounge, across the street from the studio. Whole
cubic yards of darkness and indifference beckoned me there.
It was a good place to get lost in the corner and pick French
fries off a grease-soaked napkin and wash them down with a
beer or whiskey and baste your broiling self in your own
misery.

I'd naturally assumed upon arriving months ago that the
Ponytail would be mobbed at quitting time every day. That
was the way it had been back in New York. Where you

packed bars with your fellow scribes and editors. Where you met friends for brunch and wound up catching a midnight movie. Where life was measured, properly so, by what you had all survived together.

But at the end of my first day as a Hollywood writer, I'd literally stood at the studio gate waiting to cross the street with my comrades in pencil, only to watch my cohorts jump into their imported autos and whiz by me for the freeways.

Quickly and unhappily I realized fraternizing didn't exist in Los Angeles, a city where the dread of personal obligation hangs over every conversation in every restaurant and gym and theater lobby in town. It was part of my education into the business. Where nothing was personal, although you exchanged the most personal parts of yourself all day long while creating something. Whatever happened, however banged up it got you, and whatever it drove you to—pick one of the following (or combine them) if you spent more than one season in TV: divorce, intestinal disintegration, heart attack, angioplasty, adultery, substance abuse, hysterical deafness, obesity—it wasn't personal. As they say in the Mafia before the spent shell casings rain down on the pavement in their tinkling toll: It's just business.

I didn't want any companionship that fateful night, anyway. I wanted to be alone and at a bar and having to address myself to nothing other than the crescent water marks revealed when I picked up the glass. Because I was feeling desperate. I needed something to please Messrs. Werner, Ostrow, and Jarvis. But whatever it was I needed I somehow lacked—an innate knack for storytelling and construction that a seventeen-year-old car thief, master of a life of well-wrought alibis, might have and that no amount of education or vocabulary could provide to an obedient sort like me. Whatever the cause, I lacked the capacity to engender the mental mitosis that would allow what I'd put on paper to split away from me and live. Creatively, I was impotent.

I got drunk and searched my brain for something to pitch to Mark. I closed my eyes and pleaded. Pleaded and wrung my hands trying to summon Caddigan and Blue. I would have given anything for them to come to my aid, to live and act for me and save me from being fired and branded a failure.

But the two of them refused to respond. They lay slumbering in two rickety cots in a dark bedroom of some decrepit hunting cabin in the northern Maine woods. They would not move. They snored—rasping, hacksaw cuts in a deafening duet. A feather floated up and down, up and down over Blue's mouth. I banged on a cast-iron skillet and yelled at them to awaken and help act out a script my life depended on writing. But they never opened an eye. They merely rolled over. Caddigan farted, a long, wet blanket raiser, and pulled the pillow over his head to drown me out.

I OPENED THE DOOR AND DROPPED MY BRIEFCASE TO THE HARDWOOD FLOOR IN our entryway. Dayna came around from the living room. She held her sketch pad and pencil.

"How was your day?" she asked, although she didn't have to. I was a terribly easy read, though not much of a page-turner, so predictable had my story become.

"I'm sorry I missed dinner," I said. "I needed to work."

"It's late," she said.

"I know."

"You didn't answer. How was your day?" she asked.

"Not so good," I said.

I trudged past her and went out into the backyard. It was dark and a little chilly, but I flopped onto a chaise by our shimmering blue pool and stared off into space. It was quiet back here. I could let the rest of the poison I'd absorbed that day go all the way down to the pit of my stomach. Maybe it would get sealed off from me somewhere down there.

After a few moments, Dayna came out. She stood over me.

"It was so bad you had to miss dinner and sit and stew and not even bother to call me?"

"You don't want to know," I said.

"I do," she said.

"No you don't," I said, knowing that later I would coax her into coaxing it out of me. "I don't want to talk about it."

"Ostrow?"

"I can't even talk about it." I shook my head in unendurable weariness.

"You have to quit," she said abruptly.

"I can't. Hopefully I'll get hit by a bus."

She looked down. Exasperation had begun crimping her features when she stood over me witnessing my haplessness.

"Do you want anything to eat?"

Drunk and in this sort of mood, no. All I wanted to do was maybe watch television. Not eat. Not do anything. Not even talk to my wife. Just sit there alone until the torment had worked itself all the way in and been absorbed. Just let my eyes glaze over watching kick boxing or bass fishing.

"My ovulation test was positive today, in case you're interested," Dayna said.

"Good," I said.

"I wish you were in a better mood," she said.

"Why?"

"Because we have to do it." She frowned, not appreciating having to spell things out.

"Don't worry," I said.

"It would help if you were in a better mood," she said. "It would help me."

She left me alone after that. I listened to the hum of the electric wires strung along the poles lining our back alley. The faint conversational drone from television sets in neighboring houses. Birds flapped through the clear sky. Farther above, the distant, winking lights of aircraft tracked across the stars. The cool breeze from the nearby ocean fanned me. The palm branches overhead waggled and shushed. But that barely distracted me from trying to think of what I would say to Mark so I wouldn't be fired from the best job in America. The ferret that had been foraging in my stomach wall the last few months woke up.

Then I heard: "I'm ready."

Dayna was calling from the bedroom.

I took this call from my mate, a call to bliss and to fulfill our growing yearnings to start a family, as one might the morning steam whistle shrilling its summons from the plant roof. Clamp up the old lunch box and straggle toward the gate.

The boudoir lights were low. Dayna lay in our ash sleigh bed looking trusting and beautiful and hopeful. She was wearing white panties and her "lucky shirt," a pink-striped cotton T-shirt with spaghetti-thin straps and a small, crumpled pink bow in the middle of the scalloped neckline. Above the left breast the word TUFTS was printed. That was her alma mater. She'd held on to the shirt for all these years. It was the shirt she'd been wearing when she met me and swore to herself we would one day get married.

I won't claim it was the greatest sexual encounter of my life. In fact, I won't say that for my wife it was any better than a rabies shot. But one way or another, as tired and liquored up and preoccupied as I was, I managed the deed.

It was after midnight. Dayna lay in my arms for a few minutes and then turned over to sleep.

Sleep I gladly would have. I was exhausted and drained. I felt like an oversteamed pea. And I had to be up and back at the studio in seven hours.

But I roused myself from my postcoital swoon. I reached for my nightstand and grabbed the pencil and paper I always kept there to transcribe my increasingly rare moments of lucid thought, and slipped out of bed. I didn't turn any lights on. I didn't get anything to eat. I didn't dare blink an eye. Because somehow some fleck had fallen like a flower petal out of the universe and landed in my skull as I lay beside my wife. Whether it was booze or testosterone or an answered prayer in the form of a dying boy I don't know, but I didn't dare do anything except reach the den, sit down in the dark, and put the tip of the pencil to the paper, and scrawl three words. The few words I knew I had to remember and commit to paper or die.

And then I turned on the light and looked at the pad. And when I could read those words clearly enough to believe I'd be able to make them out when sober in the morning, I turned out the light, went back into the bedroom, and lay down on my bed.

It hadn't been a very good day. In fact, it had been the worst so far. I had been humiliated in public. I had been told I was about to be fired by my boss. One of my other supervisors, my mentor, had toyed with my remains like a jackal.

Yet as I settled back on the pillow, I could smile.

I'd gotten a great idea for my A story. It was right there on the pad on the night table beside me.

For the first time in months I wasn't afraid to get some sleep.

Three

THE FIRST DOZEN OR SO THINGS I DID EVERY MORNING BEFORE WORK I could not have done in greater lockstep or with less variation in routine had I been doing them at gunpoint. After my shower and shave, I threw on the green Scotch plaid robe my wife had gotten me for my birthday and padded toward the kitchen for two bowls of Cheerios, my only peace of the day. The classical music station was on, a station so proud of the classical music it played it spent so much time demanding listeners' money to continue playing classical music that it played almost no classical music at all.

Dayna sat at our dining room table wearing a blue-and-white skirt and jacket. Her black portfolio book was wedged into a chair, looking like something a giant had dropped. Pencil in hand, lips compressed in concentration, she was listing on a pad things to do. Whereas I liked to disappear within a newspaper in the morning, fleeing to distant date-lines, Dayna was already losing no time.

Her list making could be disconcertingly compulsive. But I mostly admired it. There are few things more reassuring about a person, after all, than such hard evidence of their impulse for self-improvement.

Dayna had scattered some sketches about on the table. She always sat straight-backed in her chair like that, the picture of the perfect schoolgirl, ink unsmeared and hair never in her eyes. But the real reason, I thought, for her regal posture was that she'd spent nearly a year in a body cast when just thirteen. She had curvature of the spine, scoliosis. That was the year her parents had moved west to Oregon from Ohio. She was unable to play on her new school's field hockey team, a squad she was a shoo-in to star on. She missed giggling by the hallway lockers and was not privy to lunchroom intrigues or notes passed in class, but whatever she missed—however more difficult that made her social transition in the throes of being thirteen—nothing was more problematic than simply feeling so unbearably odd in her cast. The new kid in town, sticky with adolescence, and some physical weirdness that stood out to boot. She'd spent much of that year peering out a window by her bed, where she took up a pad and pencil and began to draw.

So the cast had shaped more than just her back. It had molded someone more wistful and expressive. It had also left her less tolerant of restraint. She was careful but devilish, refined yet ornery.

One of the first things she'd ever told me about herself was that in the wake of some high school football rivalry turned violent in her Gresham, Ore., hometown, authorities had imposed a dusk to dawn curfew. Nobody under eighteen was allowed out of doors. But restive Dayna wouldn't obey. She brazenly slipped out of her house and toured the streets seeing what she wanted and courting arrest.

She wanted nothing to impede her freedom of movement. She traveled east for college, then studied at the Rhode Island School of Design. Her migrations took her to New York. When we met, she was teaching at the School of Visual Arts. Even though no job awaited her when we picked up stakes for Los Angeles, she didn't complain. She bought herself Rollerblades and sunglasses and a membership at the gym. She learned to drive a stick shift and to leaf unerringly through a thick Thomas street guide. She'd return at night, walking crisply through the front door from parts of town I'd never heard of, clutching the *L.A. Weekly* and free concert tickets she'd been given by someone or other encountered while taking her portfolio around. I'd beg off our attending. I was too busy.

"What're you doing?" I thrust my chin toward her sketches as I made for General Mills.

"Set designs for a music video. Josie knows a friend who manages some rock group. They want someone to do a video. I'm going to try for it."

"You're thinking of rock videos?"

"Why do you say it like that?"

"I don't know. . . . Rock videos?"

"Sure. Why not? I mean, I can't keep on just doing print design and photo shoots. There's no future in that. We're in Hollywood, right? Showbiz central. I want to try art directing. Get a job on some soap or something. I know I can do that just as well as anybody else. So, anyway, why not music videos? They make tons of them out here."

"I didn't think you were such a big music fan."

"I love music. Anyway, I'm not a big furniture fan, I design furniture catalogs."

"What's the name of the group?"

"Don't laugh. Craterface."

"Some swell visuals there. Have you heard them, at least?"

"Josie gave me a tape. I listened last night, and I watched

a lot of MTV while you were out getting drunk. And I decided. They're good. Heavy metal meets alternative. What do you think of this? I thought they could be inside this sort of alive frame-type thing with all sorts of stuff springing up out of it. And then that turns into something like this. Or it could look animated, even."

She stroked at the paper with her pencil. Ribs and billowy loops and arches spun in ribbons from it. Beautiful shapes, shaded and lovely. With the sort of effortless emergence that confounds someone from the stick-figure school like me. I draw trees. Trees or people wearing bell-bottoms. It depends on how wide I draw the pants. If the pants come out accidentally too wide, I turn it into a tree trunk.

"Craterface'll be a breakout hit," I said.

She continued sketching, focused on somewhere within herself. I always found her incredibly sexy when she was a captive to the discharge of her talent. Something powerful in the unguarded purity of her. In such moments of utter unself-consciousness are people first loved. I watched Dayna sketch the New York skyline during a softball game one afternoon in Central Park unaware that the bases were loaded and she was up next, and I was smitten.

"I was worried about you last night," she called into the kitchen, where I'd begun foraging for my breakfast. She stared at me after I'd plunked down into a chair and wrangled the sports section free from the newspaper. "You think you can stop crunching long enough to tell me about yesterday?"

I didn't like talking in the morning. My bowl of Cheerios was, in effect, my daily Last Meal before the world kicked out the trapdoor and my neck snapped. I sighed and shoved the paper aside.

"Same old song," I said, dribbling some milk down my chin. "Only Mark throws my pages across his desk. Like they were maybe giving off poisonous fumes or something. Like maybe they carry the AIDS virus. Maybe he oughta call the

Centers for Disease Control. It was a nightmare. Y'understand? For a writer? Tossing the pages back at me. You ever have someone do this to you?"

I mimicked Mark's contempt, flinging the metro section at her.

"I mean, tell me this isn't some sort of cosmic joke. God's candid camera."

I tore back into my Cheerios. Dayna watched me. She tapped her pencil against her thumb.

"You have an ulcer, you know," she said.

"What?" I looked up and put down my spoon.

"Doctor Levin called with the results of the G.I. series you took last week."

"Yeah?"

"I didn't want to tell you last night because we had to do what we had to do and I didn't want you to be distracted. Anyway, he said you had an ulcer. You're supposed to call him and make an appointment."

She had an almost unreadable expression on her face as she delivered the news. Only the faintest softness around the eyes betrayed anything.

"I've got a fucking ulcer?"

"A small one. In your duodenum. He said it didn't look too serious, but it had to be treated. He already called the drugstore with a prescription for some pills. I'll pick them up. You have to take one every night."

"That's it?"

Dayna sighed and shrugged. And then leaned forward and solemnly emphasized her message: "Isn't that enough? You have an ulcer." She shook her head in unhappy contemplation of events.

"A Madison Avenue–type ulcer? How the fuck could I have an ulcer?"

"How the fuck could you not have an ulcer, Billy?"

Indeed. There had been an animal with irregular habits

and viper fangs prowling inside my wheelhouse for the past few months. I felt lousy. I looked lousy, too. In California, I hadn't acquired a tan, I had acquired wattles. The result of cramming tons of snacks down my throat during my nervous hours at work. My once angular features, with their keen and even occasionally voltaic effects, had swollen into a caricature of Benjamin Franklin on cortisone. I'd shot from 160 pounds, carried not ungainly on my formerly lithe, six-foot frame, to 179; a former panther, now a pants seat waiting to rip. My deep-set blue eyes swam around the shaving mirror in a red glaze. My black hair, lush and wavy, didn't get up with me from the pillow each morning. Of course I had an ulcer.

"You have to stop drinking alcohol," Dayna said. "The bar is no longer the answer to your problems. Not even a beer."

"Great."

"Doctor Levin said you have to stop eating a lot of things. No pepperoni pizza, no spicy stuff."

"Great."

I got up from the table and dumped the cereal bowl and spoon into the sink. I reached into the pantry for a mug.

"And you can't drink coffee, either," she called to me. "No caffeine. In anything."

I went back out into the dining room, my hands finding their way to my hips.

"Well then, what the hell am I supposed to start off my day with?"

"Why not tea?"

How could optimism get so damn infuriating?

"Tea?"

"Herbal tea. No caffeine. I think we have some way back in the second drawer somewhere."

"Some mule piss like chamomile tea?"

I hated tea. Particularly herbal tea. I associated drinking it

with a handful of other primitive health regimens my otherwise modern-minded mother had foisted on me whenever
I'd fallen ill. Chamomile tea. Like vaporizers and cold plas-
ters. Somehow on occasion a copy of a magazine like *Good
Housekeeping* would appear on a table in our house. And for
the next weeks we would turn into test dummies for the
debut of some horrifying, vitamin-rich casserole like breaded
pineapple loaf or homemade whortleberry-and-fish-oil elixir
gleaned from the journal's homespun columns and hordes of
letter-writing, put-up pros.

"I'd rather drink boiled lawn mower catch bag. Is this guy
sure?"

"Listen to me for once, Billy," Dayna said. She blinked
hard a couple times, and the skein of light freckles on her
quick-to-color cheekbones snapped like a jump rope. There
was always a contrast between the practical, gritty, list-
making wife and the numinous person I also lived with, the
one who sketched new worlds with a pen stroke and a sparkle of those huge brown eyes. But when Dayna blinked
hard, like she was doing now, and did only rarely, grace
disappeared from her face. Her eyeballs became obsidian bullets. Each blink was a gunshot.

"You have an ulcer, Billy. An ulcer. Get that through
your thick skull. And I don't think changing your eating
habits is all you ought to do. I've been doing a lot of thinking
about this."

I sat down.

"What's that supposed to mean?"

She took a deep breath.

"It means that there is something going on that is causing
you to eat your insides out. We both know what that is, or
at least we think we do. Although sometimes I think it's
partly me."

"It's the job," I assured her. "It's my great friend Ostrow
and them, it's not you."

"Either way, you can change the circumstances or change yourself. Those are the alternatives."

"I am not quitting." I pounded the table. "I can't quit my job. What am I supposed to do, go back East and announce to everyone that I was a washout?"

"Fine . . . great," she said, her voice rising. "I knew we couldn't talk about this. You are so immature. You can't go back to New York. 'Everyone will know.' But none of those people gives a damn about you. Why don't you care that you're killing yourself? And if you weren't so self-absorbed, and if you cared just a little bit about me, you'd understand how much that hurts me and pisses me off!"

She stopped shouting. We glowered at each other across the table.

"If you won't quit, I think you should see a shrink," she finally said, lowering her voice.

"Why the fuck do I have to see a shrink?"

"Because you're unhappy. And you can't deal with things in any way other than to eat a hole in yourself. And I've got news for you—I can't deal with it either. Not anymore."

"Well, I'm not seeing any fucking shrink."

She abruptly stood from the table and slammed her coffee mug down on it hard. Coffee spurted all over the place.

"Why the fuck did you do that?"

"Because you don't listen. Because there is going to have to be a change around here. Whether it's you or the job. Pick one. I don't want to live like this. I don't want to spend the rest of my life with you in a state of permanent depression. I'm supposed to respect you. I'm supposed to admire you. But you're making it impossible to. And if you won't do something, then I'm going to. You've got me thinking about just moving out."

She turned and stormed off through the French doors that gave onto our backyard. I watched her make her way to the chaise lounge by the pool. She lay down there, staring off into the brilliant blue beach sky, right on the same green cushion where I sought peace every night coming home from work with the fevered despair that was punching a hole in my guts.

She'd never threatened to leave before. I'd never even sensed the thought in her head. But I didn't go out there and console her. Even though I should have. As I'm painfully aware now. Men cultivate the ability to survive hurt, which is a far cry from being able to offer consolation. But I should have at least made a gesture, which is usually all a wife wants. Instead, I dumbly stood there smarting from her simple logic —like walking into a glass door you should have noticed.

So I bounced off that glass door and didn't go out to Dayna. Women embrace alternatives; men gird for torture. Certain voyages have to be ridden out, I rationalized. Certain battles have to be fought, wherein surrender is no option. They might fire me, but to quit *Under the Law* would have been forever to brand myself unworthy.

Especially not today. Not when I had come up with one really fine idea for my solo script. Not when, finally, I had an A story.

I turned away from my wife and retreated to the bedroom. The message I'd scrawled to myself the night before was right where I'd left it. Maybe, if Mark Werner didn't like this idea, I'd listen to Dayna's suggestions. Maybe I would quit. Maybe I'd see a shrink. Maybe I'd do both if Mark pissed on the best idea I'd had.

I GOT TO THE STUDIO, WENT UPSTAIRS, AND IMMEDIATELY SAW LIZ TO ASK WHEN I could see Mark.

"He's at breakfast with Carlin," she said.

That was Carlin Alemo, the president of our television network. The Titan whose chest thrust above the clouds, whose mighty fists clutched the threads that jerked those of us below into stupor or movement. The man who decided what the American people saw on the air.

I imagined Mark munching eggs and sausage with the Titan in some coffee shop, deciding the world—the Treaty of Tordesillas on wet Formica. Who would be moved up, who would be moved out. Who was someone to be watched, who to be disdained. This invocation of Mark's power dissipated whatever jauntiness I'd been able to husband for our encounter.

Mark walked in and casually made his hellos. He wore a windbreaker, a pair of perfectly faded jeans, and expensive sneakers. His hair was an immaculate slicked-back and dried-out coiffure, its effect that of a man perpetually turned into the wind and sun. As if having forgotten the thrust of the previous day's meeting, Mark put his arm around me and ushered me into his office.

"I laid such a beeyootiful dewey this morning," he said, hanging up his windbreaker on a hook behind his door. "A ten. Magnificent. Brown and even and round. Snipped off perfectly at the end. Went down into the toilet and made this perfect circle. Like a hula hoop. You could swing it around your waist. I tell you, every morning like clockwork."

He made a finger-kissing gesture like one of those French chefs who's just pulled a masterpiece from the oven.

"So what can I do for you, dahling?"

"Well," I said, "you know I'm working on my first solo script."

"I'm aware," he said.

I took a breath.

"I've got an A story I want you to hear."

Mark sat down and looked at me a little more seriously than usual. Because I had addressed him far more confidently than usual.

"Tell me," he said.

He nodded. He waited.

"I got the idea yesterday. I think we do a story about one of those terminally ill kids who has one last wish, okay? And his last wish somehow is to spend a day on patrol with two cops he knows and loves, Caddigan and Blue. And so the people from this foundation come to the station house and lay it out. . . . And he does ride around with them. And at first Blue is bent out of shape a little because it's against the rules. And Caddigan's thinking, Why'd the captain stick us with this pip-squeak? Okay? But they both fall in love with this kid. And I think this kid has always wanted to be a cop. Okay? And so somewhere, they're on a call and one of them gets taken hostage. The other is injured and helpless, he can't do a thing. And so the kid, who always wanted to be a cop, puts himself on the line—and, y'know, what does he have to lose anyway? And he saves Caddigan, probably, or maybe Blue, only, of course, the kid gets killed."

That was the most I had ever said in one gulp to Mark. As incoherent as it was, it was the most coherent I had ever been with him. He creaked back in his chair.

"I love it," he said.

"I'm not exactly sure how you end it, but you've got a great scene there between the kid and the cops when he dies," I gushed.

"I love it," Mark repeated. "Why don't you do this: Beat it out a little, we'll talk a little more in the next few days— or, who knows? Maybe you don't feel the need to—and you'll hand me a script in a couple weeks. Okay?"

"Sounds good," I said.

"Meanwhile, I'll authorize a story payment to you," Mark said.

Even more success. He not only loved it, he was officially buying it from me. I had made a sale!

"Attaboy," Mark said, patting me on the back as I left his office. I was ecstatic. Bells were ringing. In those few short minutes I had been turned into another person. A qualified person. An inbound player. I had been enfranchised. He'd said "attaboy." To me!

I floated down the hallway and into my office. I closed the door and as quietly as I could for the next few minutes celebrated the final out of the World Series and the final gun of the Super Bowl all rolled into one. Times ten. I leaped onto the sofa and jumped for joy and thrust my arms wide in the air. I'd begun proving I was worthy. That something could come of me.

I was about to hop off and call Dayna with the good news when onto the sun-blanched plank of my happy porch Ostrow's boot now suddenly, ominously clanked. He stood in my office doorway.

" 'Ey, looks like Billy sold himself a story to the boss man. Mark just told me. Break out the champagne!"

Jarvis appeared behind him. Ostrow pushed into the room and clapped me on the shoulder.

"Congratulations. Hey, you got a minute?"

I moved behind my desk while Jarvis sat on the edge of the couch near me. He wore chinos with an untailored buttoned-down white short-sleeved shirt. His arms—two narrow, underutilized pipes that dangled from his shirtsleeves —he dripped across his chest. He crossed his emaciated legs and rocked one over the other. There was nothing so sickly looking as Jarvis's bony, unmuscular legs.

Meanwhile, Ostrow perched on my desk.

"So . . . this is great news, kid. When'd the boss say you had to deliver?" he asked.

"Nothing definite. He wanted the script in a couple of weeks."

"Y'oughta take the missus out on the town tonight. Celebrate. Go to one of Wolfgang's joints. Want me to get you in? Say the word. Uh . . . listen. . . ." Ostrow stood and patted his belly and smoothed his mustache. "I get in about seven. You get yourself in here and I'll work with you on the story."

I was confused. Some sort of defensive hormonal proteins had been instantly released in my body. I felt a tug on the other flank of the gazelle I'd just stalked and killed.

Ostrow had congratulated me, then leveled an offer of assistance. Yet he was sitting in my office with his partner, which smacked of something "cooked up." Or was he just being a pal?

"I don't know," I said. "I mean, Mark said he really liked the story. He didn't seem to think there was a lot to be worked out." I shrugged, laconically resistant.

Ostrow and Jarvis exchanged a pregnant look, one which meant to convey sympathy for my naïveté and concern for the resultant immolation I failed to foresee.

Jarvis piped up.

"What we're trying to say here, Billy, is this is gonna be your first solo script. Maybe you could use some help."

"Well, I appreciate that," I said.

In the absence of any further response from me, they looked at each other once more. Ostrow lowered his voice and planted two hands on my desk. "See, the thing is, Billy, frankly, Mark don't think you're up to it."

A terrible cold stillness settled inside me.

"Now, maybe you'll prove him wrong," Ostrow continued, "but once his mind is made up about somebody, it don't change. And you could really turn things around if you ace this script."

"I didn't know his mind was made up about me," I said.

"It's not totally yet," Jarvis said. "But—"

"But—" Ostrow echoed.

"But what?"

"We're just thinkin' maybe you could use a little help," Ostrow said. "There's nothin' wrong with sharing a credit on the script."

"So the money gets split three ways." Jarvis shrugged. "So what?"

"It's not the money. This was supposed to be written by just me, y'know?"

"Mark thinks you're a wanker," Jarvis said finally.

"A wanker?"

"A jerk-off," Jarvis said.

"You sit around here playin' with yourself, kid, bein' funny, but you can't deliver the goods. And that's the bottom line. You deliver the goods, he'll make you a rich man. And right now Mark don't think you can deliver the goods. He thinks you're a wanker. And frankly"—Ostrow twisted his head toward Jarvis, then back—"you gotta face facts. You gotta look the truth straight in the eye because that's what it's all about. I mean, we all like you, and we're all pullin' for you. But we're dealing with the truth here, and the truth says you can't deliver."

That fanged ferret began eating at my gut.

"Look," Jarvis said, "maybe you go out and deliver a great script. That's great. But if you don't, you're history. You're damaged goods. And when Mark goes thumbs-down, you don't work anywhere. You come in here and your furniture's been cleaned out."

"So think about it," Ostrow said. "We'd be delighted to share the script with you."

"Thanks," I finally managed. "I'll let you know."

"Okay," Ostrow said. "I'm offering. You got a friend here."

Then he and Jarvis left the room.

I mulled this over for a long time. An hour ago, Mark had pounded me on the back and bid me Godspeed. Now, I had just been assured he was lying. I felt like the victim of some tornado, flung to rest in a tree by the pitiless whirlwind of Ostrow's friendship.

Then I made two decisions. First, I realized I could not

entrust my emancipation to those who seemed so well contented to keep me down. And, second, I'd better spend as little time in the office as possible.

WITH EVERYTHING ON THE LINE, I CONFINED MYSELF TO HOME AND THREW MYself into my writing. I got up every morning. I sat across from Dayna for a bowl of cereal and some herbal tea. Then I attacked my script as soon as she'd left.

Shrapnel fragments from my skirmish with Ostrow and Jarvis were still lodged very near my heart. Inoperable, they were. The sort that might forever resist the physician's hand, might never clang into a basin, dropped from drippy forceps. Maybe in a convulsive sneeze twenty years from now, they would heave out of my nose in a bloody drizzle.

But even so, I fought my insecurity to a standstill.

There was a small alcove off the dining room. Here I installed a few file cabinets, atop which I set a long pine slab that served as a wide, comfortable desk. I composed the script in longhand on yellow legal pads, filling the margins with notes, scribbling story arcs, character names, and pieces of dialogue that came to me during the day or night. Occasionally I would look up and out the window at the flashing blue-and-white disk of our pool and the palm tree bowing and scraping in the brilliant sunshine. Though it was neither a view of a snowy meadow and stone-fenced fields nor the teeming streets of New York—both of which envisionings were my more accustomed scribe's fantasies—I felt like a writer again. A pure writer. I reinvoked to myself the restless, solitary rhythms of the last place where I'd spent so much time at home writing—the damp, unfinished, windowless basement room of my New York apartment.

Dayna came home late. She usually spent the day at job interviews trying to crack the music-video world. After a stop at the gym, she'd return in a refreshed mood, and for once I added some sparkle to it. She saw me absorbed. Content. Sitting there in my sweatpants and T-shirt, still cradling that legal pad.

We'd head out for dinner and not really talk about the script or me being tortured, but chat about her for a change. Most of all we'd talk about her deepest hope that we'd have a baby soon. Much of what she wanted to impart to the world had to do with raising a child and having a family. For Dayna, the *locus amoenus,* the happiest place, was the dining room table round which a family—toss in aunts, cousins, grandparents—could argue and laugh and with each spoonful of dessert or shuffle of the cards sculpt life into the most enduring art.

At evening's end, I would take my Tenzac ulcer pill and retire beside my wife, the two of us reading in bed by each other, framed in the amber, consolatory glow of our shaded reading lamps. We would make love. We would fall asleep in each other's embrace. I'd not thought it possible, but it occasionally occurred to me during that time that I was happy.

The writing gathered momentum. There were, of course, stops and starts, but at first it was a smooth mountain climb. Steep grades, to be sure, narrow paths through boulder-strewn meadows, but I'd run into none of the unscalable, thousand-foot rock faces I'd usually encountered in the perilous ascents of my previous scriptwriting expeditions. Plot holes way too chasmic for me to get across usually now seemed only brook-wide as I picked my way along.

There was just one main snag: I felt very comfortable with the character of the terminally ill sixteen-year-old, whom I called Ted, but I needed a scene for the aftermath of his death, a wrenching, goose-bumps-the-size-of-hailstones scene where a somber Caddigan and Blue could deliver the heartrending news of Ted's demise to some authority. That authority couldn't be a parent, because a recent episode had had our guys delivering the news of a daughter's death to her folks. Mark wanted to avoid that repetitive story beat.

I didn't mind that; it meant Ted would be an orphan. All the more poignant, no? But I needed someone who stood in loco parentis for little Teddy. An aunt, say, or an older brother . . .

And then I had it! Like any terrific idea, it seemed so perfect at the time I didn't know how I hadn't thought of it before. Perhaps the instant of Mark's cruel threat as he strode up to accept his Humana Prize had been burned into my brain. Or a glimpse of the Reverend Monsignor Lawrence Connolly. Or perhaps I'd done so much "praying" over the last few weeks the idea was obvious.

The character would be a religious man, the head of the charity that had sponsored little Teddy's dying wish.

It would be Father Joey O'Dell.

He was the character I needed!

Simple.

My thinking about Father O'Dell quickly jelled: I didn't want him to be saccharine. That would be predictable. I decided that Father Joey O'Dell, the head of the Dream Come True Foundation, would be hard, leathery, angry, fallen. A bit of a tippler. A navigator of the blasphemous margins. He would exhibit an irascibility about Ted and his other terminally ill charges. Such seeming heartlessness that Caddigan and Blue would lose their reluctance and take Ted under their wing while wondering whether O'Dell was fit to be a man of God and whether he was a drunken brute and whether he cared a fig for the poor lad.

In the end, though, the tough street priest O'Dell would get the news of Ted's death in his church and become a blubbering spigot of tears.

That was the copestone. And with it finally in place in the story outline, all I really had to do was write. Which I did. Line by line. Scene by scene. Until the night before it was due I put the script in Dayna's hands and waited in the kitchen while she read it.

When she was finished, I said preemptively, "I think I'm going to get killed."

"Don't be stupid," she said, coming toward me with a big smile. "It's great. It's terrific. I only have two or three little notes."

It would have made no matter what she said, actually, but when she pointed out merely two or three places where she suggested I change punctuation, her lack of objectivity was plainly, if sweetly, apparent.

"There's a Russian proverb: 'The first pancake is never good,' " I said, waving my script after we went over it. "This is my first pancake. And they're gunning for me."

"This is like hell week at some fraternity. They're trying to wear you down. You were a terrific writer back in New York—it's not like suddenly you're not a terrific writer anymore. You're the smartest guy I ever met. I mean, what other television writer reads French literature in his spare time? Look at how you just sat down and wrote a spec script and got it to Ostrow and Werner and out of all the hundreds of scripts they're on the phone to you. Don't you realize you've got twice the brains all these other people have?"

I just looked at her levelly, trying to say in my look that even if what she said were so, none of that mattered, that out here you could be a certifiable moron, and a felon to boot, you could be a sociopath or have to consult your astrologer before picking a urinal, but the only legal tender was the quality of your pages and not your character or IQ or what your eating club was at Princeton and that was actually a good thing.

And after a moment she put her hand upon my chest and rubbed soothingly over where my heart was and she said: "I love you. Doesn't that help?"

"Of course it does," I said, but the words raked across my heart like a lie.

AFTER HANDING IN MY SCRIPT, I RETREATED TO MY OFFICE IN SEARCH OF SOME brief, prefunereal moment of satisfaction at having finished constructing the pyramid beneath which I would soon be buried. At least I had delivered it. And there was something good in that.

There I sat, knowing that Mark's secretary Liz would instantly make a copy for Mark to read and next take the script to Xeroxing, where roughly two hundred copies of my work would be made and circulated to everybody I currently knew in Hollywood, including everybody who had any say over my career, all the way up to Carlin Alemo. Beneath me, the floor vibrated with the sudden exertions of the Xerox room. The huge, computerized animal had come to life and was now spitting out and stapling my draft, collating it in a bin. Runners were taking piles of copies in their hands and dashing across the parking lot to the editorial building, the soundstage, the wardrobe trailer, the prop truck, delivering it to the drivers in the Transportation Department who would take it over to the network headquarters.

Below me, through the floor, I could hear the Xerox machine booming: Ca-chunk-a ca-chunk-a ca-chunk-a.

I wanted to be able to wait there calm and self-assured, knowing that the machine was stamping out something that would be met with hosannas.

Instead, within minutes I was on the freeway and turning into the dirt parking lot of a local amusement center where there was a batting cage. And soon I was pressing a helmet onto my head, hefting a bat, and standing in at the plate waiting for the ball to come rocketing at me. The constant rhythm of the incoming ball and the flailing bat could block all other concerns from my mind. There was just me making occasionally solid contact. Just me and that ball spitting at me and the memory of a time long ago when I'd triumphed. When I'd come through in a pinch.

It was a high school game against our archrivals. The bottom of the last inning. The bases were loaded. Two were out. We were down 1–0. And suddenly the coach was motioning for me to pinch-hit.

It was a freezing day in early April. I was cold. My hands felt like wet newspaper. I picked up a bat and stood in. The count reached 3–2, and part of me stood there, even at that moment, almost wryly observing myself in such a mythic situation. A big part of me prayed the pitcher might throw an obvious wild one for ball four and force in the tying run.

But no such luck. I remember his face as he threw. He was more terrified than I was. Terrified of throwing a ball, he had aimed the pitch. It came in high and inside, possibly a ball but too close, I quickly decided, not to swing at.

So I swung. And I hit it. Nothing great, but a solidly spanked ground ball raising dirt as it shot by the pitcher's mound. And I could see the distant shortstop rushing to his left, then waving at the ball as it disappeared into center field for a clean hit. Two runs, the winning runs, scored.

I stood on first calmly, somehow not surprised. My teammates mobbed me.

I stayed at the batting cage for an hour. It was the only person or thing or activity in the vast desert–turned–shopping mall into which I'd moved that offered even the least chance of shoring me up while Mark Werner sat in his office deciding my fate. Rapping out baseballs. Listening to the whoosh from the pitching machine and seeing the ball expelled toward me, hissing as it came, and then stepping into it, occasionally making sweet contact, remembering my great moment. Finally, when the blisters on my hands were too raw to continue swinging, it was time to go back to the office and see just how much real pain I could take.

I drove back onto the lot and trudged upstairs. I headed down to Mark's office and up to Liz's desk.

"Has he read it yet?" I asked her.

"Could be," she said. I knocked and opened his door and stood, heart thumping, on the threshold, not daring to draw any nearer. Mark was sitting at his desk, not facing me. I didn't want to enter, instead just stood there and said with as much blood in my voice as possible: "So . . . whatdya think?"

He swiveled around to face me. "Seems to be in the ballpark. We can get into the notes later."

He swiveled back away from me.

There was little to gauge from what he said. The real clue lay in what he hadn't said and in his flat tone. His message was: "I'm not thrilled." And, for those working under Mark, not thrilled and enraged were, in effect, one and the same. In fact, with each footstep down the hall, my heart sank deeper.

I turned into my office. I stopped in my tracks. It was bare.

No desk left. No couch. Denuded, the way, I instantly recalled, they told you you were fired, gone, cast out. A typhoon tore through my heart, sucking everything out of me.

So this was what they really thought of my script. I'd been cashiered.

I felt light-headed. Tears collected in my eyes. Hot, hot tears. Waxy, milky tears. I turned on my heel. I headed down the stairs. I had to get away.

There was an old Western set in the back lot, a Dodge City–type main street with the wooden false fronts of saloons and shops and a sheriff's office and a blacksmith's sitting on a dusty street lined with hitching posts. I stumbled down this street, now vacant, the only sound that of traffic on the not-too-distant freeway, and I slumped onto a bench outside a cantina.

Shortly, I saw a figure loping toward me from around the stable.

It was Ostrow. He was grinning from ear to ear as he jogged up.

"Kid . . . kid! It was a joke, for Chrissake!" he puffed. "A joke! Jeez, kid, you're not fired, willya get a sense of humor, for Chrissake?"

I had no voice at the moment to respond. It had been swallowed by injustice.

"We didn't know you'd react like that, Billy." He scrutinized me with what seemed like genuine concern and alarm. "Y'okay? It wasn't my idea, kid. Mark and Elliot're a bunch of assholes, and I told 'em so, but I didn't stop 'em, that's true. But I'd gladly go upstairs with you right now and rip their fuckin' lungs out. I don't blame you if you want to. You wanna take a swing at me? C'mon, take a poke. Stand up and let me have one. C'mon . . . be my guest."

He stuck out his chin as a target for me, planting his substance in my path, his blue eyes inviting a blow that would only have revealed even my fury wanting in effect. I tried looking off past him. Focusing on something else, something that wasn't a part of this, like a mountain or a tree. But the tears wanted to gather. They insisted.

"You gotta admit, though," Ostrow said finally, his own laughter breaking through, "we really had you going. 'Ey, c'mon, kid. . . . You wanna slug me or what?"

I finally sucked in a deep breath.

"Y'know, things haven't been so easy for me around here," I managed to say. But it felt like I was talking into a bottle, my voice was so hollow. "I'm not so stupid I don't know the score. I know the score."

"It's not about knowing the score, kid."

Ostrow paused a second.

"So whatdya wanna do now? You wanna hop on a plane and leave this hellhole behind you forever, good riddance? I've got a lot of contacts all over. I have a friend runs a mail-order house in Minneapolis. He's always looking for people to write his catalogs for him. Six figures. It's beautiful up there. It's clean. They got the Guthrie Theater. You like to hunt? I could drop a dime. You decide."

"Just beat it, okay?" I spat out.

"Sure, kid. You got it," he said.

He ambled away. And I sat there, and, while still unable to assume I'd ever rehabilitate myself enough to write another word, I at least finally managed to catch my breath and to beat back the tears.

I stayed on the Western set for a long time, staring out past the hitching post and sizing up the dimensions of my failure. There had been a duel fought here today. A gunfight almost as deadly as anything with live six-guns. Me against myself. I had summoned everything I had and every talent at my command. I had done my dead-level best and it was not good enough, not top drawer. It had been decided, the way some important things will get decided a few times in your life, try as you might to sidestep the conclusions that don't turn out your way. But from this one there was no escaping: For what I wanted and hoped to achieve I wasn't good enough. And the rest of my life would have to be a dodge.

I got up and made my way back to my office. They had put all the furniture back in. I stood there trying to decide whether I should just pack up my New York Yankees plate and my snowy skyline and move out.

Just then my phone rang.

"Yeah?" I said irritatedly.

A brusque voice at the other end spoke words that nearly knocked me over:

"Will you hold on a moment for Mr. Carlin Alemo?"

The network president! Wanting to talk to me? There had to be some mistake. I didn't know the shit could rain down from so high. Would the head of the whole network trouble himself with firing a staff writer on one of his shows? I didn't think so, but, given the nightmare I was living, it was conceivable that a precedent would be made in my case. My very existence seemed to arouse thoughts of homicide in those around me.

Soon—unbelievably—the president of the network was on the phone. The conversation was brief, but it amounted to this:

He wanted to see me as soon as possible.

Four

AS SOON AS POSSIBLE TURNED OUT TO BE THE FOLLOWING MONDAY MORNING.
Which left me all weekend to stew about the impending
meeting. What I envisioned involved a long lever by Carlin's
desk and, beneath my chair, a chute. At the bottom of the
chute? I never dreamed that far—I didn't have that much of
a future.

Dayna and I escaped town that weekend. Her best figuring
was that she was due to ovulate then. She had decided that a
romantic getaway offered the perfect prospect of insemina-
tion.

She was beginning to approach the achievement of that
miracle with an all-consuming calculation. When we'd first
begun trying to conceive, just before moving to California,
she'd greeted her periods with some nonchalance. But nonchalance had long since been replaced by the beeping of the
digital thermometer she kept on her night table. She started

buying ovulation tests, mixing up their solutions, and chart-
ing their results as if she were the Bureau of Weights and
Measures. She got to the point of figuring when the follicle
of her egg would rupture within her ovary and when that
egg would be caught by the fimbria of her fallopian tube,
thence to begin its centimeters-long, uterus-bound journey,
with the minute-by-minute precision of a space mission.

I wanted to start a family as much as Dayna. But I was a
little slow apprehending her urgency. For one thing, I was
too consumed with work. Also, Dayna characteristically
viewed all things and mentally sounded them out well before
I did. A positivist, she perpetually scanned the horizon, fixing
on all life's turning points and sighting opportunities, and she
navigated toward them. Not in a social-climbing sort of way,
but because she thought a person could make life work.

I didn't. The course I charted was a series of crazily veering
avoidance maneuvers out of the Murmansk run—rudder-
shuddering hard starboards and panic-stricken full reverses—
meant to bypass life's deadly shoals and murderous torpedoes.
The destination of my seasick meanderings? Make for that
blissful bay—viewed perpetually in the here and now as just
a sunset glow on the far side of the ocean—where one was
met at the dock by "peace of mind."

On Saturday we headed up into the mountains a few
hours outside of Los Angeles. We hadn't experienced the
countryside out West before, although I use the word
"countryside" advisedly since to neither of us did what we
were passing look like country.

This was desert. Sagebrush and bare, speckled, sandy waste
that stretched away in desolation. Far off, treeless mountains
heaved cobalt blue knuckles into the sky. Even when we
began to climb, reaching altitudes the scorching desert heat
couldn't reach, the slopes didn't display the grassy meadows
and tree-canopied bowers lush with mossy-banked brooks,
wildflowers, and vines we'd been familiar with back East, the

kinds of hillsides that beckon you to lie down and sleep for twenty years. No, these mountains weren't for nestling or drowsing. They teemed only with fir trees, brigades of which stood against the sun at stark, tense attention and failed to hold the gaze of passersby.

We finally pulled onto the mountaintop and into the town of Idyllwild in the late afternoon. Dayna had reserved a space at a hostel named, ingeniously enough, The Mountain Lodge.

My history of such accommodations in places like Vermont had been one that stretched the term "rustic" to the breaking point and rendered the word "charming" meaningless. I can still recall the cryogenic crypt into which we'd been cheerily led one leaf-season weekend near Manchester. I can almost feel to this day the lancing breath of the subzero gale that—finding the yellowed, ten-year-old want ads section of the *Bennington Banner* an ineffectual plug in the cracked Thermopane window—threatened to leave me with frostbite of the ear as I shivered in my squeaky bunk all night, my limbs entwined and braided upon themselves like some Eastern European pastry.

Those New England inns were also invariably vast storehouses of unswept cat dander. I was acutely allergic to cats. After only a few minutes spent inhaling dust and pet fur, I'd wind up in need of an iron lung. And the remainder of my weekend would be spent fighting off pulmonary edema and desperately pounding late at night on the shuttered doors of rural pharmacies, grabbing at stunned druggists' lapels and demanding with felonlike vehemence that they promptly empty their stores of all epinephrine and that if they mentioned I didn't have a prescription again I'd burn their testicles off with a hot stick.

The Mountain Lodge of Idyllwild promised a much more comfortable respite. We were shown to a spacious, clean, unattached log bungalow with its own fireplace and kitchen.

Dayna must have seen me standing in the doorway and gap-
ing at the colorful appointments—the twin bentwood rocking chairs, the shelves of hardcover volumes and carved
bookends, the hooked rugs, the antique photographs, the
quilted comforter on the bed. As the porter stowed our bags,
Dayna whispered to me with satisfaction, "Isn't it great we
can afford this?" She smoothly folded a lavish tip into the
porter's palm. It was a show of plenitude, as if that might
fool the future into thinking we were fruitful in all things.
The nineteen-year-old tucked away the ten-spot and left.
The little metal latch on the door clinked closed, and we
stood frozen for that odd moment in the porter's wake when
you have to begin living life all over again.

We spent a few hours tramping around, relaxing,
lunching. Then we hiked. The sun fell low in the sky and so
cast a less unseemly light on the landscape, not showing up
its starkness so much. The shadows of the tall fir trees length-
ened until their hatch-work bars of blue-gray covered the
hillsides, lending the hollows a solemn but much less inhos-
pitable cast.

"We should do this every season," Dayna said as we as-
cended the trail. It wasn't very daunting. But in spots we
were forced to find sure footholds and to wedge upward on
hand and dusty knee. "Something physical and outdoors."

She awaited a response. Women always do.

"A getaway," I grunted, clambering up beside her.

"Remember when we went trout fishing and you hooked
your head?"

All too well. It was one of Dayna's Outward Bound canoe
expeditions, a vestige of her childhood in the countryside
around the Columbia River. On the second day, perhaps
revealing my lack of familiarity with the intricacies of Zen
fly casting, I nearly found my way into the sport's annals
when I offered a monster steelhead I'd seen rising across
the river a furry two-inch strip of my scalp. He must have

thought it the mother of all caterpillars. He took it in one huge gulp. Unfortunately, I dropped the rod. I was yelping in pain. The trout worked out the hook in seconds.

"The wind gusted."

"Come on, you hooked your head. And then you made us hitch into town to see a doctor. Remember that one-armed drunk who picked us up? Screaming about how his wife was cheating on him and he was going to settle the score? Lighting cigarettes and steering with his stump?"

Dayna laughed.

"Why is me almost bleeding to death the high point of your life?"

The trail was narrow here, falling away sharply to our right. Up to the left, far atop the bald peak of a mountain, I could make out the swaying shadows of two climbers on rope belays. The wind piped through the trees. I tried to forget Hollywood and Ostrow and Dayna shouting that she wanted to leave me. I stood next to Dayna on an out-cropping above the valley. I put my arm around her to show her I was glad we'd come. She smiled fleetingly my way, then looked off, and I realized she was preoccupied by other concerns the way I was.

"Billy, remember that day we went up to Santa Barbara and we went to the beach and we stood out on those rocks and then we ate at that restaurant right on the sand?"

"Yeah."

"We wrote down everything we wanted to do if we got pregnant? How you couldn't wait to go sledding? And I wanted to get ice cream cones?"

"I remember, sure."

"Well, I figured it out. That was in early August."

"Yeah. What about it?"

"How many weeks is that? All the way back to August."

"I don't know—twelve, fourteen?"

Her arm dropped away from my shoulder.

"Well, I haven't looked at the napkin I wrote on since then."

"You still have it?"

"It's in my drawer. Right there . . . every time I open it up. But I don't read it. I've stopped fantasizing about being pregnant. I know I plan this and that and I take those tests . . . but I can't imagine a future with a baby in my arms anymore. It hurts too much. The last time I looked out the window and tried to see us doing all those things on the list . . . I saw somebody else with somebody else's baby. Someone luckier than we are."

We were standing on a granite ledge that overlooked the range and, below, the fir-fringed bowl formed by the mountainside from the bottom of which the church steeples of Idyllwild village poked. Above, in a nearly cloudless blue sky, hawks wheeled over the valley.

We stood there for several minutes, me gripping her in my strengthless arms.

"We've got to give it a little more time," I said.

It almost seemed as if she didn't hear me.

"Let's do more of this," she said. "Okay?"

We drove into the village that night for dinner. Although not a ski town, this was an alpine retreat, so it was dotted with the requisite number of crummy pasta-and-beer joints with Chianti bottles in wicker containers hanging from shiny, shellacked pine crossbeams. At least the one we chose had a fireplace in the corner.

Complying with my doctor's orders, I ignored the wine list. I asked for a Diet 7UP, not even a Diet Coke, which I would have preferred, because I'd been told 7UP didn't have any phosphates to upset my stomach.

"Are you relaxing, cookie?" Dayna asked while I sipped my soda.

"Trying to."

"Maybe if you didn't try so hard, you would. You look

like you're about to explode. Are you aware that your eyeballs keep darting all over the place and your nostrils keep
flaring? Relax your eyebrows."

"Spending a weekend right before you think you're about
to be fired by the president of the network isn't the best way
to relax." I picked up some toasted bread slathered with
butter, garlic, and melted cheese. "I hope this is okay for me
to eat," I muttered glumly.

"You can be such a pill," she said, shaking her head.

I look back now and realize how right she was. I should
have been joking, goofing, clowning. Making her laugh.

Anything to bring a smile to her face. Dayna's smile was
electrifying. She has an angular, questioning face dominated
by those brown eyes and a wide mouth, and when she smiles
it's as if a dozen immense crystal chandeliers have been
switched on in a grand ballroom.

Once, we were returning to our Manhattan apartment in
the late afternoon and we passed a sad old man who lived in
our neighborhood. He was listlessly walking his arthritic little
terrier. Dayna stooped to pet it and then looked up at its
dyspeptic owner and smiled that smile and I watched decades
melt away from the old man. His eyes glowed probably like
they hadn't in fifty years, since he'd tangoed till dawn with
a paramour at some long-since-vanished rooftop nightclub.
Dayna smiled at him and he heard Dorsey again. His heart
awoke and pounded against his sunken chest and his saggy
balls snapped and his blood licked at extremities it hadn't
washed in years. And he grinned toothlessly back at her and
turned to me and said merrily: "She smiles with her eyes."

And I knew what he was telling me, that I was the luckiest
man in the world to bask in such a smile.

Dayna leaned forward across the table. "What do you say
we make a nice fire back in our room after dinner? I brought
a bottle of champagne. Ostrow sent it when you were hired.
A little alcohol. Just this once."

"Fine," I said.

"You look like Mr. Universe tonight."

I saw what direction the conversation was taking.

She resumed, in a low, suggestive tone: "How are you feeling?"

"I'm not sure."

"You're not sure?"

"I'm not sure if my dick is still down there," I said. "Maybe it's not on anymore. Maybe it fell off back at work. I ought to hire somebody to trail around after me with one of those Igloo ice chests. So after they cut if off we can store it in there, you know? Get it surgically reattached."

"Microsurgery." She smirked.

"Good joke."

I took another sip of soda.

"Do you think you can do it twice in one night?" she whispered.

"Twice?" I tried not to sigh. The great male boast—nightlong capability—had never really pertained to me. As a rule, after showing up to honor its end of the contract just once, my spent member entered the federal witness protection program disguised as a circus dwarf.

Dayna apprehended my uncertainty.

"Well, two times is better than once. I can feel the ovulation cramps right now in my lower back. If we can do it once when we get back to our room and again at about four or five in the morning, it should be perfect."

"Four or five in the morning? Am I allowed one night's sleep on the one weekend off I get before I'm fired?"

"Fine, we don't have to do it at all, Billy. You go ahead and get your sleep, and we'll forget about having a baby. I'm the only one making an effort around here anyway." She blinked her hard, angry blink at me. "I could sit here and complain just like you. At least you have a career to complain about. I get up every day and take around my portfolio. But do I walk around crying because nobody's patting me on the back? 'Boo-hoo. Life is terrible, I'm terrible. How do you expect me to come home, a big failure in my career, and try to make a baby?' "

We glared at each other in the candlelight, and then I threw my new platinum credit card on the table.

SHE'D PLAYED SOFTBALL WITH OUR MAGAZINE TEAM ONE BRIGHT, SINGING AFTERnoon in Central Park. The *Matte-Finish Tile* gang had gone out for drinks afterwards and, later, for more partying in the loft owned by one of the commercial photographers who worked for our book. And just like that we'd crumpled together on the hallway floor of his studio, locked in deep kissing, friends literally stepping over us as we lay there swooning, discovering the new feeling that we'd known each other our whole lives.

Now she fairly hissed at me in a strangled voice as we drove back from the restaurant to our mountain lodge. "You complain because I force us to have sex on a schedule. But it seems like you don't ever want to do it at all. Forget about my chart. Couldn't we have sex tonight just because it's fun?"

Dayna was a plain speaker, and she was unused to shaded sarcasms or taunts when she raved. But she was getting plenty of chances to practice. She looked off out the car window, fuming and trying to contain herself. But she went on. "You have become such a drag. Either you're consumed with your work or you're holed up in the den not answering the phone, not talking, too tired to go anywhere or do anything, reading some fop like Rousseau. You know what? Take me out. Take me bowling. Let's shoot some pool or go to a party for a change. I want to have fun. Let's go Rollerblading. Let's go to a rock club and dance and get drunk and go home and fuck and maybe then I'll get pregnant."

The rest of the ride was silent. We didn't speak because

that would further foul the already fouled business at hand. Back in our room, Dayna exited the bathroom in that "lucky" pink Tufts T-shirt of hers, then removed it and lay on the bed in a lacy black bra she'd obviously bought for this romantic weekend. I undressed and got into bed beside her and listened for the call of her body, of her large, untanned breasts and the port of sweet oils between her legs.

But all I heard was the distracting, soul-flaying cacophony of voices from work. Doom lay across me.

I was dead, not susceptible to touch or thought, and when, sensing that, Dayna took me into her mouth to urge me, I was not susceptible to that either.

I threw off the covers and bounded upright and began banging my head against the wall and slapping my skull with my fist in an orgasm of fury and loathing. Then I slumped down on the bed.

"I hate this," I said wearily after a while. "It's not you, you know. It's just . . . always having to perform."

"How do you think I feel?" she said, tears beginning to roll down her cheeks. "I plan everything, but I try not to tell you about it so you don't get nervous. I'm afraid anything I say will set you off, so I walk around on eggshells. And then, look what happens. You think I like this?"

We sat there in the dimness for a long time, rubbed utterly raw. Dayna fell silent. Luckily for me. Dismasted as I was at work, I was at least spared her spoken recriminations for its equivalent between the sheets.

I looked over to her when she'd stopped crying.

"Let's try it again," I said, hoping to hide as I spoke the bland resolve of a teamster trying to rock his truck's rear wheel out of a muddy ditch.

So, since passion and desire and love had about as much to do with what was at hand as branding a steer, we persisted. I tried and tried and I banged my skull against the wall, and after an hour I bucked my seed inside her. And fresh from that joyless victory she set to work: She tilted her hips and legs way over her head, propping her backside up with cushions. A chastening, fearful silence rained down upon us at first as she lay there in that awful, ungainly position. And then a strange thing happened amidst our wrenching desolation—we began, once more, to hope.

THE HALLWAY LEADING TO CARLIN ALEMO'S OFFICE WAS LONG AND GRAND enough for a king. Which Carlin no doubt was. He had taken over control of the network a few years earlier and had begun making it profitable. Even more incredibly, he had made it also critically noteworthy. He had shown uncommon patience with so-called quality shows—such as *Under the Law*—which had mortally low viewership when they premiered but which he left on the air until they found an audience. And lo and behold, in some instances they did, and Alemo had begun getting a reputation as a man of some taste, a man of parts, an urbane Federico, duke of Urbino, amidst the meaner duchies of the other network kingdoms.

To his court countless writers and producers caravaned to pitch their ideas for new shows, hoping he would consent to produce their ideas, hoping ultimately to make it on the air, becoming one of the hour dramas or half-hour situation comedies that got everybody rich.

I spent a nerve-racking five minutes nestled in a leather armchair in his anteroom trying to gain control over my extremities, lips, and tongue. A forest fire had been eating its way through my innards ever since I'd awakened that morning. I was farting flame in the car the whole way over. My mouth was starting to feel paralyzed, devoid of suppleness. I'd barely been able to mumble "hello" and my name when approaching his receptionist.

One conclusion about the intention of this meeting jostled all others out of my mind. The scenario I invented went something like this: So colossal a failure had I turned out to be, so deformed was the sixty-page baby I had given birth to, that my hiring called into question Mark Werner's ability to administer his own show. Perhaps Carlin had some feud under way with Mark and I was good ammunition. Maybe not. Still, in the television world I was the equivalent of some crime against nature, some sideshow freak, and therefore an object of intense curiosity in immediate need of study before being put to death and disposed of.

At best, perhaps I was a joke. Carlin probably hated Mondays. He probably had asked me in to get his week off to an amusing start. He'd close the door after meeting me and shake his head and call his friends. One night later this week, he'd probably sit at a window table at Spago with Werner himself, the establishment's most expensive cabernet gushing out of their noses as they shared tales of my ineptitude. Well, perhaps my sudden speech difficulty would add to his amusement.

I sat there trying to relax my mouth with exercises, the way I'd seen actors do on our set.

"Mraaaaaaww . . . Mraaaaaww . . . Yi yi yi yi yi," I said as quietly as possible to myself lest Carlin's secretary overhear and have the security guards called. I was plying my mouth this way when I heard the secretary say, "Mr. Ziff, Mr. Alemo will see you now," and I stood and trudged toward my fate.

Alemo's office was becomingly unostentatious. Its trappings bespoke corporate prudence. There was the corner sofa–and–coffee table setup, soft Berber carpeting, a mahogany bookcase. A large painting dominated the wall above the sofas. It was one of those grave postmodern ones composed in grays and browns, this one consisting of a figure—or was it a bicycle pump?—seeming to step beyond a black door and into a blob of light.

Carlin Alemo came around his desk to greet me. He was

a smallish, well-scrubbed man. Pictures of him don't tend to capture a certain bouncy quality he radiates. He wore a beige sweater thrown over his shoulders, and a night blue button-down shirt displaying the studied ruralism of the Ralph Lauren line tucked into dark khaki slacks. Smallish blue eyes and tortoiseshell glasses. Some people think he looks a bit chipmunkish, but the thing I found most distinctive about his features was his jutting, enthusiastic jaw.

Carlin was the quintessence of cordiality, sporting a pleasant smile and an unlined, well-tanned face that made him look even younger than he was. He was thirty-eight. His brownish blond wisps of hair were brushed across his high forehead, which appeared to have gotten a little too much sun over the weekend.

He took my hand in a firm grip. Lucky, I thought, that my hand was somehow dry at that moment. I'd expected to present him with the sensation of plunging his paw into a fishbowl.

Carlin pointed me to the couch, ordered some mineral water for us on his intercom, and pulled up a chair opposite me.

"I've wanted to meet you ever since you went to work for Mark," he said, being nothing but friendly. He had a high, nasal voice. "I don't make that my business with all our shows, but at *Under the Law* I figure anyone working there is someone I ought to know. How long've you been there now?"

"About six months," I said. I wondered to myself if that was enough weeks to get unemployment insurance.

"Uh-huh." He nodded. That seemed to be important to him.

His office door opened, and in came his secretary with our drinks. Two other people bustled in right behind, and Carlin introduced them as Thad Tittle, the network's director of prime-time something, and Joan Silvester, who was the vice president of some other kind of something. Thad was a larger, darker, more rotund sort than Carlin. He wore jacket and tie. Joan was tall, almost my height, with long raven locks that stretched down her back. As Thad and Joan took seats on the sofa opposite me, I grabbed a swallow of water and prepared myself for trying to talk. Somewhere inside me a voice began advising that were I about to be fired, these onlookers would not have been asked to attend. But that presupposed some common decency.

"Bill was just saying he's been at *Under the Law* for six months," Carlin said. His director and vice president for somethings nodded friendly smiles. He looked back at me.

"You enjoying it there?"

My mouth managed to work. "So far. It's been an incredible learning experience for me."

"Mark's great," Carlin said.

"Great," Thad agreed.

"Absolutely the best," Joan said.

"Terrific." I nodded, smearing myself with offal.

"He can be a goddam butt-busting sonofabitch sometimes." Carlin chuckled.

Thad and Joan chuckled.

"But I respect that," Carlin said.

"He can be exacting," I said.

"Exacting," Carlin said with a bigger chuckle. "Good one."

"And where did you work before Mark hired you?" Thad quickly asked as soon as Carlin had subsided. Not for Carlin the job of eliciting my CV.

I shrugged. "Writing in New York. Some magazine work, this and that."

"So this is your first job in TV?" Carlin looked past me and briefly met Tittle's gaze.

"That's right," I said.

Carlin sat back in his chair and clasped his hands.

"I asked you here because I read your latest script. We were very interested in it."

The course of this conversation I'd thus far not been able to put my finger on, yet as they spoke I suddenly realized: I'd ceased tingling with relentless alarm, even as I scanned down the tracks trying to spot the onrushing freight train.

"I was very taken with that Reverend O'Dell character and that whole—what was it?—Dream Come True stuff," Carlin said.

"Thanks," I said, and I suddenly stopped looking for that onrushing freight train and found the voice to venture: "I just thought that was a good area for a story."

"The O'Dell character was your idea?"

"Yes, that was. I don't know, I thought it would be interesting to have a priest, especially one like that—you know, a cynic."

Carlin nodded and smiled. "We agree. We liked the situation very much. I thought he was a fascinating character. Throbbing with life. Lots of stories to tell there." He paused. "Tell me, have you ever written a pilot before?"

"No," I said.

Carlin looked again at Tittle and Silvester. They were smiling.

"Let me tell you what I'm thinking," he said. "I read your script and I saw that priest and it jumped right out at me. I thought, Wow, what a great TV show!"

"Great TV show," Tittle echoed.

"Got all the makings," Silvester said.

Carlin continued, "You know, each week the story of this priest, trying to make some dying kid's wishes come true? I think there's something there." He paused, and then added with gravity: "I think there's a lot there."

"It's as pure eight o'clock as I've seen in a long time," Thad said. "It's eight o'clock dynamite."

"Or even nine o'clock," Joan said.

"Maybe nine," Thad said.

"I don't even rule out ten," Carlin said, with a thoughtful tilt of his head. "Doesn't have to be just kids dying, y'know."

"Everybody dies. Better." Thad nodded, scrunching the flesh above his tight collar.

"Pick your demos," Joan said. "I'd love ten o'clock. Smashville, USA."

I sat there for a moment. I felt dizzy. And then, somehow, words started coming out.

"I obviously didn't write it with the idea of a series in mind, but actually I think there's a lot there too. I mean, you know there *are* a lot of stories to explore. Great stories. And against that you have O'Dell, getting tougher and tougher and crankier to avoid the pain."

"Good idea," Thad burbled.

"We can get the rights to the foundation's name," Joan announced, then offered, "if you want it. I just got off the phone with them."

"I'm not sure," I said. Somehow, saying those words made me feel strong in my shoulders. And then I realized: I'd made an executive decision.

"That can come later," Carlin said. "For now here's what I'd like you to do: I'd like you to write a pilot for us that hopefully we can shoot and you can produce for the network. I'm thinking one hour, probably not two, huh?"

"Probably one." Thad nodded.

"Yeah. Anyway," Carlin said, "how does that sound?"

It sounded a lot better than The boss thinks you're a wanker. And tons better than Who the hell wrote this shit?

"Sounds good," I managed.

"Do you think you'll have time to fit this in while you're at *Under the Law*?"

"I don't see why not." I shrugged.

"Fair enough," Carlin said. "And when you've got some story ideas ready, we can sit down and spitball. Okay?"

"Great."

"Great." Carlin smiled and he stood up. We all stood up and smiled at each other.

"Great," Thad said.

"Great," Joan said.

We shook hands.

"I think we've really got something here," he said. The crinkles beside his eyeballs were taut with sincerity.

"Thanks," I said.

I said good-bye and hustled down that long hallway.

I hadn't been fired after all.

Five

HE LAY WHERE HE'D FALLEN. ON THE WOODEN FLOOR OF HIS TINY STUDIO, halfway between his sagging foldout cot and the bathroom, toward which he'd been lurching when he must have tripped over something. The ottoman. He could feel it with his foot.

He'd been dreaming. Of a lakeshore. And of light. Of water gently lapping. And of his family, mainly his brother Sean: in white slacks and rolled-up white shirt, the boater at a jaunty angle on his head as he strolled slowly toward him across the sand, arm outstretched in greeting, the strands of Sean's black hair outlined against the pale tufts of dune along the shore behind him. And in that dream of light and watersong and Sean came the distant drumming of the war his brother had gone off to fight in and never come home from. The war he'd joined as well, but not to fight: to kneel over the shattered fallen and usher them beyond the pale of violence.

The violet light of a neon sign blinked in through the wooden shutters. It fell across the rickety card table and onto the worn gray rug by his bed and finally onto his damp brow. Through the gloom and the liquor daze that swaddled his head, he could not see the clock on the table. He knew it was the middle of the night, though, sensed something was calling him to get up. But movement was difficult. He ran his tongue across his parched, tacky palate. Try to wake up. Below the room's sole window, the metal radiator began its wretched bugling, emitting a few gasps of weak heat that were of little use against the chill enfolding him. He rolled over and a sick feeling roiled his gut and suddenly he realized what had summoned him to his senses: the phone.

He crawled toward it on the chilly floor. He sat up against the bed and grasped a tall, thin green bottle. He flipped the cork out with his thumb and took a mouthful of whiskey. Warmth spread down his gullet and into his gut, and his mouth was suddenly smoothed.

"Yeah?" he rasped into the phone receiver none too cordially. Whoever was calling ought to know it was late. He felt something cool and runny on his head. Bringing his fingers down from his scalp, he saw blood.

"Father," the caller said in a tremulous, faint voice over the phone. "Is this Father O'Dell? They gave me your number."

"This is Father O'Dell," he croaked, feeling around for more blood.

"It's about my boy Eddie," the woman's voice said. "The doctors . . . he's sick, very sick. . . ." The voice dissolved into choking sobs, finally shuddering out the word: "Cancer."

Father Joey O'Dell took a long pull of Jameson's and settled back against his mattress in the dark.

"A filthy disease," he said. "A goddam pestilence." He took another pull on his whiskey and let out a sigh. "What can I do for your dying boy?"

"Fantastic!"

"Fabulous!"

Thad Tittle and Joan Silvester looked up from the script pages I'd given them. Their cheeks glowed with admiration. They were the first two people, other than Dayna, to read what I'd done with Joey O'Dell, to see how I'd brought him to life in the pilot of the show I was creating. I'm not saying their reaction is anything on a par with Vasco da Gama's first sight of the Indian Ocean or, say, the moment in 1933 when, crossing a London street, physicist Leo Szilard first construed the possibility of sustainable nuclear chain reactions and an atomic bomb, but I will say that *TV Guide* once called this meeting a "historic moment."

"I've not seen anything like this on network television," Thad said excitedly.

"I love the choices you made," Joan said.

We were in Thad's office, across the hall from Carlin's. Thad and Joan sat there reading and avidly sucking down little bottles of Evian. The more they liked what they read, the more absently they felt for the bottles. The feline Joan tucked her legs beneath her on the sofa as she went along. She swatted her bangs from her forehead.

"I'm sorry, Father, I have no pass here. Without any authorization I can't let you through."

The MP looked down at Father Joey O'Dell from his guard shack.

"Son, God doesn't need a pass. I'm asking you to make an exception."

"I'm sorry, Father. Have you tried calling our community affairs officer? He could help you get authorization."

"I've got the highest authorization there is, my son."

And with that, Reverend O'Dell jammed his jeep into gear and it lunged forward, snapping the wooden gate in two.

"HALT! Stop right there!" the MP bellowed as O'Dell roared by. The sentry unsheathed his holster and drew a bead on the accelerating jeep. But before he could squeeze the trigger, a fellow MP knocked his arm downward. "What're you, crazy? You can't go shooting a priest, for Chrissake!"

"Any unauthorized entry onto base shall be met with force!" the MP said, reciting the rules.

"I still say you can't just plug a priest like that."

The two of them stood there watching the jeep head toward headquarters. The MP uncocked his gun and reholstered it.

"I'm gonna be court-martialed for sure," he said.

Around an oval mahogany conference table some of the navy's top brass were in ultrasecret strategic discussions. Suddenly the door to the room burst open.

Father Joey O'Dell stood in the doorway.

"Which one of you is Admiral Broughton?" he demanded, advancing toward the table.

The assembled brass looked up in bewilderment.

"Who the hell are you and who let you in here?" one of the admirals thundered.

"I let myself in here because that's the only way to get your attention. I'm Father O'Dell from the Dream Come True Foundation."

Torrents of soldiers, their guns drawn, rushed into the conference room and seized Father O'Dell.

"I've called and written twenty times," the pastor said as the soldiers began dragging him out.

"Hold on a second there," one of the admirals said suddenly. "Let him go."

The soldiers quickly unhanded him. The room fell silent. An imposing, florid-faced man with rows upon rows of medals stood up.

"I'm Admiral 'Blackie' Broughton, Father," he said. "Is this about that young boy . . . whatsisname? With that crazy request?"

"His name is Eddie Manzari, Admiral," Father O'Dell said. "And he may only have weeks to live."

"I sympathize," Admiral "Blackie" Broughton said, "but there are simply no regulations in the United States Navy permitting an unauthorized ten-year-old civilian to captain a billion-dollar nuclear submarine. The only person who could authorize such a request would be the president of the United States himself, the commander in chief."

Around the table the other admirals snickered derisively.

Father O'Dell advanced to the table and leaned in close, close enough so that some of the brass might have been able to smell the liquor on his breath. The woolly brows above his dark eyes clashed as he thrust his chin down toward the sitting officers. He picked up a red telephone on the table and dropped it with a ringing thud in front of the surprised Admiral Broughton.

"Then I suggest you call him, big shot," he said.

UNLESS YOU SPENT THE LAST THREE YEARS LOST AT SEA AND GUZZLING YOUR OWN urine to survive, you know that scene, the one *Entertainment Weekly* called "epic." Chances are you can even recite the lines. But for those deprived souls who missed it, I thought it only fair to reprise the pilot script.

"My only note, really my only one," Joan said. "Maybe when O'Dell breaks through the gates, they could actually shoot at him. I think there's a real opportunity there for some action. You know, gunshots, he swerves his car around, bangs some other cars. It depends on how eight o'clock we want to go."

Thad nodded gravely, in measured agreement. "Let's not sell a young audience short. Maybe he's hit, the car rolls over and explodes, bursts into flame, one of those fireball-whoosh things. He crawls out of the wreckage—y'know, bullets still flying, puzatt, puzatt, be-wang, bodabodabodaboda—cut to the admirals' office, blood dripping from his arm but he's still pounding the table, wincing in pain, fighting for that poor little dying kid."

"Something to think about." I nodded.

"CAN I TAKE HER DOWN NOW?" EDDIE MANZARI BEAMED HIS DARK EYES HOPE-fully up at the gruff old medal-bedecked sailor, Admiral Broughton. Beside him, by the conning tower of the USS *Flint,* stood Reverend O'Dell, the ship's captain, and other executive officers. It was nearly dark inside the sub's control room, the only lights those that flashed from the sur-rounding, pinging instrument panels and sonar screens. The light from little Eddie's eyes was the brightest of all.

"Anytime you say, son," the crusty old admiral said.

Eddie looked over at Reverend O'Dell. Joey O'Dell nodded.

"Okay. Take 'er down," Eddie commanded.

"Yes, sir," the admiral said, saluting Eddie.

"Aye-aye, sir," the sub commander said. He hit some buttons, and a siren commenced blaring, and in the distance sailors could be heard shouting: "Dive, dive." And the sub began rattling and thrumming.

Eddie's features were incandescent with the thrill of it all. And soon someone shouted: "Depth fifty meters, Eddie."

Eddie looked over at O'Dell, who smiled at him.

"Level 'er off," Eddie commanded.

"Aye-aye, Captain Manzari," the captain responded.

"Leveling off at one hundred meters, Captain," said a voice from the shadows by the control boards.

"Good work, son," Admiral Broughton said, draping his

arm over Eddie's shoulders. He fitted a submarine commander's dark blue cap over Eddie's head.

"Son, there's someone special who'd like to talk to you," said Admiral Broughton, and he nodded toward the instrument panels. Within seconds, a swabbie had brought a telephone to Eddie's ear, and the tinny sound was piped over the loudspeakers:

"Hello, Eddie, this is the president of the United States."

"Gosh, good morning, Mr. President." Eddie glowed.

"How do you like the ride down there? Pretty smooth, is it?"

"It's just swell, sir," Eddie said.

"Glad to hear it. Glad to hear it, son. Now, Eddie, you make sure the crew follows your orders to a T."

"They gave me a hat, Mr. President."

"Great, Eddie. I'm hereby making you an honorary member of the submarine corps. Now, I have one direct order for you as your commander in chief. I want you to do what your mom and the doctors tell you."

"Aye-aye, Mr. President."

"And one final order, Eddie: Promise me you'll never give up."

"I promise, sir."

"Good. Well, I've got to go now. I've got a pesky Congress to deal with. Good-bye, Eddie."

"Good-bye, Mr. President."

The grown men in the dark, hard-bitten sailors all, had lumps in their throats as Eddie handed off the phone.

"Wow!" Eddie exclaimed.

Father O'Dell pulled a handkerchief from his pocket and passed it over Eddie's head to Admiral Broughton. The old salt nodded gratefully and daubed at his eyes surreptitiously so none of his subordinates would see.

Eddie was having a ball.

"Up periscope," he commanded.

"Aye-aye, sir." The call went out. And quickly the steel sheathing slid upward. Eddie gripped its handlebars and peered into the scope.

"Wow!" he exclaimed. "This is so neat! There's a big freighter on the horizon, Father. I bet he has no idea we're down here."

Eddie continued surveying the sea surface, swiveling the periscope to sweep 360 degrees, his small knuckles whitening as they gripped the conning bars.

Suddenly, Eddie's grip loosened. His arm dangled at his side. His small body swayed.

Back onshore, Eddie's mother waited anxiously for her son's return as the sub tied up at its mooring. Behind her, as a precaution, an ambulance waited, its motor idling, its siren lights twirling. She squinted up at the dark bulk of the ship, looking for her boy.

Then she caught sight of Reverend O'Dell, walking solemnly down the gangplank, carrying Eddie's limp body like a badly wrapped parcel. As he got closer, the men from the ambulance scrambled into action.

Reverend O'Dell carried Eddie toward the ambulance as, behind him, gruff old "Blackie" Broughton fought back his emotions, stopping by Mrs. Manzari. Admiral Broughton stood at attention, tears running down his cheeks, his broad shoulders heaving, as the men in white took Eddie. He snapped a salute as the ambulance roared away and then turned to Eddie's mom. "I've served with a lot of brave sailors, ma'am," "Blackie" Broughton said, "but your son there is the bravest I've ever known."

THE JAMESON'S SPLASHED OUT OF THE SHOT GLASS AND OVER THE CHEWED BLACK oak bar top. Joey O'Dell topped off yet another drink. It was two in the morning, and the bar was empty now save for .

Paddy O'Binion, who mopped up the tattered linoleum floor behind Father O'Dell. He lifted a chair and turned it upside down on the tabletop and shook his head at his good friend O'Dell's quivering hand as he poured himself his drink.

"This'n musta been a corker, huh, Father?" Paddy asked.

Reverend O'Dell threw the drink down his throat and let out a sigh.

"No more'n the last one, no less'n the next."

He poured himself another.

"Man of the cloth shouldn't be drinkin' the way you do, Father, if you don't mind me sayin'."

"Oh, and why shouldn't I, Paddy?"

The portly Irishman wiped his hands on his soiled apron. "It just don't seem right is all." He wielded his mop once more.

"Right?" Father O'Dell swiveled around on his creaky red-leather-topped stool. "Right? You want to tell me what the devil right is? Throwin' a party for one of those little ones, takin' 'em to meet their favorite movie star or ball-player or ridin' a submarine before you kneel down to give 'em last rites?"

He threw back another shot and wiped his mouth with the back of his hand. "What a funny word that is. There ain't no right. Ain't no such thing."

He took a long pull on the bottle.

"That's just the liquor talkin'. You better pray the good Lord don't hear you sayin' such things."

"Screw the good Lord, Paddy."

And with that O'Dell angrily hurled his shot glass against the wall. It shattered into a thousand pieces.

O'Binion gasped in shock. Father O'Dell staggered to his feet. He grabbed the whiskey bottle and began weaving his way out of the saloon.

"Good Lord's as good as you say, he'll tolerate a complaint from a drunken servant. How much I owe you?"

"It's on the house, Father," Paddy O'Binion said.

"Well, let's call it the good Lord's tab."

"Where you goin'?"

"Chat with my Maker, Paddy. Chat with my Maker."

And, bottle in hand, Reverend Joey O'Dell banged through the swinging bar door and out into the night.

"I CAN'T BELIEVE IT, I'M ACTUALLY WEEPING," JOAN SAID, LOOKING UP AS SHE closed the script. "Feel." She grabbed Thad's hand and pressed it to her cheek. "My eyes are wet." She reached for the Evian bottle but knocked it over, soaking Thad's couch.

"Very strong. Very strong," Thad said, clearing his throat and putting down the script. He looked up. "You've got one helluva series here. Standards and Practices may ask you to tone down the booze and the 'screw the Lord' stuff, but never mind. You should feel very good about it."

"Thank you. I do. It feels like it's popping, you know?"

I couldn't believe they were reacting this well. Even looking back on it now, knowing how positively everyone else reacted.

"Oh, absolutely popping," said Joan, daubing at her eyes with a hankie.

"So what's the next step?"

"Next step," Thad said, "is we get Carlin's notes on the script. Hopefully, it'll be nothing major, just a few tweaks and potchkes. But, it's Carlin, so—"

He shrugged and looked over at Joan.

"So who knows," she said, translating the shrug. "He's totally unpredictable. We never know what he'll like. And he hates a lot more than he likes."

"Uh-huh." I didn't like the sound of that.

"But, really, there's no use worrying about it," said Thad. "Meanwhile, let's roll the snowball a little. Casting: Let's come up with some Joey O'Dells."

"I'll get the script to Cissy Storm, she's our casting person," Joan said. "Let's let her draw up an availability list."

"Why not," Thad said.

He stood up. The meeting was over. I stood to shake their hands.

"With a little luck we're gonna own the night," Thad said, pumping my hand and smiling. "Start looking for houses."

"You're a great writer," Joan said.

When all the mania was at its zenith, I got a letter from a fan in Jessup, Md., asking me to describe Thad's office and if the details of this encounter were accurate as reported. It seems he was constructing a homemade museum dedicated to the series right behind his house. Inside he wished to hang artifacts from the show. And the centerpiece of it all was to be a series of dioramas, one of which re-created this revelatory instant, when Thad and Joan, in the debased equivalent of Keats's first looking into Chapman's Homer, set eyes on the new world I'd put before them.

DAYNA AND I MET FOR AN EXPENSIVE DINNER THAT NIGHT. I FELT, WHY THE HELL not pop some corks? By any reckoning it had been a good day, a very good day.

Bounty was the restaurant at which to celebrate such tidings. Lights strung in the bushes by its brickwork entrance glittered as you approached from a courtyard off the curbside. The room inside exploded with high-decibel gaiety and the beat of loudly piped music. It wasn't loud enough or raucous enough or happy enough for me.

Joey O'Dell, that sullen but softhearted holy miscreant, had sprung from my loins onto and then off the typed page. He drank the liquor I wanted him to; he said, thought, railed, and acted in accord with my thinking. Unlike Caddigan and Blue, those recalcitrants, perpetually recoiling from my imagination's lash. Unlike anybody else I had ever attempted to create. Somehow, through me, Father Joey O'Dell was alive, and he was mine. And what I wrote of him lived and breathed and, to judge from this afternoon's reading, worked.

I was mighty. And I was immune. Something had at last worked after months of feverishly drafting and redrafting the pilot script Carlin wanted. Ostrow and Jarvis had attempted to dissuade me from the escape tunnel they perceived me digging, but I had not let them. Oh, I'd jumped on pages to rewrite for *Under the Law,* and I'd attended all the story meetings, but when Ostrow or Jarvis opened the door to my office to make their terrorizing bunk checks, they'd been deceived, because what they'd seen had really been pillows stuffed under my blankets.

"This's really not working, kid," Ostrow would say, the pages of my *Under the Law* scene crumpled ruthlessly in his fist. Normally icy darts, those words melted before even reaching me, for I'd turn and apologize for my ineptitude and absorb his insults knowing that pages of the budding script for *Father Joey* stacking up in my desk felt anything but unworkable. As he hacked at me, they sang loving cantos from my drawer.

Ostrow and Jarvis did their worst. And when that didn't get my goat, they sank even lower—Ostrow plied me with friendship. Redoubled buddyhood. Lunch invitations. Laughter at all my jokes. Solicitude for Dayna. Praise for my abilities. Ostrow trotted out a plan for the two of us to write a movie together. Then he insisted that I meet him incognito late one evening in the parking lot behind a supermarket. As if we were acting out some sort of espionage drama, he instructed that I drive up with my headlights off and park in a predesignated corner of the lot behind Vicente Foods in Brentwood. He stepped from the shadows after I'd gotten out of my car. I suppose it's all right to reveal what he told me.

"Can you keep a secret, kid?" he whispered, glancing around. "A lotta agents shop here, is why I'm bein' tight-lipped."

"I can keep a secret, sure," I said. I was bemused at this sudden turn in my treatment. It was perhaps the only time in my life I didn't know which to prefer, being held in contempt or being taken into confidence. Ostrow whispered: "Mark's planning for you to take over the show."

I laughed at the absurdity.

"Serious, kid. The three of us are leaving after the year's out to develop a new series, and they're gonna need somebody to run *Under the Law*. You're the guy. The man. Just say the word to Mark. You're gonna be a multimillionaire."

I'll admit that a part of me wanted to believe him. But this was ridiculous—they'd just finished spending a year grinding up my bones and using them for tile grout.

"Gee, I don't know, Pete. I mean, I've got this pilot to do."

"Pilot?" He laughed and shook his head at my stupid assertion. "Am I hearing right? You're talking about a pissant little pilot script? Someone's handing you a Rolls-Royce."

He wheeled and marched away quickly. But then he turned and toddled back. "I'm tellin' you, you should think about this seriously. The show is yours. Mark wants you to have it. I can't believe you got no idea what that means. You want me to set up a meeting with you and Mark tomorrow? You say the word, we can conference you, Mark, Carlin, and Dan Thompson—he's head of the affiliates—he's already signed off on the deal. Go home and get packed. You're flying to New York tomorrow. Shit, I can't believe they never told your agent."

The more I deflected, the more came my way. Until

Ostrow and Jarvis had become exasperated with resistant Billy Ziff and his pilot.

"You're blowing the deal here, kid," Ostrow admonished me one morning, having hustled me off to breakfast with Jarvis.

"Mark is the wrong guy to piss off," Jarvis chimed in as he scraped up his omelette. Breakfast here was Jarvis's favorite meal of the day—the $1.99 special.

We were in a café near the studio, but we were really in an alley, the one holding me up while the other whaled at my belly, bouncing me off the garbage cans.

"You may think you're writing your own ticket with this here pilot, but lemme just count the things could go wrong before anything you wrote gets on the air," Ostrow said. "They could hate the script, or not find a time slot for it, or maybe not be able to cast it, or they make it and it sucks. There's a zillion things. Then where're you gonna be?"

"They'll probably bring in someone else to run the show anyway," Jarvis continued. "Million-dollar car, ten-cent driver, you've never even been in an editing room, just being honest here. What do you know about producing a series?"

"Or Mark could put the kibosh on the whole deal," Ostrow said. "Right now, Mark don't believe you can piss your name in the snow. You couldn't get him drunk and make him believe it. He drops a dime to Carlin, you go splat."

"We're telling you for your own good," Jarvis said. "As friends. We don't want to see you fuck up."

"Not now, when you're on the verge of gettin' the show if you'd let me help," Ostrow said. " 'Cause you make Mark happy, you work in this town for life, you lick all the pussy you want and die a rich man."

"In this business you fuck your mother before you fuck Mark," Jarvis said. "You ought to be working on a script idea for Mark, showing him you want to do his show."

"And you ain't doin' it, kid. If you're worried you'll get

behind with your thing, I'm willing to help. I'll come in early and go over your pages with you. Or if you wanna come over to the house, the wife'll make us a nice brisket, we can sit and work on it."

"Same goes for me," Jarvis said. "You buy some takeout, bring it over, we can spend a few hours."

But I was getting all the help I needed from Joey O'Dell. As he grew, so did I. He became my companion in the dark cell within which Ostrow and Jarvis had imprisoned me. His obdurateness, his belief in what he was doing, were mine. Standing upon his shoulders, I could glimpse the sunlight. It was Joey who finally knotted together the sheets that made the rope that was my only hope in clambering to safety and freedom. Sheet by sheet, page by page, he and I breathed life into our souls. I was becoming—like Ostrow, like Werner, like Jarvis—capacitated.

Joey O'Dell was making my dream come true.

I looked up to see the lithe, black-suited Bounty maître d', his hair slicked back and tied behind in one of those ponytails, escorting Dayna through the restaurant to my table. She smiled as I caught sight of her, that luminescent smile, and I watched her come my way and she stopped a couple of conversations as she did. She wore an off-white linen dress and a necklace. Simple and elegant.

"I think I've got a job," she said the second she'd been seated. "I saw some guys today. I think I'm finally going to get to design a music video. They flipped for my stuff. We got along really well. They said they wanted me if we could make the deal work out and I would sign off on a budget."

"Are they reliable?"

"I think so. They have a small production house, Dancy Productions. They've done dozens of videos. This one is for a female rap group. From Cleveland. My budget would be fifty thousand, which is decent for one of these things and for someone doing it the first time like me."

"Great," I said, taking her hand. "That's terrific." The music was loud, thumping. A singer was howling about feeling fine and hanging her heart out on the line and hoping someone whose lips tasted like wine wouldn't end up being a swine.

Dayna sat back, unfolding and draping a napkin over her lap, letting out a deep, satisfied sigh. She rolled her eyes playfully at me. "I almost can't believe it," she said. "I was beginning to think I wouldn't get a shot like this."

"You're too talented not to. I've always told you. Maybe we both are. Guess how much Thad and Joan liked my script this morning?"

"Really?"

"I've never gotten a reaction like that. They were raving. They went nuts. If you dreamed up someone reacting positively to your script, you couldn't dream up something this good. They loved the characters. They loved the dialogue. They loved the paper. They loved the brads . . ."

"That is so fantastic, Billy. It's a good thing you didn't listen to me and quit. Boy, that was some stupid advice."

"Let's get some wine," I suggested. "I'm sure a little won't hurt me too much."

"Not for me." There was a mischievous little smile on her lips. "Here's the best news: I'm two days late. I don't want to jeopardize the baby."

"Two days?" This was bigger news than anything. Big enough to lift my heart up into my throat. "You're actually late?"

We were interrupted by the ponytailed, slit-eyed cuisine-o-morph, who bent over our table brandishing a magnum of Dom Pérignon and producing a slip of paper for my inspection.

"Complimentary," he said of the champagne.

"Who's it from?" I asked as the cork submitted to the insistence of the server's thumbs.

He nodded, directing my attention across the crowded room. Leaning back and waving at me, I saw none other than Carlin Alemo, flashing a smile and nodding my way. I waved back. Then I inspected his note. Later, I had it framed. I hung it in my office. Now it's lying around somewhere here in the back room in Vermont. It says:

I read it. I love it. Let's make it our Dream Come True.

Six

TONY PARIS'S NEW HOUSE LOOKED LIKE AN AWARD. IT JUTTED UP LIKE A Lucite cube on a granite plinth from a hilltop high above the star-dusted basin of Los Angeles. Pink and white floodlights stuck into the ground played across its curved glass contours. Music pounded from within as Dayna and I drove up. Our car was received by one of a half dozen bustier-clad females serving as valets.

Neither of us was prepared for the size and tumultuousness of the housewarming party which had announced itself from a block away. A momentous bash was in progress, judging by the noise and the important industry pashas de-Benzing by the curb. It had the feel of the place to be in town that evening. It had the rhythm. It had the wiggle.

Lloyd Wells, Tony's squat, owl-faced agent, was there, of course, prominent right near the entry, his fretful eyeball flickering toward the doorway every time someone entered.

Also on hand was the president of his agency. And the vice president of the agency. They ringed Tony Secret Service–like, guarding their meat like a pack of wild dogs from the marauding agents of other, bigger agencies who would inevitably be darting and circling, dangling big promises from their claws and eager to feed Tony's ego with them.

Ralph was already there. He was a retiring sort who chose not to lend himself to all this frippery. He was given to bolo ties, soft chairs, cha-cha music, and not straying far from where the bourbon was poured. This seems the way with many line producers, who are wranglers and bred to keep things in order, and certainly at this point in his life, when he had paired up to elder me, showing me, a neophyte, the ropes of the TV series business like you would a kid a Tinkertoy, hell-raising and waste-making enticed Ralph not at all. But he seemed to be putting up with Tony's ruckus tolerably well, sipping at his drink as if he were on a country-club veranda some Sunday afternoon, dismay never once crossing his face no matter how loud it got. Ralph's long experience in the business and all-around equanimity had rendered him difficult to impress, but as he surveyed the crowd from a love seat in Tony's den, even he nodded grudgingly.

"High octane," Ralph drawled. He pointed out executives from movie studios and TV networks on hand. And some of the really big agents. These nodded toward me in respectful salutation, apropos of my perspicacity in cooking up such a hot property as Tony, although the gesture contained none of the diffidence it might have had they felt I owned a stranglehold on the talent. To those agents I was just TV, a bag of airline nuts; they were megamillion-buck movie guys. They were slumming tonight in the new TV star's house, crisscrossing the room with the kind of steely finesse that would send Count Dracula crying for Mommy. Speckling the throng was the inevitable deluxe sampler of models and actresses. Mute, blank-eyed does in the forest of plunder.

Tony had quickly sliced through them all to greet Dayna and me. He was shiny-faced with excitement and booze. He wore a white tuxedo, underneath the jacket a tight black T-shirt. His protruding eyes seemed glazed. His buddy Beans looked attached to Tony's shoulder like some epaulet. I thought I glimpsed the leather strap of a holster peeking out from Beans's jacket. But I couldn't be sure. I couldn't see straight. The music was making my eyeballs reverberate.

"You know Sky Van Dyke," Tony hollered over the din, introducing the film director as he encircled both Dayna and me in lavish bear hugs. He was tottery and loud. "My godfather. My main dude! Will you marry me!" he cried impetuously, clinging to me and tossing off introductions to a cluster composed of the somber-faced former DEA agent turned movie executive Ben Paradise; the English music producer Rory Bly, who was bare-chested beneath an ankle-length rhinestone-studded taupe duster; and Fiona, who was introduced as "the lingerie model," and who had been married to both of them. She was Tony's date for the evening.

Tony led us on a tour of his new digs—all twelve rooms, with views of the San Fernando Valley on one side or the city on the other. Every room had an attached sitting room. And each sitting room had an antechamber. It seemed Tony had to leave four rooms just to get out of his water closet.

Hand-painted tile. Italian rugs. Sculpted sconces. A meat locker. A cook's study. An indoor lap pool. The pièce de résistance was a fully equipped recording studio that had been meticulously designed, sparing no expense, to look like a cheap garage. Old gas station pinup calendars dotted the walls. Paint peeled artfully. An ancient red Coke machine squatted in the corner, the kind with the top you flip open and you get your wrist wet yanking an ice-cold bottle from a metal bracket. There was a brilliantly devised crack in one of the ceiling's acoustic tiles, from which water steadily dripped—plink plink—into a fixed, empty, rusted, dented Bardahl can on the floor.

"The water's recycled," Tony said proudly, demonstrating the switch that turned off the drip during recording. "The whole house is environmental. I'm serious about the earth and the trees. They need the air too. Now watch this."

He suddenly reached into a cabinet and within an instant was drunkenly brandishing a shotgun.

"Whoa!" We flung ourselves out of the way.

"Ka-blamm!" The shot exploded into the far wall, commencing a deafening ringing.

Dayna and I held our hands over our ears and winced.

"It's lead," Tony hollered, laughing at us, pointing at the wall as we tried to recover from the shotgun blast. "It's built special so I can do that. All I want. It's a helluva release. Gets the tension out."

"Incredible, Tony," Dayna and I said politely over the painful clanging in our heads. We must have said "It's incredible" a couple dozen times on the tour of Tony Paris's new house.

It was impressive. Nearly overwhelming, actually. A bet on the future I would never have dared.

"All thanks to you, my man," Tony said when our tour deposited us downstairs, where the melee was, if anything, in fuller revel. Ralph had left. I was immediately snared this way and that by congratulatory producers and agents. The sincerity in their eyes! Some touched hand over heart as they spoke:

"I watch the show all the time—I think Tony's great in it."

"You and I should get together and come up with something."

"I absolutely adore the series."

"You should call me!"

"Well, how do you like our old friend Tony now?"

"How does it feel to be the most talented producer in town?"

Tony had whisked Dayna out among the dancers. I caught shadowy sightings of her joyously wriggling about as I drifted, drink in hand, through the mayhem about me.

Spending as much time as I did with Tony and feeling as close, even—to be honest—proprietary, as I did, I hadn't allowed for that part of his life that lay outside my purview. Now I felt a palm pressing at my chest, as if thwarting me, stating a limit: Tony's "private" life. People he had known before me, people he would know after me, after I would cease to be important to him downrange along his launch trajectory. Other priorities, not what he and I shared. In all its writhing, rock-and-roll abandon, Tony's life suddenly seemed foreign and unmannered and reckless. I assessed it and him with a new wariness as I sipped my drink—my noncaffeine Diet 7UP—and had my chats and watched Dayna and Tony and the fabulous bodies in this fabulous house and listened to the ear-splitting music.

A far cry from the day scant months before when we'd waddled nervously outside the network's audition room hoping to convince Carlin Alemo that this unknown, who I'd plucked from a five-line supporting part in *Johnny Mayhem,* should be cast as the lead of a new TV show and welcomed into twenty million living rooms each week. Though Carlin loved my script, my pilot was what is known as "cast contingent," meaning that the part of the lead was deemed so crucial to the successful execution of the show that if no suitable star could be found, the show wouldn't be made.

So nobody that day was more nervous than me. I was still only one "no" away from being dropped back into a huge, boiling kettle while Messrs. Werner, Ostrow, and Jarvis danced around me in aboriginine ecstasy, tossing onions and carrots into the stew, on the verge of retasting a fricassee so fragrant and delectable the spittle flew off their lips in anticipation.

Carlin sat in a back row of the theater flanked by Thad and Joan and other network executives. Carlin pursed his lips and looked none too pleased as he scanned Tony's black-and-white picture without even a hint of interest. Obviously, it wasn't with relish that he met a nobody. I was nearly contorted into a fusilli from the tension.

Tony was finally brought into the room to read for the brass. Introductions were made, but there was about as much small talk to be bandied about as there would have been had everyone been gathered there on the promise that I was to unwrap the Hope diamond from a velvet cloth in my back pocket. When the question in the air is an impending fortune, a burp is too fucking verbose. But we were ready. We'd endlessly rehearsed the long speech the irrepressible O'Dell makes to a startled president after sneaking little Eddie into the White House. Tony cleared his throat and started in:

"You see that man over there, Mr. President? The man with the briefcase? They call that 'the football,' don't they? That's Doomsday, isn't it? The plans to blow up the world. Dogging your footsteps wherever you go. Well, little Eddie here's being shadowed every day too, Mr. President. Every place he goes. Every second, Doomsday might tap him on the shoulder. . . ."

Suddenly, Tony paused. A pause he'd never "played" before. And his face flushed. His forehead expanded, as if a big sign saying BLANK was blinking on it. He looked over at me in the front row.

"I'm up," he said to the room, shaking his head and looking helpless.

"No problem," I said, although I was instantly seized by panic. I flew out of my chair and turned to Carlin. "Just give us a second."

Wrenching a script from my briefcase, I steered Tony off to one side.

There was a time bomb ticking.

"I'm sorry, man, I'm blowin' it," Tony muttered disconsolately to me. Somehow he'd turned into a big bowl of mush. You could have sprinkled him in the hog pen.

"Don't be ridiculous," I said, trying not to fall apart myself. "You're doing great."

"I'm doin' lousy and I'm blowin' it. Aw, jeez . . ."

"They love you. Here."

I forced the script under his nose. Like smelling salts. He cast his eye back and forth on the page.

"I dunno, man."

"Be quiet and read this and concentrate. Blank everything else out and concentrate."

"I'm sorry, man, I'm gone. This never happened to me before."

Pathetic! My guy was decomposing right before my eyes. Turning into clay and shoe gunk like a vampire caught in the sun.

"Tony, just shut the fuck up and concentrate on this. You're doing fine! Do it like you've done it a hundred times before. Just you and me in the office," I hissed as inaudibly as I could. This seemed to bolster Tony. Behind me, with the suddenly acute 360-degree awareness of a fly one gets in such situations, I felt the air going out of the network brass. I could hear haunches shifting weight impatiently in their seats. I could hear breath slowly exhaling and turning into a low, dissatisfied mumble. I imagined Joan and Thad reading some other writer's pilot and telling him or her how great it was and to buy a new house.

"Y'okay?" I whispered to Tony, trying to coax equanimity from him.

He tilted his head noncommittally.

"C'mon, let's go. You want to do it with the script? How do you want to do it?"

"No no," he refused, pushing the pages back at me.

"All right. All right."

I returned to my seat, trying to appear nonchalant. But my heart was plummeting. Snapped elevator cable time. What a catastrophe, one that would no doubt be bandied about with much delight among the hooting trio of Werner, Ostrow, and Jarvis: Young fool wheels trained bear into the king's office—but the bear ain't trained! Yes, this would be the story that Carlin would relay to Mark over breakfast latte. Bust-a-gut time. Unable to get it out. "So after this big intro, the clown just stands there . . . just stands there, can't even manage a fart. I'm sittin' there, waitin', nothin'. . . . I'm goin', What kinda producer is this guy, bringin' in a mutt like this? He just stood there, I'm tellin' ya . . ." Milk and coffee would be spurting from Carlin's mouth, dribbling over his chin. Mark would choke, a quick, violent upthrust of his shoulders, as his designer oatmeal splurted out from between his puffing cheeks, gurgling: "Billy's a joker, whatdya gonna do? Brings in a guy who poops on the rug. Kid's a wanker, I told you." That's what he'd say. They'd be toweling each other off at some power breakfast. At my expense. Because I brought in a guy who pooped on the rug. I was trying to save our careers, but Tony Paris was pooping on the goddam fucking rug!

Tony stood there another moment, muttered an apology, and then collected himself. He looked at me as if that were helping him to steady and focus himself. I had the feeling in that long moment that everything was now at stake on this roll of the dice. There are no exceptions made at the network. No allowances. Perform. Sell. You want understanding? Understanding is the waste product of failure. So much methane.

Finally, Tony began the speech again. A little severely, maybe at first a little too much reproach and not enough anguish, but he began. And he built up speed and started to glide and work. Tony knew how to work his head with great outrage and sarcasm and sincerity, knew how to punch words.

"You see that man over there, Mr. President? The man with the briefcase? They call that 'the football,' don't they? That's Doomsday, isn't it? The plans to blow up the world. Dogging your footsteps wherever you go. Well, little Eddie here's being shadowed every day too, Mr. President. Every place he goes. Every second, Doomsday might tap him on the shoulder. Thank the good Lord you never get that tap, Mr. President. What's in that briefcase stays locked inside. But that briefcase following Eddie around? . . . That briefcase is gonna be opened, Mr. President. Someday soon they'll spin the lock on that briefcase and it's gonna open in young Eddie's face. All we're asking, Mr. President, you're a powerful man, maybe you could help keep it locked just one more day. . . ."

You could almost see Tony's muscles rippling as he tossed off that speech. I thought of him as a boxer at that moment; strange, you might think, but there he was, scrapping, furiously repealing any existence other than himself, dispatching the disbelief that would fell him should he be deserted by his art. And in its wake, after he'd finished, there was a pool of silence, pure as a knockout, dappled by slow, low breathing. Whatever happened, I knew that in a moment of crisis I had massaged a skittish actor into shape, given him the time to collect himself and maybe save the two of us. I held my breath. And then, after what seemed like years, Carlin pronounced: "I love him. What's his name again?"

Here, in twelve rooms off Mulholland, was the result. Bigger than I had foreseen, and a bit vulgarly so. I decided to revisit the bar if I could push my way to it, and a glass of white wine seemed not only fair but warranted.

"Do you like it?"

I turned toward a diminutive man, no more than a few inches above five feet in height and with reedy legs and a broad barrel chest, all of which combined to suggest some sort of cortical abnormality. He wore a white T-shirt beneath a sheer, shiny silver jacket whose sleeves he'd pushed up high, revealing his forearms, which were his most normal and powerful-looking attribute. His gray hair was slicked straight back and fell down below his collar.

"I painted it especially for Tony."

He'd thought that I, lost in musing, had been absorbed in the artwork I'd been half-turned toward.

"This is your work?" I said after a moment's hesitation.

He smiled and nodded toward a bottom corner of the canvas. I leaned in toward the signature.

"Liam Bunch."

"Bunch," I said. I knew little about art. I'd been to the Met in New York, the Uffizi in Florence with Dayna. I therefore harbored some skimpy knowledge of the traditional, requisite Renaissance stuff like the Adoration, which I knew was the Magi looking at the Christ Child; the Annunciation, which was the Angel telling Mary she'd been chosen as the mother of God; and the Approbation, which was, if I recall correctly, Christ making the New York Yankees.

Other than that, I couldn't tell you the difference between a fresco and trompe l'oeil. But I did know my eyes had come across the name Liam Bunch in at least two magazine articles I'd read recently. Flavor-of-the-moment-type squibs. Either an exhibition at MoMA in New York or something about his divorcing a porn actress. Maybe it was both.

Feeling some substantive critical response required, I peered more closely at Bunch's painting through the dim light. I made out a woman or, more precisely, the torso of a woman, for her head was cut off the frame. Her limbs were at grotesque angles. She was falling from the sky, from a great height, her legs splayed, her clothing shredded from her body. She wore black high heels, a black long-line bra and panty girdle. Floating beside her in the air was a textbook, *Principia Mathematica*. Below her was some kind of destroyed institutional building, its top apparently blown off.

"Girls' school, eh? She is the science teacher," Bunch half-grinned, and his bulbous nose bobbed.

"Interesting subject." I nodded, compressing my lips and trying to emit the sort of erudite-sounding grunt of a latter-day Clive Bell. I wondered how much the United Federation of Teachers would appreciate this piece, say, hanging in the entry of their union hall.

"Tony has commissioned two more in this series," Bunch said. "The next I call . . . *Valedictorian*."

Around me the music vibrated off the walls. Shadows cavorted on the dance floor. Misery fled. Tony waved and cackled. A great roar began building. People reeled and wobbled and rocked. Everyone got caught up in the sort of cataclysmic group frenzy you find only in a great party or a platoon of marines hurling themselves over barbed wire.

DAYNA AND I HEADED UP THE COAST THAT EVENING, CHECKING INTO THE BILT-more in Santa Barbara well after midnight. I had to shanghai her from Tony's dance floor, where she'd been disporting herself like Mitzi Gaynor for three hours.

"Ovulation time, honey," I'd whispered in her ear, coaxing Dayna into the car, where she sat with a faraway smile on her face for the next two hours, saying little as the wind whipped through her hair. The dark bulk of the mountains hunched to our right. Around each elbow in the highway there was the silvery flash of foam as the waves pounced onto the sand in the moonlight. An odd realization stowed away in the car as we drove: For the first time I was the one tugging on her sleeve and issuing reminders.

For the most part, I'd endured our childlessness armed merely with hope. And armed with that all-too-human odds-making by which we calculate as impossible calamity's knocking on our own door.

But Dayna had exhausted denial a long time ago. Months before we set out for Santa Barbara, Dayna had sat down across from me one morning as I was bent over my bowl of cereal and tummy-friendly herbal tea and announced: "I'm making an appointment at the Center for Reproductive Study. It's time. We've got to find out what's going wrong. Don't you agree?"

I could hardly object. No matter how mighty the arm I raised at work. No matter my seemingly limitless power to command and array the world I had begotten. No matter how I had peopled the airwaves, sending my seed into every home in America. At my home I was no father. Each month her period came and the pages of a blank diary began to accumulate, the thickening journal of our bereft voyage.

Friendly environs, the warming comforts of everyday life, had fallen away. Instead, what we saw was unfamiliar to our eyes, what we experienced foreign and perceptible only to each other, and, ultimately, as boring to people who were not childless as having to endure slides from someone else's vacation.

We developed a language—self-referential, guarded, so-licitous—the way travelers do, invoking experiences particular only to us and concerned with an itinerary only we possessed and followed. The language was minimalist and best whispered demurely, as two diffident wayfarers whisper to each other in the pension breakfast room amidst a table of jabbering strangers. One that constantly sounded out on the road in a terse, repetitive echo, sonarlike, to fix the other's position, to summon the other's notice.

Our everyday compass useless, the mundane become momentous, normalcy impossible to assert, what had we become if not travelers? And like any travelers unable to arrive at their destination, we were getting irritable. We turned moody and bitter with each other, fretful about the fate we felt clamped around our legs and each to the other.

"Billy? Are you listening to me?" Dayna asked impatiently that morning.

"Huh?" I said. My attention had wandered back to the ball scores.

"Don't you want a baby in this house?"

"Yeah, sure I do. You know I do. I want a baby as much as you."

"You say you do, and I want to believe you, but all you ever talk about is work. Maybe your biggest thrill is being on the set and giving orders and everybody fawning all over you. It seems like it lately. Maybe you lap it up so much you're afraid a kid will cut into it and spoil it. Maybe you've changed. But you have to tell me. I feel like I'm being ignored. Like I'm alone with this."

"That's not true," I said. "I've just been busy."

"Too busy to live your life? We can't go on with me with the thermometer and you fitting this in between your big-shot meetings. We can't keep on with that. Our marriage can't endure it. That's why I've got to know. Are you sure you want to have a baby with me, Billy?"

Of course I wanted one. At the schoolyard where I'd shoot basketball on weekends I'd stare at the peewee soccer games, envying the dads who stood on the sidelines, their eyes pinned by pride to the figures of their kids. My gaze lingered ruefully at our friends—they might holler at their children as they stooped to pick up food thrown onto the floor, but I longed to be so exasperated. People without kids —I'd never even thought of that for myself. Grown-ups who didn't want kids were guys in turtlenecks, who lived in condos and, sure, got a helluva two-seat convertible to compensate and maybe a lot of stamps on their passports, but they wound up opening cans of soup at night and drifting into the absorption of odd pursuits. Despite the freedom and vitality that seemed theirs to enjoy, they were slowly foiled, quieted, overtaken by the early encroachment of an immense silence—the knowledge they were the last in their line. Not for me.

Dayna had to know I wanted kids. Wasn't that patently obvious? Why did the drawing board have to be taken out every morning, every conversation? Why did it suddenly seem like the works that had so smoothly sustained us were in such visible disarray? Clashing at each revolution. Demanding attention. Requiring exhaustive study. Maybe even dismantling for full inspection. Total rethinking couldn't be ruled out between bowls of cereal. Modifications, wholesale changes, might result before the tea had done steeping.

In a sense, I see now, Dayna's irritation was no different from the way she grew cross even when the trip before us was just a picnic on the beach. Because the best way to avoid the obstacles on a journey is never to embark at all, I characteristically ignored what needed to be done. Even with as big an issue as this, I hadn't prepared. And until Dayna braced me with the question I hadn't thought needed answering, I can't say how many more months I might have sat there, dully spooning toasted o's of oats into my mouth.

"Yeah," I said, trying not to sound testy, but at the moment of fathering my TV show, feeling so stung by the pricking badge of barrenness she insisted I wear. "I'm sure I want to have a baby with you."

Into the doctors' hands, me cursing every step of the way,

we put ourselves. And they determined that Dayna needed a look-see.

"It's a good thing. I want to do this," she said, the night before the surgery. A tooth pressed into her lower lip as she spoke. I locked up the house, turned off the lights, popped down my ulcer pill, and got into bed beside her in a swish of sheets. I took her hand.

From a distance, the roar of a freeway reached our ears. In Los Angeles you try to fool yourself into thinking it sounds like a far-off waterfall. In L.A. you spend all your time trying to fool yourself about something. Until you forget what you're fooling yourself about. Then you get into therapy to help you remember.

We sat in bed together quietly for a while. The silence contained every possibility and every regret.

"Things will get better now," she said, finally breaking the silence, for a moment seeming like a magician, putting her hand through the curtain of worry that surrounded me and pulling out something pleasing.

"I dunno. I mean, I'm drained from this already. Aren't you? Our nerves are shot. We're both at the breaking point. Don't you worry about that?"

"No," she said. "I don't worry about that. But I'll tell you what I do worry about." She lightly played her fingers over mine.

"What is that?"

"I worry that tomorrow when they look inside me they will find something they can't fix. That my tubes are blocked or damaged and no good. And I'll never be able to get pregnant. And then this will all be my fault."

"It's nobody's fault."

"How will you not blame me if that turns out? If it turns out that I'm the reason you can't have a child?"

"That's not going to happen. Has Wilder said anything like that?"

"No."

"Well, then."

"But if it does happen, you'd blame me. Unconsciously. You'd hate me because I couldn't give you a baby."

"No I wouldn't," I said.

"You'd turn away from me, maybe even find someone else. Out of desperation."

"Don't be silly."

Tears pooled in her eyes. Her breath was wet, slushy.

"I can't go through with this unless I know that if worse comes to worst we'll still have a baby and that you'll be happy."

"You mean not our own child?"

"Not our own biological child."

"I want my own kid, is that so terrible?"

"If it's just to have a little Xerox of yourself. I'm praying to God tonight, Billy. Whether or not I get pregnant, let me be a parent."

"I just want something that nobody can say isn't mine. I don't think I'm asking so much."

"I refuse to be the reason you can't be a father. See? I'm right to be worried. You'll never be happy. Can't you make the most out of the shit that comes your way?"

I sat there thinking about that, thinking about making the best of things. How you did that without feeling like they'd suddenly thrown all the furniture out of your office.

"Dayna, I don't want to fight."

I let my voice trail off so we could be still and let the silence overtake and run to ground our conversation. Which it did.

After a while I said, "Just remember, it's nobody's fault, okay? Whatever happens, it's nobody's fault. We're gonna survive this."

I reached over and set the alarm clock for one of those ungodly times doctors like to make you have to get up.

Surgery and fishing-trip times. Then I listened to the far-off waterfall and watched over Dayna as she closed her eyes and went to sleep. At the foot of the bed she'd already prepared and packed a small black carrying bag for her trip to the hospital. I stared at it and at the pink fold of a nightgown that swelled through a not-quite-zipped-up hole in the valise top. At that moment in the dark I loved my wife very much for her tidy fortitude. It convinced me that we were deserving and that she would survive her operation and mend our frayed nerves and send Chaos tapping on some other windowpane.

And at least part of that prayer came to pass in the cross-hairs of Dr. Wilder's laparoscope. He'd made Dayna "good as new." Now her tubes were "clean as a whistle," and she was ready to get pregnant. And that same little valise she'd taken to the hospital was tucked in our trunk as we drove up the coast trying to resume our journey on the road to all-is-well.

Dayna still seemed giddy from Tony's party as she undressed for bed after we'd checked in.

"Guess what—Tony wants to hire me. He's doing an album," she said. She widened her eyes and smiled, appreciating how that would take me by surprise.

"An album? What the hell sort of album do they want Tony to make?"

"What kind do you think?"

"Since when is he a musician?"

"He's got that recording studio."

"So the fuck what," I snorted. "I've got a kitchen, nobody's hiring me at the Four Seasons. Besides, what's he going to record, gunshots?"

"He's been making music for years, you know that. He and Beans used to have a band back in Chicago. They call themselves the Bopulator Brothers."

"The Whatthefuck Twins? What was that?"

She laughed. "The Bopulator Brothers. Blues."

"Jeez." I laughed too. "Tony Paris goes from pointing guns at people and saying, 'I wouldn't do that if I was you,' to selling his sweat for $15.95 a bead. So you're going to design the album?"

"Not the album, the video. I'm going to do the whole shoot."

"No kidding? That's great."

"You don't sound like you think it's so great."

"I do. Really. The Bopulator Brothers, holy shit." I couldn't help shaking my head. "One small question: Can he sing?"

"Croaks, is more like it." She shrugged. She unclasped her lacy bra, pulling the white satin cups free from her breasts. "I hate to say it, but does it matter? It'll sell a million copies anyway. Tony's a star, he'll get a lot of promotion. There'll be a big budget. The video'll get tons of play. It's a great gig for me."

"Definitely. Congratulations. When did you start using words like 'gig'?"

She smiled. "A great job, all right? Anyway, Tony says they're already talking about shooting the video somewhere out in the desert. The album's got a release date. They're putting together a tour, weekends when he's not shooting the show."

"Oh. I'm glad someone told me."

"I thought you would be happy about this."

I parted the curtains with my finger and peeped out. Below, on a cement path along the lawn, a staff member pushed a clanking room-service cart; the jostled silver settings and trays atop it tinkled furiously. A vibrating tray cover slid off and clattered to the ground, and, quickly, half of some sandwich I was too far away to make out the particulars of spilled onto the sidewalk. The waiter stooped down to the cement, saw nobody looking, remade the scattered sand-wich, and replaced it on the cart. He rolled on.

"You know, I think I'm actually jealous of the guy," I said, turning back to my wife. "Y'know?"

"Jealous?" Dayna looked amused. "Of Tony?"

"That house. That party. All of a sudden this guy is the hottest actor in town. Did you see who was there? He's got movie deals. He carries a tune about as well as a tracheotomy patient and he's got a record contract."

"And you're threatened?"

"I didn't say threatened."

"Whatever word you want. Give Tony some credit. He's got talent. He's magnetic. Whatever you want to say about him, he at least showed you that you could be a writer again."

"True," I said.

"What am I telling you for—you saw something, that's why you cast him. A couple months ago you didn't seem to mind that mob scene at Rose's. Anyway, his success is only good for you, it only feeds back into the series. It all helps you in the end."

"Yeah . . . well. It's all due to me in the first place."

"Who doesn't know that? You've got pucker marks all over your ass, Billy, come on. You're acting like you created the guy or something."

"Well, I did."

She looked at me. One of those looks ablaze with the pithy diagnosis of insanity a wife delivers to her man. "That's a little bit twisted."

"Well, I just told you, I'm jealous of him."

"I think Tony should be jealous of you," she said.

Dayna posed provocatively for a second, standing there in her panties with a coy smile on her face. Her long legs swept gracefully up to her hips, her filmy crotch. She bounced under the covers. Happy as I'd seen her in, well, ever.

The moon was full. It floated high in the clear night sky. Its reflection, a white train, stretched from the ocean's dark horizon nearly to the window where I stood watching the sea, sniffing its saltiness, listening to the gentle tumble of the low, rhythmic surf.

"Come over here," she said from the bed, "and let's make a baby."

Seven

RECOUNTING HIS FIRST STEPS ON THE ROOF OF THE WORLD, SIR EDMUND Hillary didn't describe the icy pinnacle one might imagine. Not some spire hooked by his fingernails, one leg straining to heave up and over the lip of the summit. He first mounted an icy hump, then proceeded onward, only to realize that further progress lay somewhat lower and that he'd already topped the crest. He'd reached the peak without knowing it.

And so, as I reflect now, the next few weeks and months seemed to me: blindly charging forward, somewhere inside sensing things no longer seemed beyond reach, but not yet realizing the triumphant circumstance I, indeed, had attained.

Lest it seem all glory was funneled only in Tony Paris's direction, I hasten to add (and herewith indict myself for my earlier scratchings of envy) that buxom, stiff-nippled Praise had rubbed warm oil onto her hands, straddled my back, and begun kneading my naked torso, pausing occasionally to whip her long blond hair across my shoulders.

Over lunch at the Bistro Garden, my small, freckled African bee of an agent, Go-Go Bernstein, pollinated my career with offers from this or that movie executive. She was scouting out properties and scripts for me to write, even, perhaps, to direct. Almost every day at the office a messenger would drop off more stuff for me to read. Rewrite this, consider so-and-so, produce that.

Presents packed with so much corporate-logoed leisure wear I could have been Sweatsuit Man the rest of my days were regularly borne into our offices. It got to the point where via one gift club or another I received weekly replenishment of fruit, wine, fruit juice, beer, bread and muffins, smoked meat, fresh flowers, cologne, CDs, videos, and books. Needless to say, affixed to all this tribute were the adulatory little missives of sundry wheeler-dealers who now thought it worth their time to establish themselves in my good graces.

As the show's success grew, I found myself a guest in the premium seats at sporting events, sitting amidst Hollywood royalty. The courtside seats I accepted. I spurned those in the "luxury boxes," this American phenomenon being unfathomable to me. What moron would fork over a hundred grand for guaranteed seats so far from the action you could only make out what was happening on a TV? And only if you stole a glance away from the overdressed idiots surrounding you, a bevy of sports know-nothings. I'd like to sell you our newest ultraluxury box—you pay a cool million for the privilege of sitting at home in your underwear and listening on radio.

The newsweeklies and papers sought my opinions, and not just on the state of television but on topics like affirmative action and campaign reform and ethics in American culture.

A story about me appeared in *Gentlemen's Quarterly*. Along with a full-page picture.

USA Today reported the first upsurge in ten years in applicants to the priesthood, chalking it up to the burgeoning popularity of *Father Joey*.

While church officials decried O'Dell's occasional blasphemies and his drinking, they grudgingly welcomed the show. Pulpits around the country found important consolations in Father Joey O'Dell's flinty professions. Imagine my philosophizings coming out of the mouths of ministers talking to their congregations! As if I had some seminal take on women in the priesthood or the doctrine of the Holy Trinity and the Filioque controversy. Me—urbi et orbi.

Dayna and I were driven in a limousine up to Carlin Alemo's Santa Ynez Valley ranch for the weekend. This was a huge tract, stretching from mountaintop to the farthest valley floor opposite. There was a round-robin tennis tournament on Saturday morning on Carlin's private courts, followed by a picnic. We packed into the hills on mounts from Carlin's stable, then dined on cold lamb and stuffed rabbit legs served by Carlin's help. On Saturday night I learned how to play whist. Sunday morning was skeet shooting. By the time the afternoon rolled around, we were all feeling that it was maybe, oh, 1896, and just about full enough of ourselves and our way of life to flog any servant caught pilfering so much as a sugar cube. At which point we gathered outside the main house to ejaculate in outsized whispers as a helicopter airlifted in a huge piece of expensive sculpture—a large, bulbous sort of a growthy-looking piece of eruption-pocked dark rock that might well have been entitled *Venereal Warts* —which Carlin crowed he had just bought for half a million. The rest of the time Dayna and I indulged in a little baby making by our own private hot tub in our own private bungalow. And the other guests included the wealthiest, most formidable people in the industry. I'm not a name-dropper, but, what the hell—"Bronco" McTubbins, Earl and Anastasia Vask, Jim-Jim Blaine and his girlfriend, Candy Bible.

Requests, awards, citations, each more flattering than the next, showered me. Such vindication! I was so intoxicated by everything that I hardly blinked when Go-Go cackled to me one afternoon over the phone what was perhaps the best vindication of all.

"Carlin wants to move your time slot, doll," she cawed, "and guess what you'll be replacing—*Under the Law*! It's a fading show. Stale. Carlin no longer believes in it. He wants to dump it and kill it, but in an honorable way. Carlin's putting it on hiatus until another slot opens up. But they want you in there instead. Isn't it fabulous? Let Mark eat his little heart out. Fabulous!"

It was the first last laugh I'd ever had. I imagined Ostrow and Jarvis, recalled the treachery of their attempting to thwart my pilot. Now their guts would be pretzeled in impotent torment (just as mine had been) as the network jettisoned their show and replaced it with mine. I pictured Ostrow and Jarvis out of work, cast to the winds on the hobo's lice-ridden meanderings, sorting through back-alley garbage pails for dinner slop. Forced to boil their own shoes for supper.

When Go-Go and I got through laughing, I hung up the phone in my new car. I'd purchased it the week before, one of the indulgences I'd allowed myself. Each sniff of my new leather interior grayed the hairs on my temple a distinguished degree more and inspired thoughts of confident drives through misty mornings to important meetings. The car had every option short of a CAT scan. The day was glorious. My hand-painted tie was perfect, as if Matisse had just finished a final brushstroke and handed it around my bedroom door. My linen suit hadn't dared wrinkle yet. My socks held and hugged my calves with the unwavering constancy of slaves bearing a king.

I was returning from a luncheon sponsored by the United States Olympic Committee. I'd really broken bread with the gods there. I'd sat on the dais in my wonderful socks next to the governor of California. If anyone felt as invulnerable as I did at that moment, it was the governor, who was also enjoying public esteem, though not quite to the extent that I was. Like every other successful American leader in the last half century, the governor had reassured the people which group of fellow citizens it was perfectly all right to hate. This made them feel so good they'd rewarded the governor with another term. Plans for the White House were already under way, since no state offered such an abundance of people to hate as California. In the backseat of my new car was the plaque the governor had just presented me while everyone applauded. It was a token of gratitude for our episode about the dying, vomiting, bald, teenage ice-skating queen, which had portrayed "the highest standards of the Olympic spirit."

Yes, I'd let Success have her certain saucy sway over me. She dandled me, chucked my chin—I purred. Why not? But I'd been successfully vigilant, I felt, despite all the tribute and vainglory, in fending off a swelled head.

Back on the lot, I eased into my parking space. I breezed into our production offices, which were as usual fluttering with activity. On the walls of the waiting room we'd hung many of the magazine covers Tony had appeared on already. Phones were jumping on the assistants' desks just down the foyer. PA's, the production designer, accountants from the budget office, and casting people were hustling about. The Xerox machine hummed. Life was being collated.

Mona, my secretary, read off from my lengthy call list. It was almost a page long in just the two hours I'd been at lunch. It contained the usual cavalcade of agents, including Lloyd Wells, and ended with one unusual note: The Smithsonian Institution had rung up.

Ralph was grinning from the door of his office, which was opposite mine. "Yeah, can you believe it? They want Tony's collar."

"His collar?"

"Yeah. Joey O'Dell's clerical collar is now an artifact of American culture."

"You mean like the *Spirit of Saint Louis*?"

"Uh-huh. Just like John Glenn's space capsule. They want it for their collection."

I almost patted my belly.

"Let's get it to 'em."

"Got a minute?" Ralph asked, crooking his finger and motioning me toward him.

I went into Ralph's office and sat down on the couch, draping my arms grandly over the backrest. It felt good to have created an artifact of American culture.

"How's it going? We get the first shot yet?"

"No. That's why I wanted to talk."

"Really?" The clock on Ralph's desk said it was 2:49 already. When you're in production, shooting a fifty-odd-page television script in seven days, the most important thing is to "make the day," that is, the pages scheduled by a prudent producer like Ralph that constitute that day's work. You don't want to fall behind.

Ralph and I daily monitored two key things to make sure we reached our filming goal. First, when the crew reported, customarily around 6:45 A.M., get the actors onstage for a rehearsal and get that first shot of the day going. Second was the first shot after lunch, when there might be a tendency to straggle back to work.

I shot Ralph a quizzical look. He half-shrugged, turned up his palm, and wordlessly shook his head.

"Tell me we're not getting into a bad habit here."

"Tony's having a few problems with Alan," Ralph said.

Alan Crabbe was a new director we'd hired. We'd over-looked one monstrous peccadillo when we put him on our payroll—his preposterously presumptuous habit of standing behind a lectern when speaking. This podium was constantly carried around beside him by his tight-lipped, tight-sweatered assistant, whose only assisting expertise besides po-dium holding, one assumed, involved rolling smooth latex up and onto engorged flesh.

Anyway, I'd hoped the company would merely laugh at this auteuristic fillip of Alan's. It was impossibly silly for a TV director to get away with such behavior, because on a TV set, unlike in film production, a director is typically little more than a traffic cop and frequently barely more than a bum trying to keep out of the way of honking traffic.

There is perhaps no more difficult job in the business than being an episodic TV director. You are injected into a company, a crew not of your choosing, to deal with actors who are sure they know their characters better than you and probably do. You are expected not to fall behind schedule while turning out an episode that is both exactly like the show's other episodes and distinctive. It is a brutally tall order. Apparently, something about Mr. Crabbe wasn't going down too well with my star.

"That accounts for Lloyd Wells on my call sheet?"

"A pretty fair guess," Ralph said.

"Tell me I'm crazy to get worried about all these little delays lately. What was it last week, this mysterious head-ache? Then the car breaks down one day? Then, what, he was forty-five minutes late last Tuesday because he couldn't find contact-lens solution at the drugstore?"

"My opinion?" Ralph said. "Tony's getting a little fried from the grind. This is what?—episode fifteen? He hasn't had a day off in months. And making that record album sure isn't helping things any. Not to mention the video. You can see it. The man's dog tired. He's helicoptering between here and Two Bunch Palms every night, running on two hours' sleep. I keep hearing stories about how crazy the video's getting."

"You do? What do you hear?"

"Nothing too specific. But a business affairs friend of mine over in the recording division that's paying for it—he had to go out to the desert and smack a few heads. Tells me the shoot's totally out of control. Two hundred thousand dollars outta control."

"Jeez—"

"Lotta carrying on and partying. Like it was spring break or something. No one's in charge. And no one's saying no to our friend Mr. Paris. I'm surprised—Dayna hasn't been talking to you about it?"

"No," I said, shaking my head. Truth to tell, I had spoken to her only once since she'd checked into her hotel for what was supposed to be a two-day shoot. We'd both been maniacally busy, and the only contact we'd had was a pile of message slips. "We spoke I guess it was day before yesterday. She said things were fine. She was right on budget."

"Fine? They're on location for a piddly little music video going on a week? The record company is ready to call out the National Guard. Anyway, much as I hate to say it, it ain't Alan," Ralph said. "I can go hang out on the stage, play principal if you want. But Alan, say what you will about him, is no slouch. He's just trying to do his job. He's got his shot list. He's prepared, once you can get him to stop playing Oxford don. Best face I can put on it is I think what this is about is just exhaustion. We're all exhausted. I'm exhausted. You're exhausted, too. What's wrong with your eye?" Ralph squinted at me. "Your right eye's all red."

"Really? I don't know."

I got up and checked myself in a mirror hung on the back

of Ralph's office door. Sure enough, the eye was streaked with strawberry milk. I hadn't been rubbing it, as far as I could remember.

"Too many two ayem's in the editing room, I guess."

"That goes for everybody," Ralph said. "Lookit, as far as Tony goes, I'll do whatever you want. If we're lucky, he wraps his video, gets a nice weekend rest, and we're fine."

"Tony out of makeup?"

"Should be. We better get that shot done pronto, or we'll be a half day behind."

I left Ralph, went down the stairs and into the bright sunshine, and headed for Tony's trailer by our soundstage.

Actually, Tony was housed in more than a mere trailer. Because Tony was the star of the series, Lloyd Wells had negotiated for him, in addition to his $35,000-a-week salary, a deluxe, fifty-foot-long motor home that came equipped with a kitchen and a private bedroom and all the comforts of the QE2.

Outside it, polishing the Mercedes in which he squired Tony around, I found Beans.

"Your Bopulator Brother in?" I inquired.

Beans nodded toward the Cunard flagship.

I knocked on the door. The star's trailer was always a tricky little enclave to negotiate. It existed as sort of an independent duchy, an embassy that lay in some tacit sense immune to the sway of the influences beyond its gates. There was the de facto aura, though not yet perhaps tested before the Supreme Court, of sanctuarial inviolability around it. No one entered without knocking and being screened. Not me, the boss. Not the first AD, who regularly fetched Tony from it. Not his masseuse. Not his personal trainer. Not Beans or any of his other old Chicago friends who'd visit occasionally. Not the delivery man from the Ivy who came by with the two-hundred-dollar take-out orders Tony's assistant or Beans regularly phoned in. Not the bookie whose visitations

I'd gotten wind of in the last couple weeks. And not any of Tony's paramours who popped in and out discreetly yet never unnoticed.

"Come in." Tony's assistant, Genevieve, peered out from the door. I entered. She left.

Tony was right there, reclining on a sofa cushion wearing a white Bopulator Brothers T-shirt, a John Deere cap, and jeans. There was a bottle of mineral water beside him. He wore a pair of headphones and was listening to something on a Walkman and humming along to it.

"Yo," he said, looking up, then looking back down, murmuring along with the music.

His eyes were red and filmy.

"Hey," I said.

He took off the earphones.

"How's it going?"

He shrugged, as if that was all he was able to mount out of his weariness. "Fabulous, Willie," he said in a hoarse, tired voice. "In-fucking-credible. We're putting together a tour. 'D I tell you about it? I'm listening to some of the tracks we got so far. Here."

He got up, making a great braying sound to clear his sinuses, and handed me the earphones to put on.

Boom-whack-a, labba labba, back-a whack-a bagga whappa . . . com-a come come . . . boom-whack-a labba labba, back-a whack-a bagga labba . . . gedouda mah face . . . whack-a labba labba back-a lack-a whack-a labba . . .

"Sounds like fun," I said. If fun sounded like about a thousand sixteen-penny nails turning over and over in a dryer.

"I wrote it," he said. He grabbed another bottle of mineral water out of the refrigerator.

"So things are going great." I handed back the earphones with what I hoped wouldn't seem undue zeal.

"I'm whipped, man."

"You don't look it," I lied. "Hey, how's Dayna? I'm starting to miss her."

"Dayna?"

"Your production designer?" I chuckled. "My wife, remember? Tall, big eyes . . ."

Tony flashed that sideways smile and drawled, "Oh yeah . . . great legs, nice"—his hands dialed the air at breast height—"right . . . yeah. She's great, man. Doin' a great job for us. You got one great lady."

He plunked himself down wearily.

"So listen—why the fuck'd we hire this fuckin' asshole to direct?" He took a pull on the bottle of water.

"You don't like Alan?"

"He doesn't know his ass from a hole in the ground," Tony rasped. "He's a fuckin' jerk. I could direct better than this idiot."

There was a pointed irritation in his tone I hadn't heard before. Very grouchy.

"You're in the mayor's office today?"

"Right."

In case you were hit on the head by a toppling construction crane and spent the last couple of years relearning swallowing and how buttons work, let me remind you that this was the episode about a beautiful housewife, a former circus performer, dying with advanced Parkinson's disease. She beseeches O'Dell to help her fulfill one wish: to perform as a catcher on a high-wire trapeze act. Aware that the woman has lost most of her muscular control, the mayor of Chicago had refused to allow a permit for the event, a benefit organized by O'Dell in which the woman would catch a flier coming off a quadruple somersault ten stories above the Loop with no net below.

Tony grumpily seized the script pages for the day's work, flicking them with the back of his hand.

"It's this scene, man. The same scene we've done over

and over again already till I'm blue in the face. I say I don't care about all your damn rules, fuck you, we gotta do this bullshit . . . blah blah . . ."

"Yeah," I said.

He kind of whined and pouted here. "Well, I go to this fucking jerk Alan with an idea how to do it differently and I'm not gettin' anywhere with him . . . like he's deaf . . . y'know, like I'm nobody around here."

"Tony, those are our bread-and-butter scenes," I said. "They're what the audience likes about you, the way you shake things up, go after the officials, y'know? . . . don't stand for any bullshit . . ."

"I know, but I'm tired of always doing it the same way all the time."

"What's your idea?" I asked.

"Well, y'know how I shook that doctor up in the ice-skating thing? Well, here, talking to the mayor after I barge into the City Council meeting, it's still more of the talk . . . yak yak yak . . . I don't care, you better do this for that poor woman . . . blah blah blah . . ."

"And?"—I was trying to keep words out of my throat, actually, because I felt an onrush of resentment at Tony's dismissive yak-yak blah-blah characterization of the dialogue which had been written and published in the script and to which I attached no little pride.

"And I'm saying to that fuckin' jerk Alan, let's just quit all this bullshit, y'know? No more talk. Or maybe I say some of the bullshit and the mayor ain't listenin' so I just fucking haul off and whack the motherfucker."

"Whack him? You mean—"

"Punch the sucker."

I eyed him a moment while he took another gulp of water.

"You want to deck the mayor of Chicago?"

"Why the fuck not? Just cold-cock the sucker. Like I'm

tired of all this fucking talk. Like, you know, he's being an asshole, and he's insulting my cause, so I just fuckin' slug him. Bim, bam, flatten the fat fuck. Lay him out cold. Which nobody will expect."

"Uh-huh." True, nobody would expect that. Nobody would expect a priest to slug somebody like that.

"Because I'm not some no-balls kind of guy, right?" Tony asked, a challenging note in his voice.

"Right."

"I mean, I'm a priest, but I'm also a man with balls, right?"

"Definitely. That's the whole wonderful thing with you. You have balls."

"Because without balls, forget it."

"I would think so," I said. "No question."

The quintessence of refined artistic debate, this was becoming.

Tony struggled up from the couch and began pacing.

"I mean, I gotta be a man sometimes. I'm always walking around in this fuckin' collar with God on my mind. God this, God that. I mean, where does it say a priest can't get out of that fuckin' monkey suit once in a while and wear some real clothes, y'know what I'm sayin'? Like a normal person. I mean, I'm supposed to be an attractive guy, we got a huge female audience, I'm gettin' fuckin' bras and panties in the fuckin' mail, and so where does it say a priest can't look cool, be a rock-and-roll guy? Who says I can't wear a nice sharkskin suit or somethin'? Some Italian linen, y'know, a little Armani, somethin' double-breasted. We're supposed to be on the cutting edge with this show. I mean, where does it say a priest can't have a little fun with the ladies, even. Get it on once in a while. I mean, what am I supposed to be, a Catholic priest?"

"Yeah."

"Well, why can't I be a Methodist priest or a Lutheran

priest or a Jewish priest or something like that, get a little pussy goin' on the show—get fuckin' laid. I mean, doesn't fuckin' Joey O'Dell ever get his rocks off? C'mon, everyone knows priests get laid all the time. The audience isn't stupid. We're underestimating them. Y'know, maybe this babe doesn't want to be on a fuckin' trapeze, maybe she falls for me and just wants a good fuck and I take her out for a beautiful dinner, a horsey ride around the park, a little dancing, then we go up to some incredible hotel penthouse overlooking the city lights and I just throw this one titanic fuck into 'er and she dies happy, y'know, stops shakin' right there in my arms and then I give her absolution. I mean, I don't know—you're the writer."

"Yes," I said, trying to inject into the word all the sense of respectful consideration the syllable could allow while simultaneously, in my mind, not feeling that way at all about what Tony had to say. Actually, picture a man (me) holding a shovel, repeated clanging sounds, and a body on the floor not much more than a spreading glob of battered goo beneath the raining shovel blows.

"Maybe I'm a priest, man, but I've got to start bein' more of a man," Tony complained.

"You are a man."

"Well, it don't seem like it. . . ."

"You're a man of the cloth, Tony. Which, since we've established you as a Catholic, kind of makes the lady thing sort of a hard sell. For you, sex is . . . well, it's a distraction, an annoyance. It's like having athlete's foot, know what I'm saying? That's what kind of a minor nuisance sex is. It's meaningless to Joey O'Dell. Like athlete's foot. It's a nothing. You're bigger than that. Think of yourself as beyond sex."

He took another swig and shook his head. He slumped back into a seat and didn't look at me.

"I dunno, man," he said, "you're the genius. I'm just

tryin' to keep it fresh. As it is, I'm really starting to feel like my hands are being tied behind my back as an artist. I'm bein' robbed o' my gifts.''

I sat there trying to maintain an impassive facade of cogitation. I pursed my lips. Inwardly, my brain was a horror house of flashing banshees. I looked at Tony, who'd slipped on his headphones again and begun blithely snapping his fingers. In just these few moments, he'd started changing in my eyes, something like that time-lapse dissolve in the werewolf movies. Not all the way yet, but little fangs suddenly had appeared, peeking from his lips, the ears had pointed and sprouted hair, the forehead now flattened backward, the beginnings of a canine pate.

"Whack-a labba labba tabba . . ." I could hear faintly dribbling out of the headphones.

"I'm on your side here, Tony.''

Actually, the side that claimed my allegiance now was the production report. No matter how I did it, I had to get his ass out of this trailer and onto the stage to work.

"What?" He took off his headset. He looked at me blankly, almost as if we hadn't been having the fairly heated conversation we had just been having.

"I said, I'm on your side, man. I hear you, okay? We're on the same team here. I'm sorry if Alan gave you such a hard time about trying that punch on the mayor. . . . Alan doesn't work here again.''

"I gotta punch somebody once in a while, man . . .''

"I understand," I said. "I think we ought to go out on the stage and I'll call in the stunt coordinator and see if we can make it work.''

"It doesn't have to be the mayor, man. It could be one of his aides. Or it could be the mayor and all of his aides.'' He brightened at that thought. "We don't have to show a lot of blood if you don't want, y'know, to keep it religious.''

"Well, let's go out onto the stage and try it."

He regarded me. He nodded provisionally.

"As for the other stuff, the ladies, let me check that out. I mean, I think there can be a great romantic tension between you and some beautiful woman, which can be almost as good as you actually doing it, y'know?"

He shook his head slowly. "I gotta be able to fuck some babes on the show, Billy . . . ."

"And I'm saying, let me think about it, that's fair, right? . . . I want to keep things fresh like you do. Let me noodle it around."

"We gotta shake things up."

"I agree. I completely agree. Without using you and what you can do as an actor, we're nowhere. The ball issue, we're in sync. We lose that, we're in the dumper. I'm with you totally on the ball thing."

"That's all I'm saying. You can't tie my hands behind my back."

"And I didn't want to tell you about it, but I'm working on a great idea for a new episode for us which, if you don't get an Emmy for, then fuck them."

"Yeah?"

I got up and began pacing.

"I didn't want to tell you too much about it, but just think what would happen if the person who came down with the fatal disease was someone you didn't expect. What about if that person was . . . you?"

I tried to leave space for a bass drum beat and cymbal crash there. His eyes widened a little with surprise. The notion seemed to tug his lips back upward. Those onion eyes of his lit up all moon yellow for a second.

"Maybe," he said.

"You think you could act the shit out of that?"

"Possibly, bro'," he said with a sudden giddy confidence.

Then his face flashed puzzlement. "But I can't die, can I? I mean, or can I?"

"You dying is something to think about," I said, with a big, big grin.

"It could be amazing," he said, nodding as he thought about it, but completely missing any irony.

"I'm working it all out. That's why I didn't want to tell you about it yet. But I think that's our big episode of the season. Maybe a cliff-hanger, y'know? We get the network to promote the fuckin' hell out of it. I'll solve the death thing."

"Fabulous."

"And you'll get a fuckin' Emmy."

"Beats a fist up your ass, bro'." He cackled.

"You'll go in a fuckin' limo and walk up that red carpet with some beautiful debutante and sit there in the audience and they're gonna call your name and you'll go up onstage in this incredible thousand-buck tux and get a motherfucking statue. You just better mention my name," I joked.

I let a moment go by, watching Tony look off out the window while he drank deep from the visualization of his thank-you-to-the-Academy speech.

"C'mon, let's get down to the stage and punch out the mayor," I said after a suitable interval.

He grunted with satisfaction and started to move. "I'll be out in one minute."

I stepped out of Tony's lair and into the sunshine. Beans was crouched down with a rag in hand, shining the little spokes on the hubcaps of the Mercedes.

"Hey," I said to him, "do me a favor please and go find Jimmy Bragg, the stunt coordinator, and tell him to meet us on the stage. And then go to the prop truck and get Joe Meriweather—tell him we need some breakaway bottles and glasses and a breakaway table and chairs."

Beans nodded and left. When nobody was looking, I took

my key chain from my pocket and left Tony's car finish a tiny souvenir.

I TRIED MY BEST OVER THE NEXT FEW WEEKS TO IGNORE WHAT THAT LITTLE VOICE in the pit of my stomach told me about that conversation in Tony's trailer. I relayed it to Ralph and spent a few days sitting in his office listening to his calming, logical drawl. Ralph soothed me with the benefit of his years of experience in television and the vagaries of stars' behavior. It was this record thing, this grind, he reassured me. We would work out a few days off for Tony. He could rest, come back refreshed. Less combative. Less destructive. Less obnoxious. Less presumptuous. In any event, handling your star was the job of the executive producer on a hit TV series.

But there was no ignoring the initial shock of Tony's challenging tone. And there was no ignoring in the days that followed the increasing frequency of calls from Lloyd Wells peppering me with requests. The chum beside me on the barstool had left. Suddenly, Tony demanded to direct episodes (no surprise—he had as much as said that in his trailer). Tony wanted more advance notice about upcoming story lines. Tony's record tour conflicted with our shooting schedule—could we bend? The increased dosage of two Tenzacs a day was now required to pet my growling ulcer.

I spent less and less time in meetings with the writers I'd hired going over scripts or developing story lines or meeting freelancers. I spent less and less time in front of my own typewriter.

And I spent more and more time behind a closed door in Ralph's office figuring out how to deal with our star's latest request. Or how to deal with arranging our shooting schedule so Tony would be wide awake and willing when he got to the stage. So that he wouldn't joke with the lines and would commit to the scenes. My job slowly was evolving into that of a wrangler. A schemer. Handling Tony. Not that Tony had turned into the kind of insulting bully the two stars of *Under the Law* had been. Not yet.

But I couldn't help feeling that some beast had gotten loose, had torn free from the rigging that constrained him to the creative process and commonweal. Something was out of my control and threatening us all. An iceberg adrift in the sea-lanes. A clot severed from its arterial lining and with each pump of the heart racing through the bloodstream, circulating toward a calamitous collision with the brain.

"WELL, WHY DON'T YOU TRY PUTTING YOURSELF IN HIS SHOES FOR JUST A second?"

"Put myself in his shoes?" I said, in the tone of one who'd just been told somebody'd peed in his wineglass.

"Yeah. Why not?"

From the passenger seat Dayna parried my indignant look. She might as well have stuck her tongue out. We were en route to the airport to pick up my parents, who were making their first visit west. My new car muffler had been knocked loose on a road bump coming out of the supermarket where I'd bought the provisions they'd requested for their stay (two boxes of All-Bran). The exhaust pipe had clunked to the ground, and, too late for the airport to get it fixed, I'd had to crawl beneath the car and jerry-rig some strapping. We were trailing sparks down the highway.

"You have a lifetime appointment as devil's advocate or something?" I demanded. I was in a ratty mood. "You got a tenured position? You chairman of the faculty senate or something?"

She curled her lip in distaste at my crabbiness. If the institution of marriage has come close to perfecting anything about the human species, it is the ability to look disgusted. Dayna, with plenty of chance to practice, had developed one of the world's all-time greatest look-of-disgust moves. It was like her whole soft, angelic face suddenly lifted its skirt and took a squatting crap on the curb. In a synchronous movement of sheer perfection, her lips ruffled, evincing such a penetrating vision of distaste that you could get ptomaine poisoning just witnessing it.

"Can't you answer that question?"

For the moment, she had no interest in talking to me. She wanted to let the look do the talking. Which it did voluminously, leaving me to steer the car, my head buzzing. One thing or the other preyed on me. First, Jarvis, Ostrow, and Werner, then—whoopee, the pilot—and now Tony Paris had his canines sunk into my back, his claws raking my ribs.

"I asked you a question."

"Screw you, Billy, okay? If it's getting to be such a problem, do something. Fire him. But don't take it out on me just because I happen to get along with him. You know, it's like you don't expect people to grow or change. You want Tony to stay put, just be the same undemanding person he was. But he's not anymore. And I've got news for you, you aren't either. I mean, when he makes a record, or goes out on a tour, or shoots a video, do you think he ought to stand there going, 'Gee, I don't know, let me call Billy,' or 'I can't decide, I'm not talented enough.' You know, maybe it isn't only Tony who's having problems with a big head."

Dayna stared out the window while I made agitated clucking sounds with my mouth. Success was a broken muffler. I sparked down the road in pluperfect resentment. Of everything. Of the visit from my folks. Of Dayna very much. Of her stoppered-up sympathy for me, which she'd seemed to keep very tight control of lately. And of myself for having never put the kibosh on her working with Tony and the sort of back-channel relationship they'd formed. Maybe it was just the way her earrings jangled that infuriated me. Or the

new haircut she'd turned up in arriving from Tony's desert
video shoot a couple weeks ago, her 'do clipped shorter than
I'd ever seen it, her head shaved in the back—one of those
punkoid rock-and-roll cuts that, like everything else about
her attitude lately, reminded me that I seemed to have been
robbed of her exclusive services in my corner.

Not that I felt she'd gone so far as to undermine me. I
simply resented it when I'd be home from work stewing
about the latest slight offered by my difficult actor, and in
she would walk, brow unwrinkled, fresh from presenting
him her stage design for his summer tour, which, she trilled,
he'd raved about.

"You're going to sit there and tell me in all the time
you've been working with him you haven't encountered an
ego the size of Montana?"

"No."

"I hear he was a maniac on that shoot. Bossing people
around. Getting in everybody's face. Throwing away money.
You didn't encounter any of that?"

"A little. Look, all I know is I worked like a dog. My
budget is all up there on the film. People seem to be happy.
They can see I didn't get the job just because Tony was
doing you a favor. It's the foot in the door I needed."

"So he was fine to you."

"He was fine to me."

"Yeah, well, you've apparently got a blind spot."

She sighed deeply. "Talk about not seeing clearly."

Now seemed about the worst possible time for a visit from
my folks. The two of us were so cranky with each other. It
was all the more vexing because I'd thought the one big rub
had been fixed with the surgery, even though we still had
some concern because we hadn't gotten pregnant yet in another bunch of tries.

Maybe, as that one debilitating impediment had been
lifted from our backs, something else had been ripped away

with it. A vacuum, a silence, a remoteness had been left behind where a common cause had existed.

Our baby plight had left me leery of the emotional pawing I encountered when my parents came off the plane and the inevitable stocktaking that ensued. I'd been divulging precious little about my life to the family since smuggling myself out of my own childhood at the age of fourteen. Even so, it was all I could do to withstand the heartbreaking rampage of their affection. So dammed up from the infrequent visitations. Their dimming eyes afraid to look for their grandchild, this yearned-for, late-in-the-day gift denied them. The mint not on their pillow.

We headed out of the terminal. My father, the burly bear shrinking toward koalahood, seemed ever frailer and ever more badly dressed. He wore a new short-sleeved shirt, picked for what he would have said was how "sporty" it looked. Yet all it did was reveal the luffing triceps on his mottled arms. He insisted on toting two hundred pounds of luggage and presents, a burden that seemed sure to blow his ventricles to smithereens.

"This Tony Pappas, you get along?" he queried once I'd fastened his seat belt for him and we'd gotten rolling. I'd never had to fasten his seat belt for him before. But he appeared helpless before the simple mechanism. It was a shivering intimation of a time when I'd be pushing at him, inspecting for bedsores. Nothing wrong with his vocal cords yet, though. "I have a bone to pick with you. What's with this goofy face he makes for the camera?"

"We get along fine, Dad," I said, doctoring the truth in the sort of terse stiff-arm that would have been the envy of many a Ministry of Information official. I didn't want to have to side with Tony Paris against anybody, especially my father. Since childhood, anyone I'd thought estimable he had mercilessly caricatured as a way of needling me, I suppose, for my worshiping someone other than him. Joe Montana.

Bono. My father once ran down the subject of my civics term paper—Albert Schweitzer—saying he should have stayed closer to home and been as good to his parents as he was to those African strangers.

"This face. He must think it's racy or something," my father persisted. "Why don't you tell him? Won't he listen to you?"

"The women like it, Louis," my mother broke in, tapping him on the shoulder from the backseat. "What you care doesn't matter."

"I'm just saying, if I see him doing this all the time"—my father, mimicking Tony's smile, puffed one cheek out and drew up one side of his upper lip to look like a man flinching from an onrushing projectile—"then a million other viewers must see this and feel the same way. It stands to reason. If he keeps doing this"—he repeated the mug—"he won't be a success. Not in a million years. Mark my words. What's that smell?"

"My tailpipe broke."

"On a car this new? You chump. A car like this must go for forty grand—"

"It wasn't forty, Dad—"

"The tailpipe broke. Unbelievable!" he pronounced bleakly, sounding about my exhaust system probably like God did when Jesus got sentenced. "This Tony Pappas a mob guy?"

"No evidence so far, Dad."

My father's abiding theory was not only that the most important sporting events, whose results I'd hung on as an adolescent, but the entire working of the planet—from a cancerous alteration in the p53 tumor-suppressor gene to the course of the Humboldt Current—was decided by two mob guys sitting in a penthouse high above Las Vegas.

"Believe me, the head of your network will get a call. 'You like Tony Pappas? Well, we like this other guy, Ray.

We want Ray in the TV show. Tony Pappas is out. Or on July ninth you're gonna have some trouble. Mr. Tony Pappas is going to be hit by a car.' Mark my word. Tell me something—do you remember that trip we took to Hershey, Pennsylvania?"

"That was a great trip, Dad—"

"Remember those hives you got? Those big crocodile tears. Hey, Felicia, remember? Those big crocodile tears rolling down the kid's face when he got those hives? I should have settled out here after the war. What a climate."

"Who cares about the climate?" my mother said. "Let's discuss something else."

But, as wildly scattered as the so-called conversation had been, Something Else was not what Dayna or I felt like discussing. So, since dealing with parents is as much an exercise in fending off as embracing, I lobbed defensive questions at them. Had they saved the hydrangeas? How went the old willow?

I took my folks to the studio, which, of course, impressed them. I introduced them to Ralph and Tony. Old Onion Eyes was brilliantly charming to them. No one is more polite than he who can afford to be because he holds a knife hilt-deep in your chest. My parents were smitten by the TV star all their friends were talking about. Afterwards, we had lunch in the commissary while I had one of the transportation guys fix my car muffler.

That afternoon we toured Los Angeles. I'm not sure what it says, but in what other town would the two most prominent points of interest be footsteps in concrete and tar pits? Not to mention Forest Lawn cemetery, which was the spot that, to my amazement, my mother announced she most wanted to see.

"An ex-schoolteacher like you? You come to Los Angeles and you want to go to Forest Lawn?" I was aghast. I couldn't figure it out. In the time after you leave home, do your parents keep growing and acquiring new tastes or do they just stop hiding from you the most egregious evidence of their stupidity? Perhaps you'd simply conspired to shield your eyes from it while growing up in order to keep your sanity.

"What's that supposed to mean? You always hear about it," she said, tossing her head defensively. "You know I love the movies."

"There's a difference between loving movies and being a ghoul, Mom. I think of you as being more sophisticated."

"Your sense of humor is lost on me."

"Okay. Fine. Forest Lawn. We'll go to the graveyard."

I bit my tongue and spun down the freeway toward Griffith Park. I couldn't think of anything creepier than this sort of moronic idol worship in America's Valley of Kings. In the blazing sun, hunting down the final haunt of some actor who'd probably been at least as much of an egomaniacal asshole as Tony Paris was being to me—I wanted to kill my mother. But she trudged stoically onward in the sneakers she'd donned, peering at headstone after headstone even as the rest of us were beginning to wilt. We seemed to be walking forever, up and down hillsides. Past the Vale of Peace and across the Vale of Hope. I wondered how the average dead people felt being slighted under my mother's quick, dismissive glance at their names. Oh, that was only Joseph Wilson, a run-of-the-mill dead person with zero box-office gross. And she would tramp on.

Not that the heat or ghosts stopped my father's erratic ditherings.

"I think I see Stan Laurel," he would offer, shading his eyes while he squinted against the sun, calling out as if he had sighted the New World. Then we'd reset course to hike up yet another hill. The only time he fell quiet was when he stood, seemingly awestruck by history, inspecting a life-size replica of Boston's Old North Church, an edifice that seemed quietly puzzled to find itself situated on a hill-side overlooking Disney's Animation Building. And then he quickly resumed peppering me with prattle, unraveling whatever moments of lucid comment or reflection we seemed just about to knit together. I sort of gave up and in lieu of anything else attempted to delve into family current events.

"Did you see Ellen before you came out?"

My older sister, with whom I had a perfectly convivial relationship, was married, with two kids, and was a special-education teacher in Merrick, Long Island.

"She seems well."

"And her family?"

"All good. I think Buster Keaton is this way, dear."

We set our sights on the Vale of Enduring Faith. He'd taken on my mother's zealousness now. They refused to be denied seeing the tombs they wanted. Who cared about my sister?

"How's Cousin Hoglah, Dad?"

My cousin had changed her name several years ago for reasons unknown but somehow having to do with the life-style she'd embraced after college, working the land and living in some hand-built wicki-wacki near High Point, North Carolina, right on top of a hill that was supposed to be some spiritual vortex of incalculably rich mystical energy but which, in any event, yielded pitifully small tomatoes.

"I don't hear from her. Felicia! I think I see Lucille Ball!"

We continued this insanity for what seemed like an hour, me fuming, Dayna panting wordlessly at my side and think-ing who knows what about her daffy in-laws. But our search turned up little more than the grave of someone I'd never heard of who my father thought he remembered as having appeared in an old silent film, *The Golem*. Which was proba-bly made by some mob guy.

"I thought Bette Davis was supposed to be here," my

mother finally said, pulling to a stop in the Vale of Abiding Love and looking crestfallen. Here she was, an intelligent woman in her sixties, a docent at the Met, talking like a child who wasn't getting her lolly.

"You sure this is the right Forest Lawn?" my father said, suddenly looking accusingly at me. "We're obviously in the wrong cemetery. It figures."

"Don't be stupid, Lou." My mother was running a hand-kerchief across her perspiring face.

"Don't look at me," I said, trying not to let my anger loose. "I've never been here before. I don't make a habit of tramping around looking for dead actors."

"What do you have to be such a smart mouth for?" my mother said.

"I just don't understand what we're doing here. It must be a hundred degrees out. What's the point? This isn't Lincoln's tomb we're talking about, it's Raymond Massey's maybe."

"It is pretty hot," Dayna said, fishing for concurrence.

"It's just something that interests me, is that so bad?" my mother said. "They get plenty of tourists here. Look at that beautiful mosaic—'The Birth of Liberty.'"

"Well, quite frankly, I'm amazed that this kind of bohunk bullshit somehow captivates you."

"I really don't appreciate that tone."

"I'm sorry."

"Let's everybody just cool down a bit," my father said.

"I thought you came out here to be with me and Dayna. Look, obviously we're lost. Maybe we can try again tomorrow. There's another cemetery we can try on Santa Monica near Paramount. I hear that's where Valentino and Tyrone Power are. But for now, can we just get out of here before we all have heatstroke and get buried here ourselves?"

"Let's just ask that man over there."

"What man?" I sighted along the finger my mother was pointing. "You mean that guy cutting the grass?"

"Yeah, ask him."

"Mom, really—"

"Then I'll do it myself." My mother shot me a sharp look and wheeled toward the gardener.

"Felicia, wait a second. I'm not sure I can keep this up anymore," Dayna broke in. "Maybe it's the heat or something. I'm feeling a little dizzy all of a sudden. I'm sorry, but I better sit down somewhere in the shade. I really shouldn't be out here like this . . . because, well . . ."

She put her hand to her lips, and tears sprang from her eyes.

"Billy," she said, a laugh breaking through, "I think I'm pregnant."

Eight

Yessir, I was the Proud Pappy. The Cursor and the Precursor.

The Genial Generator.

Sir Spawn.

The Sinewy Sire. The Giant of Genesis. The Ensign of Engender.

Steamboat Willie.

The Framer of the Constitution.

The Duke of Dick. The Master of Mitosis.

I was the Oompah Band.

King Ferdinand of Fecund.

Big Ben, baby, and the Colossus of Rhodes.

The Khan of Concupiscence.

The Father of Waters.

The El Cid of Seed.

The Guns of Navarone.

I beget, therefore I am.

I got the Elgin Marbles in here.

Got my Writ of Priapus.

I could procreate, promulgate, and progenerate.

Gin. Bingo. Checkmate.

I was gonna be a daddy.

WELL, SURE I WAS A BIT NONPLUSSED AT FIRST HEARING THE NEWS BLURTED OUT like that on the Forest Lawn hillside in front of my mother and father. That sort of information should have called for something a little more intimate and discreet, and maybe even a time when I was in a better mood instead of one when I was seething at my parents.

But Dayna apologized, and it quickly made no difference, of course. She'd been forced to announce it, lest we spend another three hours doing the Bataan Death March behind my necrophilic mother at the cemetery. Dayna had taken the home pregnancy test at our house that morning, and—what with the rush to get to the airport, our bickering, and the day jammed with events—she hadn't found the right moment to give out with such throat-catching news until she'd been forced to.

Lou and Felicia were delirious. In fact, we all got a little emotional there on the hillside that afternoon amidst the tombstones. We called Dayna's folks that night. My parents couldn't know and not hers. Don and Jenny Chilton still lived in a yellow clapboard house in Gresham, Oregon, where she was a school librarian and he had been a copying-machine dealer before opening his own fly-fishing catalogue business. We imagined them there, on the phone by the stairs, Jenny's apple cheeks flushing with joy, Dayna's dad cocking his head toward the receiver to share the word, his face alight in a luminescent smile (he's passed that gift down to Dayna). And that's exactly how it was.

"I'm going to go into the kitchen and pour myself a nice

big Scotch and drink to your health," he said. "Maybe I'll sit down at my bench and tie a new fly and name it after your baby."

Over the next weeks Dayna and I began telling others we were pregnant. I know you customarily wait a little longer. But after all we'd been through, we were too excited to hold back. The typical, male, dummy-headed nudge in the ribs to me surpassed the most fulsome praise any Nobel committee might accord. Poke. Jab. "Heh heh heh. You old dog, you . . ." The sly cutting of the eyes at me. Chortle. I slurped it all up, right out of the saucer. I rejoiced in every punch in the arm.

"Yeah, well, someone had to do it," I'd mutter, looking down at my shoes with deep humbleness. Maybe even rocking back and forth a little on my heels. Maybe even jamming my hands down in my pants pockets. I thought about wearing suspenders for the first time since I was five, just so I could snap them.

"You old devil, you . . ."

Expecting. Was there ever a more lovely word? Was there ever a more lovely time? There is a future we are happy about and it is coming our way.

Dayna soon was nauseated and running for the toilet nearly every morning. To hear those odd, abrupt, retching scales echoing down the hallways! As if I lived with some practicing mezzo-soprano. I'd prick up my ears at the sound of this aria and then contentedly ruffle the sports pages and settle down to my cereal to await the dramatic final chord that was the sound of the flushing toilet.

We sat side by side in bed at night, reading pregnancy books, looking at pictures of the developing little life inside her, and holding hands and redoing the world with every page turn. Oh, did we indulge in all of it! Batting around names. Imagining our tot crawling through every nook of our suddenly comfy nest. We played imaginary police-sketch artistry—combine my chin with her big eyes and wide smile; or amalgamate her nose and my blue eyes with her arching eyebrows and regally high forehead. We debated schooling and child care and the merits of boys versus girls and whether the nursery should be wallpapered with a pattern of little ducks or bunny rabbits. The boxes piled high in there, the detritus of our childless past, would be cleaned away and replaced by a crib, a changing table, a rocker, a delicate dangling mobile that played lullabies as it turned.

I glutted myself on endearing visions I'd until now hurled from my mind as if they were images of hell. Sand castles. First steps. First words. Swings. Penciling in my kid's height on the edge of the wooden, swinging kitchen door. Curtain up at the school pageant. Pushing a wobbling bicycle from behind as I taught her or him to ride. Reading *The Wind in the Willows* and watching the curls of her or his hair against the pillow and the dull, lager-colored light beating through a lampshade encircled by Mother Goose characters.

And so for a blessed while my psyche perched in a tree house even as *Father Joey* bit at the bark below me, trying to claim my attention. I had found peace of mind.

The pregnancy brought this bliss to me at a perfect time during the production season. It rejuvenated me. We were nearing the end, and we were all fried. That's the way it turns out making one-hour TV. The pace of shooting invariably overtakes the stockpiling of prepared scripts, no matter how carefully in advance the writers can break stories and draft pages. We were shooting scripts that we'd succeeded in rewriting and polishing for the camera mere days before. We began having to skimp on prep time, telling location managers and set designers and directors what we'd need without their being able to read finished scripts. By the very end of the year, I foresaw we'd be staggering to the finish, running scenes down to the awaiting stage before even the actors had a chance to read them.

This added to the stress, playing on nerves, splotching complexions, and chafing stomach linings. Exhaustion confounded perfection. I had to spend extra hours rewriting. I had to stay later and later in the editing room watching cuts of episodes. So while my mind soared happily, conjuring its nursery tales, I got to spend less and less time with Dayna side by side in our bed. Work ran me ragged. And Dayna was still working hard, too.

There was even less time to enjoy the fact that the show had become such a hit. We were winning our new time slot, the one *Under the Law* hadn't held. Tony Paris fan clubs were being started all across the country. There were tube-and-Bible parties every week when the show aired and talk about it all next day at work, and if you hadn't watched, when you walked away from the watercooler your friends made faces at you behind your back. People even began asking for my autograph.

We were cited by Congress.

A deal was struck to begin broadcasting overseas in France and Italy and Japan.

Astronauts circling the earth in the space shuttle said the only thing they regretted about their weeklong flight was that they had to miss our show. They hoped Ground Control had taped it.

Tony's appearance on *Saturday Night Live* was that show's highest-rated effort of the season.

Maybe it was this overwhelming success and the mood it fostered; probably, my happiness was due more to the answered prayer of pregnancy and impending fatherhood—but I felt more steeled against Tony's increasingly shameless behavior.

Ralph helped so much in dealing with Tony. He never seemed resentful of the primacy of my relationship with our star, that we had a crucial, creative bond. Yet my relationship with Ralph grew into an equally important alliance—a mutual defense pact. We developed ways to deal with our petulant actor.

Ralph was a wizard at rearranging the shooting schedule to give Tony the odd morning or afternoon off. Tony seemed never to appreciate how Ralph extended himself to do this. Ralph absorbed the resentment of many of our guest stars, who, as a result, had to play their close-ups not with Tony—who might be off rehearsing with the Bopulator Brothers or consulting with Dayna about the right look for the next videos they were set to shoot—but with Tony's stand-in or maybe just the script girl reading Joey O'Dell's lines.

Ralph and I teamed to ease Tony out of the trailer with a smile on his mug. A lot of good-cop, bad-cop razzle-dazzle. When Tony demanded something particularly impossible from me, I might meet it with: "Let me ask Ralph and see if it can be done." And when only Ralph was handy to hear one of Tony's requests—one time, for example, he lobbied our hiring Beans, possessed to our knowledge only of the abilities to grunt, drive, and wipe, to direct three days of second-unit action sequences—Ralph's response was a bright nod and "Gee, sounds like a good idea to me, let me check with Bill." Not infrequently—mercifully—by the time we got back to Tony with a carefully constructed counterproposal to his most unconscionable aims, his previously nonnegotiable demand had already been forgotten. That's often the way with egos. They usurp the space in the brain once taken up by memory.

"I need a mug of beef bouillon right here on this stool on the set when I'm working, and it's got to be in a clear glass mug like this and it's got to be hot, steam-coming-off-it hot, is that clear! If I blow the steam off it once and the steam doesn't come back, it's not hot enough! Hey, everybody, from now on, this is the bouillon stool. I don't care if you're the fucking Pope, nobody is to sit on my bouillon stool!"

Cut to:

"No, it can't be Acme Bouillon, that stuff is garbage. It's got to be Figg's Végétal, from Fortnum & Mason in London. I don't care, pay the motherfucking Federal Express bill, this is what I need to work! You want a hit show? No bouillon, no shooting!"

Cut to:

"Hey, who told you I liked bouillon?"

Ralph was happy just to do his job well and to counsel me. He didn't yearn for public plaudits. He never cared that he was excluded when Tony and I were asked to appear on *Good Morning America.*

It was no big deal to Tony. But I'd never been on television before. My excitement helped to make me fairly chirpy at five in the morning as I sat in the makeup chair, all bleary-eyed, Tony kidding me about now knowing how it felt to be worked over first thing in the day like this. He wore a yellow-and-black bowling shirt. I wore my best blue suit and tie.

We sat next to each other in director's chairs being interviewed on a hookup from New York by the show's entertainment reporter, a round-faced black man who was irrepressibly glib and apparently ecstatic to be doing the first live national television interview with the principals behind this new cultural phenomenon.

"How'd you come up with the idea?" I was asked. I answered the way most writers do, which is to say in halting, weak-voiced circumlocutions that arrived at no point in five seconds or less and so seemed utterly worthless to the interviewer. He couldn't switch his attention fast enough.

"How does it feel to be the hottest TV star in America?" he inquired of Tony.

" 'Ey, it's better than a Louisville Slugger in the groin," Tony cackled.

"People are just so in love with your character," the interviewer bubbled.

"Well, I dunno, I think the thing is with this guy is that he's real. And I think people like somebody who's real."

"I know, but you hear words like 'gruff' to describe you, or I mean O'Dell, and that's not the usual type the viewing public takes to."

Tony gave out a sort of dumb chuckle. He shrugged, suddenly at a loss.

"Well," the interviewer added, "the country is just really getting to know you, and there's this incredible curiosity. Particularly among women. You have some killer effect on them. Has that always been true? I mean, you're not traditionally, beefsteak-type handsome, you know what I'm saying? I mean, I think we can all admit that here."

Tony searched around some more and then tugged at his ear while emitting a high cackle, as if he'd been asked something unfathomable and not altogether welcome but he wasn't going to be cross about it. Tony hated being interviewed.

"Some reports mention a lot of wild parties and that sort of thing in your past . . ."

"I wish, man, lemme tell ya," Tony said.

"Are you religious?"

"Religious? That's kind of a personal—"

"I just mean, that sense of helping people that O'Dell has, do you have that too, that, you know, people-first deep down, or whatever, you're really caring and tender?"

Tony jerked his thumb my way. "Better ask him," he said.

"Well?" The interviewer reluctantly turned to me. "What does Tony share with O'Dell, if anything? What's he like to work with?"

What I could have answered!

What I should have answered!

I might have stopped the scourge in his tracks right then and there. Instead, Paul Revere pulled up at the first pub he passed, strolled in, and bought a round for the Brits. Truth, reality, my roiling Krakatoan ulcer, were brushed aside as I yanked out the biggest honey dipper you ever saw and began oozing.

"Oh, they share a lot—that caring you talked about . . . that loyalty and commitment . . ."

"Yes?"

"Well, that's Tony. I mean, working with him is truly fantastic. He's always considerate of others, always sensitive. Always trying to make us a family."

Tony beamed.

"So the success hasn't gone to his head?"

I laughed at the absurdity of that. "Not at all. We're both superappreciative of what we've got going. Tony's not stuck up at all about it. I mean, well, my wife just got pregnant, and the next thing you know, there's this huge, expensive bassinet and a teddy bear delivered to our door. All kinds of baby gifts. Right from Tony. And that's just one example."

"Great. Well, we have a little surprise for you two, one that I hope makes getting up this early worth your while. The American Television Watchers Awards nominations are being announced this morning, and we've got a little inside news—Tony's been nominated, and so has your show. Congratulations!"

"Well, ain't that a kick." Tony laughed. And he turned to me. And we hugged. Buddies. Rip-roaring, tear-up-the-roadhouse-Friday-night homeboys. Right there on national TV.

So I left there smiling, my six minutes of fame on tape, with just a bit of an aftertaste as I recollected my less-than-candid, garland-heaping piffle.

I didn't head straight over to the lot, though.

The bright TV lights had pained my right eye, which not

only Ralph but several others had remarked on for the past weeks as looking red and irritated. It had worsened in the last couple days. It was tearing a little. It felt stiff as I turned or changed focus. I decided I shouldn't ignore it any longer. Reluctantly, I made a quick phone call to Mona, and she set up an immediate ophthalmologist appointment.

So I interrupted my calls to duty to visit Dr. Michael Bay in Beverly Hills, on one of those four or five streets lined with medical buildings and haughty shops that seem to spit at you as you pass by.

Dr. Bay was a short, balding gent with a veiny, boxy nose. He wore a white tunic and shuffled about his examining room with little apparent enthusiasm for what he was doing. About sixty or so, I guessed, probably nearing retirement. Overseeing a listless practice in a drab, underlit suite that wanted a good deal of redecorating. Lots of cataract patients, no doubt; no longer much time spent on abashed fourth-graders who weren't seeing the blackboard clearly from the back row in class.

He introduced himself, and I followed him into a room and took a seat in a cushioned chair opposite the ordained eye chart. Dr. Bay washed his hands, then positioned himself on a low rolling stool. He took a quick glance at me, then flicked some switches by an appurtenance that he pulled toward my chair.

"Something going on there, all right," he mumbled as he did this. "You should have come in sooner." He scanned the patient information questionnaire I'd filled out, which had been attached to the clipboard he held.

"Ever have this sort of irritation before?"

"No. Once I was hit in the eye by a hardball and it swelled up and got irritated. But that was a long time ago. I'm doing a lot of reading and working in the dark and staying up very late, so I'm sure I'm not doing my eyes any good. Maybe they're just tired."

"I doubt that's it . . ." he said. "Lean your head back and I'll put some drops in your eye so I can have a look inside. You allergic to any medication?"

He glanced again at the clipboard.

"No," I said.

He held my eye and poised the dropper over it.

"You're taking Tenzac?"

"Yeah. A little occupational hazard. For an ulcer."

"Hope you're not trying to have kids. This'll sting a little."

I felt a wet burning from the drops.

"What do you mean?"

He blotted the runoff rolling down my cheek with a tissue and went for the other eye. I caught a glimpse of an orange splotch on the corner of the Kleenex.

"Side effect of Tenzac."

I blinked at the liquid bombardment in my other eye.

"Really?"

"It's used as a male contraceptive in Europe."

He wiped again at the excess.

"I didn't know that."

"You don't get the literature. And you don't have a son trying to start a family." He grunted as he turned and reached for his appurtenance. "We don't know exactly how, but sometimes gastrointestinal inflammations can involve the eye; that may be what's going on with you. Now lean forward and put your chin right on this."

He pushed an appliance up to my chair. It was a bulky metal scope that looked as if it would have been put to good use by Torquemada. He scooted around to the other side of it and began turning wheels to adjust its height.

"My wife's pregnant," I said through a jaw clenched on the metal brace of the scope, but he seemed too preoccupied to hear the defensive note in my voice.

"My kids're all grown. One's in school, the married one's a stockbroker. Talk about a crazy business. Everybody's got bleeding ulcers or worse. Now let's have a gander in there. Just look straight ahead, right at me," he said, switching off the room lights so that there was only one small, laserlike beam of white lancing at me, leaving my blood-rich retina naked to his view through my dilated pupil.

I LEFT DR. BAY'S OFFICE AND WALKED ACROSS THE STREET AND UP TWO FLIGHTS of concrete stairs to my car in the parking structure. But I don't remember crossing the street, and I don't remember taking any stairs. Into the ceaseless whine that was the twenty-four-hour Daytona of my mind, a new rattle had been injected, a low background flapping as of something unstrapped and very, very wrong.

As soon as I'd fired up the car, in midmull, the phone beeped.

"How's your eye?" Mona wanted to know. "You going blind?"

"Fine. He gave me some drops. What's up?"

"I'm not sure, but Ralph told me to tell you you had to see Tony as soon as possible."

"Why?"

"I don't know. Something's going on."

"What?"

"I don't know."

"Put Ralph on."

There was a pause on the other end. Then, in a tone of reluctant divulgence she admitted: "He's not here."

"He's not there?" This was surprising. His not being there. Ralph was always there.

"He went home."

"What do you mean, 'He went home'?"

"He went home. About five minutes ago he just got in his car and left."

"He left? To go where?"

"Home," she reiterated more stressfully. "I don't know what's going on. But I think all hell's breaking loose. Um, I think maybe Ralph just quit."

"What?"

"I think, maybe . . ."

"Are we shooting?"

"I don't think so."

I was nearing the freeway when I hung up the phone. My show was apparently in chaos. Dead ahead I could see traffic was snarled up and not budging. And what the fuck was it that Dr. Bay had just told me? I cursed to myself and screeched to a halt at the roadside. I yanked a softcover pamphlet from my glove compartment. It showed the fastest surface-street routes through Los Angeles for just such occasions, which were not infrequent in this freeway-stitched wasteland.

And then I floored it. I had to get across town to the studio. I accelerated past late-for-important-lunch speed, up past late-for-a-studio-meeting speed, up all the way past deal-going-south speed and just under show-taken-off-schedule velocity. Something like Mach 8.

I careened wildly through somnolent, split-level neighborhoods. I blurred by the L.A. byways with their meaningless Milton Bradley names. Greenview. Broadslope. Niceday Avenue. Or their Spanish equivalents with their interchangeable morphemes—Via del Sol. Avenida del Sol Via. Calle de la Rambla del Sol. No one in Los Angeles lived anywhere real. The vitamin-deprived Okies who'd settled this wasteland couldn't even think up anything to call their towns and streets. Because there wasn't really any life here to inspire it. There wasn't a High Street on a hill above a harbor that had once teemed with square-riggers and the scents and spices of the world. There wasn't a Market Street, invoking the five-hundred-year-old cobblestones where the bazaar had once been situated at harvesttime. No, in Los Angeles, if you lived in a ten-square-mile bean field with an incinerator smokestack back in 1935, it was incorporated as the City of Industry. If your bean field had a general store, it became the mighty City of Commerce. One more orange tree than anyplace else in this Serengeti and they made it the City of Orange. The whole place was a fabrication, a store-bought pack of place-names and road signs that had fallen to the ground from the back of a pickup and been glued onto a history that scarcely existed.

Horn-tooting, Art Arfons at the Bonneville Salt Flats, I blasted across the L.A. basin. Road markers were just a blur to me anyway because my pupils were still dilated wide open from the drops I'd been given by Dr. Bay. I roared around gentle curves. I flew over speed bumps. I dove through amber lights. I cut off slow-going, elderly drivers in their ancient, tail-finned sedans. I sent sweatsuited retirees— towels wrapped around their necks as they did their pathetic speed walking—diving for cover and glanced devilishly in my rearview at their receding, fist-shaking figures. It's possible that at the intersection of Via del Cañón Flores and Gentlebreeze I might have crunched six tricycle-peddling tots like tenpins. But there was no time to stop. This was more important. I had the right-of-way. The executive producer need abide no law.

The camera wasn't rolling!

I sped past the studio gate and onto the lot and skidded to a stop outside our soundstage, Number 6. A few feet from the QE2. As I jumped out of the car, I could see stagehands lolling around, reading newspapers. Yes, we were at a dead stop. At sixty thousand a day. And, yes, Ralph's car was missing from its reserved parking space.

My heart was still pounding from my road race. As I approached Tony's trailer, I caught sight of Beans. He saw me and just wordlessly nodded toward the stage.

Its twenty-five-foot-high door was as immense as the concrete blast shield to a bomb bunker. It had been rolled open. Beyond lay the inert blackness of our place of work.

I entered. I felt the crew's eyes following me, the way those who've been driven to the sidelines fasten onto the arrival of one consigned to right a failing situation. Looks of expectancy. Some with taut smiles that offered support. Some faces smeared with doltish excitement at what they perceived to be an imminent, entertaining free-for-all. It was that look—the call to a spectacle—that set my heart pounding harder. I sensed I was walking into the aftermath of some violent revolt.

From farther on, by the set where we were shooting, I heard loud music pulsating. Some strain of gaiety inappropriate for the hushed filmmaking that was supposed to be taking place.

Before I could get to it, though, I was intercepted by our first assistant director, Jim Boone. His lips were curled in disgusted disbelief, it seemed, at the sense of order that had fled. But before he could get anything out of his mouth, he was superseded by Victor Tosky, the director, who stormed up to me in a funnel cloud of outrage.

"I have never been asked to work in this kind of situation, and I have seen it all," he hissed, his stage whisper echoing so that none of the crew perched about us could fail to hear his words. He hooked an arm around my waist and angrily dragged me off to the side.

"You know what that asshole is doing in there?" He pointed toward the set, from where the music issued. "He's fucking auditioning backup singers for his fucking musical group! I don't believe it! On your goddam time! Not to mention mine!"

Victor let that condense all over my features. I felt, as it were, a large gauntlet thump onto my weejun. Since directing our successful pilot, Victor had become a big shot and moved on to what he deemed bigger and better projects.

Ralph and I had had to cough up a truckload of money to lure Victor back to direct a special two-part episode for us. This was the one wherein O'Dell finds a homeless man dying on his doorstep and the bum's request is to have one final meeting with his long-lost son, who's been told that his father is a rich diplomat. In case you've spent the past three years hiking around Tibet looking for yeti scat and never saw the show, you might want to rent it at the video store. This was the episode that was interrupted in Rhode Island by the announcement that the governor had been hospitalized and needed blood donations, resulting in so many angry viewers that he nearly hemorrhaged to death.

"I didn't come back here for this shit!" Victor thundered at me. "What the hell has happened to this guy?"

"Success, Victor" was all I could say.

"You ought to know that I have a call in to my agent and I'm considering walking," he said.

Great. I could feel sixty pairs of eyes trained on us. On me.

"Where's Ralph?"

"Ralph and Tony had a big fight. I don't know where Ralph is. I think he left."

"What started it?"

"I don't know."

"I do." Jim Boone, who'd stepped back a respectful distance, approached. "Tony had some suggestion or something like that and Ralph said no."

"Whatever it was, it would've meant pushing back at least an extra day, which I told Ralph I can't do because I'm scheduled to start prepping a pilot and I'm not available," Victor suddenly butted back in.

"That and who knows what else, the phase of the moon," Jim said, shrugging at me.

"Have we shot anything today?"

Jim shook his head.

Victor waved some rolled-up script pages in fury.

"You've got to control this fucker. This is up to you. This is the moment of truth. I'm telling you. Right now. Either you run this show or he runs this show. I mean, the word is going to get out about this guy. I want this noted on the production report. I'm not taking the blame for this."

"Jim, make sure this delay is put on the report," I said. "However the wording goes, make sure it has nothing to do with the director. I'm sorry, Victor," I said. "Let me see what I can do."

I patted his shoulder and then stepped away toward where the music was coming from.

We'd built an "alley" set where the homeless man supposedly lived. I rounded a wall and saw Tony and four women in the "alley." There was a boom box on the floor. What was yowling from it was, I quickly realized, a song from Tony's soon-to-be-released Bopulator Brothers debut album, entitled *Bop Till You Drop*.

Tony was in his O'Dell wardrobe, his black trousers and clerical collar. He and the quartet of beautiful women behind him were practicing dance steps under the eye of a female choreographer. A dozen or so of the crew watched.

Tony had taken control of the stage.

Using a rolled-up script as an imaginary mike, he took a step left and crouched over and howled, sort of looking like one of those hunched, furious godlike figures in a William Blake engraving. Urizen and the Urizenettes. They pranced and twirled behind him as he sang:

"You walk out the do' just leave the ring on the flo' . . . Got-ta got-ta got-ta got-ta got-ta ooooooowaaaaaaa. . . ."

They hunched and stomped and Tony did a couple knee drops.

Sixty thousand a day! The crew was just sitting around!

Tony saw me and nodded, and after another small nod from Tony, the choreographer turned off the music.

"I hear we're having some problems," I said, master of the

conciliatory understatement as I approached. The show at a standstill. The star in rebellion. The producer gone. The director ready to quit. A hundred people on a time clock with their thumbs up their asses. Yes, it was fair to say we had some problems.

Tony was perspiring from his exertions. He was loose, angry, unpent. He was cruising. His eyeballs glowered.

"I don't remember writing this scene in the script," I said, trying for a little levity.

"Yeah, well, the producer tells me to get fucked, then takes a walk, I figure I might as well put the time to good use for myself." This he tossed off in a glib, challenging way.

"That doesn't sound like Ralph."

"Yeah, well, that's the message I'm gettin', man. Loud and clear."

He was in a vile mood. He shifted his weight from one foot to the other, unsettled and impatient.

"From who? I'm not giving you that message."

"I refuse to be treated that way, man. I won't fuckin' have it. You can take this show and shove it! I got better things to do."

He'd grabbed a towel and was running it over his face as he paced. The crew heard every word.

"Why don't we go back to your trailer and talk about this, okay? This is not the place."

He didn't respond to that, didn't look at me. He simply wheeled and began marching off the stage and out past everybody bellowing: "You ask me to do this shit and I do it. Every single day. Every fuckin' scene. Every goddam fuckin' day. One episode after the next. And I do it. Okay? 'Cause I'm a pro. And then you turn around when I ask for anything and it's a goddam problem. Well, I can't work like this, man! I hate this! I'm tired of this fuckin' show! This is jive, man! I wish this show was canceled!"

He stalked off toward the door and the sunlight, spewing

this disheartening poison. I rushed after him past the stony-faced, hushed crew. I was conscious of adopting the role of pacifier. Which to me smelled of supplicant. I was following the beat of his tantrum. But there was no time to care about that.

He'd already slammed the door shut on the QE2 when I reached it. I barged right in. My own anger was mush-rooming not only at his unconscionable tirade and slap at the crew but at being upbraided publicly and having to chase after him like that. A dim voice inside me urged restraint over the violent anger I felt. I wanted to uproot a tree and drive him into the ground with it like a peg.

To my surprise Lloyd Wells hopped up from the sofa cushion as I entered. He scraped a napkin across his mouth, which was in the midst of chewing a greasy deli sandwich, and held out his hand. Sitting beside him was the movie director Sky Van Dyke. And between them lay an open script. Thick. A film script.

"Hi, Bill, you know Sky . . ." Wells said. A hook of rye bread and slivers of meat tumbled around behind his teeth like clothes in a washing machine.

I nodded. I looked at the script for a long enough moment so that Lloyd would note me noting it. The verb I use in stage directions when describing a character suddenly getting angry is "flared."

I flared.

"You part of the problem or part of the solution here, Lloyd?" I demanded.

I realized as soon as I said it that I was shaking with anger. I stared at Sky. He read my face. He'd seen Tony storm in and could hear the star's hoarse ravings as he banged the walls in the bedroom at the other end of the trailer. Sky Van Dyke was quickly on his feet.

"We can finish talking about this later, I think, at a better time," he said to Lloyd.

"Sure, Sky."

"Nice to see you, big fan of the show," Sky said as he passed me and ducked out the door.

Lloyd stood there a moment. He smiled sympathetically, trying to tease understanding from me.

"It's all comin' down on him," he said, pointing toward the back of the motor home. "The release date of the album, the tour, this new feature Sky wants him for. It's getting to him a little, that's what I think."

"Fuck that," I said.

Tony stormed out from the bedroom, vigorously rubbing a towel over his hair and torso. He'd taken off his shirt. Thick black hair matted his shoulders.

"We asked Ralph one little favor, that's what this is all about," Lloyd said. "This show is Tony's home. So is it so wrong to maybe work in a spot for the Bopulators? It was just a question."

"That's what you wanted from Ralph?"

"Yeah. That's all. A notion was had."

"By whom?"

"A notion. Anybody can have a notion," Lloyd said.

"This is a great showcase for my music," Tony said.

"You got twenty, thirty million people a week watching," Lloyd said. "Thanks to everybody. To you, to Ralph, to everybody. But thanks to Tony, too. A lotta thanks to Tony. So I simply thought, Hey, I'm no writer, you're a great writer, you're the executive producer, maybe there's a way those fans get to see Tony's new thing, see their star in a new light for an hour."

"You want to put the Bopulator Brothers on *Father Joey* for an hour!"

My brain had difficulty even entertaining the notion. It was so far-fetched.

"All right, it doesn't have to be the whole show. Make it half and half."

"It doesn't even have to be that," Tony said scornfully from the sofa he'd pounced on. He yanked off the top of a sandwich on the table and dropped some turkey into his mouth. He'd thrown one leg over the other and was pumping it restlessly. "I know exactly how it could be done. I could make it work in my sleep. I have the whole story line written out."

He glanced up at me.

"Just a couple of scenes. You can take a look at it. Do whatever you want with it. But I know how to make it work. I can play both parts."

"The Bopulator Brothers and Joey O'Dell?"

I was no more articulate than that. As if by repeating the notion I could make some sense out of something so hopelessly foolish. Something so hideously self-serving. The manufacture for this overblown ego of such a hollow tour de force, to insult the meaning of the phrase. A homunculus of showmanship.

"The network loves the idea," Lloyd said.

"You already asked the network about it!"

This was astonishing! This fired up my booster rocket.

Lloyd shrugged ever so nonchalantly.

"I happened to be having lunch with Carlin, and the subject happened to come up," he downplayed. "I can tell you this—he thought that Tony writing and playing and directing an episode like that was fabulous."

The air was crackling. My chest felt tight. I was enraged and kept telling myself not to lose control.

"Let me get this straight. You didn't come to me, to the executive producer of the show, with this idea. Instead, you went to the president of the network?"

"It's just a notion," Lloyd said. "I don't see what's to get so upset about."

"You don't, huh? You had the fucking balls to go over my head—"

"Wait just a second, Bill," Lloyd sputtered.

"Yeah, because I'm not being listened to here, man!" Tony erupted. He jumped from the sofa. Lloyd's right arm went out involuntarily as if to keep us apart.

"My needs are not being respected!" He stalked off toward the bathroom.

"He's not wrong, Billy," Lloyd said to me.

"Bullshit," I said.

I hustled down the passageway in pursuit.

"Your goddam needs are fucking goddam well being met!" I screamed. "Your needs on this show are good scripts and good directors and an executive producer who is an open-minded collaborator and a friend, those are your needs on this show, and don't tell me they're not being met, goddamit!"

Tony roughly slid open an accordionlike door. He was sitting there on the toilet, defecating by the sound of it. His pants were down around his ankles.

"You keep saying that and saying that, and all I can tell you is how I feel. And I feel fucked over from upstairs in the office there," he barked. He suddenly cut off his breath.

Thwick. Thwashaaastt.

"For starters, you gotta choose. Me or Ralph. He's gotta go."

Fuf. Thiiishok. Vlump.

"Ralph is a workhorse on this show," I said, turning away.

"Ralph insists on seeing me as just some other little actor on his day out of days sheet and that's it. He don't wake up, he's gone. It's him or me."

"Why am I standing here having to remind everybody that this is my show? I created it. And you have a contract."

Tony snapped off some toilet paper. He leaned forward, and his hand disappeared under his thigh.

"Fellas, decency, please, let's not debase an intelligent discussion with 'you signed a piece of paper.'" Lloyd had come up to join me in watching Tony wipe his ass. "The point is the working relationship. Making sure things run smoothly for the show. We all want the same thing. We're all in the same boat. And if Ralph is rowing in the wrong direction, you need to find a way to honor Tony's creative input and his vision. And I don't think this is working with him taking orders from a Ralph. I think Tony's grown immensely, as we all have here. And if it were me, making Tony happy, giving Tony a producer credit, involving Tony more, giving him an episode to direct maybe, is something I'd do in a heartbeat . . ."

Tony rose, hiked up his trousers, and flushed.

"All I'm saying," Lloyd went on, "is that if you went to the network and told them there were a few changes you wanted to make at the top here, I think Carlin would listen. He thinks the world of you."

"I can't believe you want Ralph off the show," I said to Tony. "It's a big mistake. And I'm not going to stand here and tell you that I'm prepared to do that."

Tony went into his bedroom and plucked up a hairbrush.

"Then just think about what we're saying for now, Bill," Lloyd said as we drifted in after Tony.

"Yeah, think about it," Tony said, preening in front of a mirror and not really meaning I was to think about it at all.

"You go behind my back and pitch an episode promoting the record album. You meet with movie directors while you should be out there on that stage shooting with Victor—"

"Victor," Tony harrumphed.

"—and then you want me to fire the producer and bump you up in his place—"

"And I wouldn't mind hearing about the story lines and directors you're discussing either," Tony said, parting his hair neatly, not missing a beat.

"Uh-huh," I said.

The trailer fell silent for a moment. I watched Tony comb his hair.

"Shame on you, man," I said.

He turned around and plunked the hairbrush down on a bureau.

"I'll be out in a minute," he said. "I gotta put on my stupid fucking monkey suit first. Go tell Victor DeMille."

I walked away. Lloyd followed me to the trailer door.

"All we're talking about is Tony should have some input," he said. "He should have what any star has. I want you two to kiss and make up later. This was good, cleared the air a little. This needed to happen. So there's no bad blood. Two American Television Watchers nominations for you bozos, eh? Heals a lotta wounds."

But I didn't want to hear any more. I couldn't. I had to get out of there. It had turned into a hellhole for me. A sulfurous pit, the taste and smell and sense-recoiling, flesh-crawling feel of which I'd once known and thought I'd left behind forever at *Under the Law*.

I closed the trailer door behind me and stood on the metal steps and at least breathed some fresh air. I squinted into the bright sunshine. Jim Boone was right there.

"Okay?" He looked up at me.

I couldn't manage any words. I simply nodded, which sent him hustling off to tell everyone to get ready to shoot.

But it wasn't okay. Not at all. I think at that moment I felt worse than I ever had working at *Under the Law*. Like some trekker who thinks he's clawed and trudged his way out of the wilderness only to find he's merely navigated some great big circle back to his starting place, I experienced the sickening flash of horror revisited.

Literally light-headed, I stood on the step of the trailer afraid to move. I tried to steady myself.

All my authority had suddenly been challenged and as

good as usurped. All that I had created by creating Tony Paris/Joey O'Dell had suddenly been shattered.

I hated Tony Paris.

I looked down at Beans crouched as usual over the Mercedes, silently, ceaselessly polishing and buffing the finish to a mirrorlike sheen.

And then I noticed a piece of decoration on the pink rag he was taking to the shiny hood. I looked closer.

A scalloped curve. A squashed, dirtied pink bow on a collar. The snaking strand of something like a snapped shoulder strap trailed the swabbing clump of cloth. And there, in small block letters squished together beneath his rubbing hand, slid the crimped word: TUFTS.

There was no doubt what Beans was waxing Tony's car with. He was using my wife's undershirt.

Nine

WHAT'S THE GREATEST MYTH ABOUT THE FEMALE SEX PERPETUATED OVER the aeons? Fidelity. As personified by the ever-constant Penelope.

While her husband tangled with sirens and sea monsters and the Underworld and cyclopes, Odysseus's wife closeted herself away from all suitors for fourteen years by cannily weaving and unweaving a shroud.

Bullshit.

If I were Odysseus, I'd want to know, Where's this shroud? Show me one strand of this so-called shroud!

She never wove any shroud. She was on her back every night. With her tunic hiked up to her neck and one leg pointing toward Troy and the other at the Atlas Mountains.

She was a slut.

Like all women.

Like Dayna.

That conclusion penetrated my brain as if driven by a nail gun when I saw Beans swabbing the car with that spaghetti-strapped Tufts T-shirt Dayna wore in the sanctuary of our marital bed. Her lucky shirt.

Tony and Dayna were cheating on me!

My unfaithful wife! With my ungrateful creation!

Death and Murder! Hell and Ruin!

In that brief moment outside Tony's trailer, some wrecking ball had bounced off my gut. And it had atomized me into countless, incoherent motes. And I discovered my own new corollary to Heisenberg's principle that misperception inheres in ascertaining the transitory: Ubiquity is not an impossibility.

So do not scoff when I tell you that over the next few weeks I existed in a thousand places at once. I lived an infinity of lives and possibilities each second and everywhere within the tempest of my being and beneath the cloud that the news about Tenzac had condensed above my head.

Had I gotten Dayna pregnant or had Tony?

Was he the father of my future or I of his?

While I wrote our show's season-ending scripts or discussed a scene on the stage with Victor or Tony, my mind was elsewhere, plotting different plots, following other scenarios.

Late at night corporeal me trudged into my home. I threw open the refrigerator and wolfed down cheese and crackers and gulped soda as was my wont; I gabbed with my missus about how soon after the impending birth she should have Jenny come down to help out or the problems she was having with a new kind of paint in the construction of a set for one of Tony's videos. I shuffled into and out of the bathroom, knotting my robe with the determined tug that seemed to put paid to the end of a man's day. I brushed my teeth and spit mouthwash into the sink; I climbed into bed next to Dayna; I touched a palm to the budding swell of her belly, bent to listen to the thump and gurgle in her womb; I kissed Dayna tenderly on the forehead and turned off the light and held her in my arms while her breathing became slow and regular and her body sank in sleep against my chest.

Yet I was in none of those places. I existed elsewhere. A chaos of preoccupations raced and quivered in my being like the dusk-freed rampage of a million bats' wings beating against the corners of a cavern. Shapeless, shadowy conclusions ransacked my brain. Horror, houndlike, hurtled wide-jawed at my throat.

Death! Death and Murder to them!

Death!

Death and Murder.

When cool my blood I could, the map of my thinking led me thus:

Okay—dream of dreams!—Dayna was pregnant. There would be a baby. But another reality gestated as well:

Perhaps—and perhaps was, well, in all probability, perhaps too weak a word—it was not my baby.

Nothing now could make that thought go away.

Those idle comments, tossed off in Dr. Bay's listless ophthalmology chambers, that my ulcer pill, which I'd taken every night at bedtime—for how long now? when would it be a year?—initially thanks to the firm of Ostrow, Jarvis, and Werner, was regularly used as a male contraceptive in Europe. . . . And I'd had to increase my dosage thanks to the onion-eyed Fiend I'd created. . . . If it was true, if Tenzac had that effect on me, perhaps I couldn't have impregnated my wife.

The image of Beans and my wife's shirt beneath his splayed, hairy, sliding hand on the mirrored car finish haunted me.

Search as I might through the mental microfiche of my mind, I turned up no evidence of any untoward relations between Tony and Dayna. No sparks. No Van de Graaffian snap in any of what had always looked to me like perfunctory tactile exchanges. Not in their salutatory cheek busses or shoulder squeezes. Nor had I seen any furtive, eye-lit love looks between them while we kept company together.

Yet . . . yet. Pace with me now in my detective's cubicle. Light your cigarette off mine and grab a cup of coffee—I take mine black, thank you—and listen. Loosen your tie.

Was there the opportunity for this crime?

Yes. No doubt, yes. They'd become friendly, meeting at the bar after shooting. Around the set when she'd visited. And at his mansion at the housewarming, where they'd danced together (was it there in some moment of writhing, rhythmic abandon that the two had reached their tacit, lust-cemented compact?). They'd seen each other in a social context on many other occasions as well, all of it playing out innocently on the face of it. I agree, I agree.

And then, of course, there was all this working together, especially that week out in the desert.

How had Ralph characterized the shoot—something about "spring break" behavior? An orgy in the air? Late, wearying hours of work alone amidst the bacchanal when aching muscles cried to be massaged. And hadn't she been noticeably out of touch with me, rushing back—and kind of tight-lipped about the experience, come to think of it—only hours before her scheduled ovulation? What sybaritic sirocco had blown hot through that Sahara? There, perhaps, they had wreaked their licentious havoc. The rivulets pouring off their bodies! The dampness! I'd been blind!

Hell and Ruin!

But let me not get ahead of myself.

That there was an opportunity for the crime—established. The means?

Yes, check that one off, too. Slash a bold, thick check o'erreaching the box, bold as Tony's seemingly indefatigable sex drive, uncontainable as his ever-ready, hemp-thick hard-on. He had the means all right.

Tony was always on the prowl for women. And weren't they literally throwing themselves at this new TV sex star? Hadn't Dayna herself commented on how appealing he was? Maybe she'd even called him sexy. Hadn't she taken to defending the bastard?

But the motive.

What might his be? No time need be wasted ascertaining that. He was a man in perpetual rutting season. And a man who, as had finally been brought home in his trailer, felt no allegiance to me.

More coffee? Let me open this window, get a little fresh air. There. Have another cigarette. I'm not through. On to her.

She wouldn't have succumbed, you say.

To which let me just start by saying other women certainly did.

But not Dayna, you say.

Not even once?

Though I had never let any of my flirtations go beyond the giggling stage (and I'd had my opportunities, now that I'd become such a big deal), who's to say Dayna hadn't let any of hers progress further?

Add in, and don't stint on this, the debilitating effect on the marriage of our childless lovemaking by the clock. How cruelly draining it had been on us. We'd been so dispirited and in such agony for so long. How easily could she deny herself a fresh, thrilling, and unencumbered dalliance? Wouldn't spontaneity, sex solely for sensual gratification, be irresistible to Dayna? Wouldn't it have been to me?

Consider merely the toll of time and the dictates of my prepossessing job on our marriage. Could she not very easily have been tempted to abjure her wedding vows?

I've heard it said that people get married so they have someone to be mean to. That's true, if cynical. Perhaps, to put it another way, the marriage vow is our most heartfelt, agonized apology for what we are, ultimately, incapable of feeling for another person.

Marriage is a long-term game of hide-and-seek that two people play. Not so much partners making common cause, spouses are competitors in this enlivening and sometimes infuriating game—two people in a quest to find each other, over the course of years closing and retreating, masking and peeling, recognizing and renewing, confounding and provoking and thus regenerating the game on and on. The more learned about the other, the more hidden and in need of pursuit.

Ultimately, though, as each in turn and at varying moments eludes the other—hiding behind a fold in time and life—one might unwittingly secrete him- or herself in a place beyond the other's reach. It could happen by accident as easily as by any conscious desire, but the marriage might be imperiled by one partner's irretrievable removal from the other's ambit.

They couldn't find each other anymore.

Perhaps this had happened to Dayna and me. We thought the crisis of childlessness had brought us closer together. And it had. But perhaps it had also insidiously weakened our capacity to be far apart.

There was so much unspent fury between us. We had inured ourselves to so much, narcotized ourselves. And in the end we had together produced nothing to show for all our efforts. That was grounds for annulment, wasn't it?

Here, have a Danish. I've got prune, cheese, peach. Let me pour you another cup of joe. I'm almost finished.

What I'm getting at is, to give her the benefit of the doubt, perhaps "motive" is the wrong thing to be looking for in Dayna's case. Was there, instead, a predisposition born of loneliness and failure? Because there seemed to her no longer any purpose to her virtue, had she stopped defending it? Was her body simply open to looting, like some beautiful temple left pristine and abandoned in the moonlight? She might not have fought off a moment's pure, untrammeled animal bliss, something if not to be excused (don't ask me to do that) then at least not unworthy of mercy or understanding.

I, as I said, had had my flirtations. I had had my lustful daydreams with this actress or that wardrobe assistant.

The sight of Dayna's lovemaking shirt turned into Tony's car-washing rag might not have resulted in anything more than denial had I not felt the smart of Tony's disrespect seconds before in his trailer. But add all I've said to Dr. Bay's offhand pronouncement and call it not unreasonable, I submit, to see if perhaps any greater insults had been done me.

Let the investigation proceed.

Confrontation at that point wouldn't have been right. No proof existed other than the telltale T-shirt, which at best was circumstantial.

There was nothing in Dayna's behavior to quiz her on. Oh, maybe there had been a nearly inaudible click, a clasp minutely undone and then reshut on a necklace that never had left the neck. But there was nothing I could check up on and nothing I wanted to stir up with her yet. I wasn't ready to go through any purses.

It was a bit different concerning Tony. At least for the moment. I was, of course, infinitely less privy to his private life and whereabouts. And at the studio his discourtesies had been nothing but "professional," however abominable. Any sort of confrontation with him about extramarital high jinks —balling up anger, piss, and suspicion and aiming one at his bare neck—would have recklessly jeopardized the show. It would have produced storms. At the very least, it would have demeaned me irredeemably. And laid the groundwork for, if not downright invited, further attacks from him on my own standing.

What could I do to address the clamor in my brain?

How to relegate the memory of that sweeping spaghetti strap on the car hood to something recalled painlessly and shrugged off with a laugh?

What would the next step be in your investigation, Inspector?

But there is another alternative, you so coyly point out. One my executive cuckold's brain refused to admit for discussion. And that is—do nothing. Yes, do nothing. Whatever was going on between Tony and my wife would blow over. Would vanish, if it had ever existed at all. And perhaps I should stop stewing, buck up, and keep my eye on the important business at hand—sustaining and safeguarding my television baby: not Tony Paris, but Reverend Joey O'Dell. Here the fine print of my voluminous contract with the studio rose up and sambaed in sixty-four-point type before my raging eyes. The show was a huge hit, ordered for a full season, and guaranteed for the next. Contractually, were I successfully to shepherd the series through another year after that, when it would unquestionably still be popular— probably more so—and when enough episodes had been produced to sell the show into syndication, I would strike it rich in the most glittery, literal sense of the term. Through profit participation in that syndication sale, I would become an instant multimillionaire. I would never have to work again. I would have succeeded at the Hollywood game. I would have shown everybody—particularly Ostrow, Werner, and Jarvis—once and for all. Shut up and keep the show going, you wisely suggest, and make a mint.

Thus I warred with myself. Enter the lists to undo gigolo Tony Paris, and, in effect, for self-preservation, slay my firstborn, Joey O'Dell?

Or rise above it and go to the bank?

Which was the manlier choice?

Where should Othello go?

WORK HAD NOW REACHED AN INSANE, ALL-CONSUMING PITCH. EXHAUSTION AND crankiness among the crew gave way to a sour feeling with word of Tony's strong-arm expulsion of Ralph. Ralph's competence and calm demeanor had earned him their deep affection.

I debated acceding to Tony's demands with Go-Go in phone call after phone call, lunch after lunch.

"Look, doll, I understand the pain you're in over this, I really do," she said. "You want me to tell you it's unfair? It's unfair. Does it suck? It sucks. All right? Has Tony Paris turned into a meanspirited person who ought to be dragged naked across a floor full of jagged glass? Yes."

I looked mournfully across our corner table at Bistro Bistro.

"Now are we through crying about it? Do you know what you're going to do?"

"What am I going to do?"

"You sent Ralph what I told you?"

"Yeah."

"From Loretta's? The deluxe basket?"

"Yeah."

"Good. Now you've shown your support for him. You've shown you're his friend. Now you're going to fire him."

"Who's running the show if I do what Tony wants?"

"That's not the point."

"That's exactly the point. I can't simply appease Tony. Ralph doesn't go around advertising it, but do you realize he's got a teenage daughter in some special-education school somewhere, she's retarded or something? She walks around in a football helmet so she won't smack her head when she has a fit and falls down? The school costs fifty thousand a year or something like that. I'm going to fire him? The fuck I will."

"Listen, Billy," Go-Go said, "buying a new football helmet is Ralph's problem. This is the reality of doing a hit show with an actor who's become a star. It's just business. He has got to be kept happy or you're nowhere. Now if you realize that, you're still the boss. Forget this business about appeasing. You're not some bozo like Neville Chamberlain running some two-bit country, you're an executive producer of a megahit show. You don't want Tony promoting his record album on the show—which I have to say I disagree with you about—but for the purposes of argument, you don't want that? You don't want to give him a bigger trailer? You don't want him misbehaving? Okay, now here's how you're the boss. You're in a position to deal. 'I make you a producer, Tony, fine, I remove Ralph and hire a line producer compatible with you—you put off singing on the show, you give me this and this and this in return.'

"It's a negotiation, doll," she said. "Two can play this game. That little schlemiel Lloyd won't know what hit him. They want, they've got to give, that's the way the world works."

Go-Go looked at me. A forkful of grilled salmon disappeared into her maw, and a self-satisfied smile appeared in its place.

And so I reluctantly found myself days later slamming my car door and trudging up the path to Ralph's house in the San Fernando Valley.

He hadn't set foot in the office for what seemed like weeks. Instead, he'd stayed home, expelled from the set, a victim of Tony's unpredictable temper because he'd insisted Tony act like a professional.

It was dark. We'd wrapped for the day, and it was after dinnertime. We were limping through shooting, flailing about, because the set was in such a state of demoralized

confusion. This, in turn, prompted only more furious bark-
ing from our star, the belled bully.

I didn't know why I was there even as I knocked on the
door. I didn't know what I was supposed to say or talk about.
I couldn't see how or why the modest, fun show Ralph and
I had begun making had turned into such a huge, horrific
mess. Least of all why Ralph in any way should be forced
from it, blamed for it. It made no sense.

Ralph's wife, Doreen, was friendly, peering amiably at my
dulled puss. She led me out back and placed two bottles of
beer down on a redwood picnic table on the patio. She
called out, and in a moment I saw a light go off in an
Airstream trailer parked in the driveway. Shortly, Ralph
emerged, ambling toward me with a screwdriver in his mitt
and a smile scrawled over his wide, friendly face.

I nodded toward the silvery vehicle after he sat down.
"You better not be planning any trips," I said. Mr. Gruff
Affability.

He smiled warmly back. "Sink needed fixing," he said.
"Gonna go up and visit Rebecca."

Doreen went inside. Ralph and I sat there listening to the
rustle of the bougainvillea blossoms that climbed all over the
latticed lanai roofing the patio. A lot of conversation wasn't
in the air. There wasn't, it turned out, a load of stuff in need
of ironing.

"I want you back, Ralph," I said, even though the re-
signed silence said things otherwise were sealed already.

"I appreciate that," he said simply.

I went on to tell him how I missed him.

"Goddamit," I said, "I'm going to pick up the phone and
tell Carlin Alemo what's going on. Get the network to back
me up against Tony or else . . ."

Ralph smiled tolerantly.

"I wouldn't make that call, Bill. Trade your star for me, a
nuts-and-bolts guy you can get for a dime a dozen, it ain't

gonna fly. Face it. You make that call, and they'll think they're dealing with a whining idiot. I appreciate it, though."

He took a pull on his beer. He tilted his head back and let the beer slide down. But he wasn't thinking of anything as far as I could see, wasn't catching my fire. He was just tasting his beer. When he lazily put the bottle back down, I knew we were parted.

"I'll be okay. We'll work together again," he said.

I didn't want him cheering me up. It should have been the other way around, not me with the job, him the guy sacked for no good reason. None of the success of the show could have happened without him, I told him. But he wasn't in need of hearing that.

"I'll be fine," he said. "I'll get another job, sooner rather than later, probably."

"The network owes you, I'll make sure they know that at least," I said.

He accepted that.

"They might not give me another hit with five years in front of it. But that's the way this business is," he said. "You're still learning."

I sat and listened to the crickets chirp out in Ralph's backyard. It was an honest backyard. There was a set of swings off to one side and a hulking, ugly stone barbecue stationed castlelike at the other end of the cement patio. The rest was short grass and a tetherball setup for his daughter when she came home and an orange tree and geraniums and a hammock. An honest backyard in a town full of lap pools and tennis courts and Zen gardens and statuary that looked like venereal warts and a million bucks' worth of nursery-bought designer trees.

I thought to myself that every multimillion-dollar deal signed by above-the-line types like me or Tony Paris or Ostrow and Jarvis and Werner ought to have a sort of personal zoning clause in it saying we'd have to have backyards this simple. You got to pick from three types of flowers: geraniums, azaleas, or impatiens. Nothing exotic or expensive. Your pool had to be oval, no flighty shapes, and had to have a plain old diving board—if you had a pool. Fuck waterfalls. Fuck fountains. And everyone, no matter how big your deal was or how many points you had, would have to have an ugly old barbecue pit. Maybe that would keep us all sane and personable and not allow us to turn into dicks, which, I realized, sitting there at Ralph's Sears-bought picnic table, was what I was turning into.

"We'll work together again, pal," Ralph repeated, and he caught my hand in his, and my hand actually throbbed. I felt a traitor to myself and the vow I'd made never to turn into Ostrow and Jarvis, who presided over barbarism while filling out their deposit slips.

Ralph threw his other arm reassuringly around me. I guess I must have looked stricken.

"Everything okay with you and Dayna?" he asked. He seemed to be making an innocent query. Yet it felt somehow awkwardly placed in the conversation. Maybe that was just hypersensitive me. Maybe Ralph was just being powerfully bighearted, turning the subject away from his own difficulties.

I peered into his eyes as I bade him good-bye. There seemed something more piercing in his look than the sort of philosophical acceptance that comes from surviving having things torn from you time and again in this business. Ralph withheld a lot from me. Maybe, who knows, he'd heard rumors about Tony and Dayna he'd kept from my ears.

But that wasn't something I could ask about right there. I had to find that out for myself.

THOSE WERE JUST A COUPLE OF HOURS IN MY LIFE THAT WEEK. CUTTING LOOSE close, valued friends. Lying to people. Lying to myself. Making up to untrusted people whom I held in contempt and who, in turn, held me in lower esteem than that. Feeling crazier and crazier, hollower and hollower. Working furiously to hire Ralph's replacement. And to finish writing what I hoped would be a terrific final script to the season even when my heart wasn't in it and I had no endurance left.

And all the while impaled on the horns of my dilemma. Horns of my own making, feeling the tick of each climbing rating point cutting deeper into my gut.

I'd finally given myself up and over to the impossible and uncontrollable gyrations of the show. And having anything remotely like fun got to be less and less a part of my day.

Despite all of that, the show became even more and more of a hit. To attract more and more of a following. Some of this you already know, but in case you've spent the last few years locked up in some sort of Biosphere isolation experiment, milling your own wheat and washing it down with rainwater, I'll spell it out here:

Time magazine sent someone out to do a cover story on us. They were considering making Joey O'Dell their Man of the Year.

I was alerted that reference would be made to the spirit of our series in an upcoming presidential speech.

A book publisher offered six figures for Tony Paris's memoirs, no doubt destined to debut at number one.

A realtor in Malibu called, inviting me to bid on an oceanfront house in the Sea Colony, right next to Robert Redford or some big star, I forget who exactly.

We were given special citations by the National Institutes of Health and the World Health Organization.

The Brazilian government offered to fly me to Rio to appear at the opening of a film festival there, where our show was causing a sensation.

There was a riot in the Women's House of Detention in

Philadelphia when the TV cable went out one night right before our show was to go on.

Paul Newman called. Not anything big, just a fan.

I was contacted by the parents of a young boy diagnosed with leukemia whose dying wish it was to meet Tony Paris.

Reverend Joey O'Dell got 18 percent of the votes as a write-in candidate for a vacant City Council seat in Baton Rouge.

The U.S. Postal Service announced it was issuing a new stamp with Joey O'Dell's likeness. You probably voted in the election to pick which of the two portraits they would use.

So whose life could have been more perfect than mine was that morning as I got ready to provide a sperm specimen at the California Center for Fertility Study (no way was I using Dayna's doctor for this)?

I was instructed on how to "provide" in the most cursory manner by a rotund, dark-complected Latina who took the information sheet I slid across a counter to her and handed me a plastic cup.

She hardly looked up from her lunch. Barely stopping the shoveling motion that stoked it into her boiler, one flabby arm holding a dripping fork pointed me toward a room in back where I could do my providing.

Plastic cup in hand, I clumped off toward a numbered doorway. The tinny drone of salsa music pounded out of a portable radio on the front desk beside the woman and seemed to follow me into the cubicle.

There was a sink on one wall, above which was taped an instruction sheet telling providers to wash their hands and then write their names down on a plastic label to affix to their plastic cups when the providing was done.

To assist in the job at hand, there was a stack of magazines. No, not *The Kenyon Review.*

I took a deep breath and tried to gather myself, tried to clear my head of all debris so I could focus on one thought, one fantasy which would pull me, like a rope tow at a ski lift, to the pinnacle of flesh and feeling necessary for specimen providing.

"Ay que bamba las pompas . . . oye no que mosquito . . . aya . . ." The tinny whine drilled into my brain with the percussive clap of many cuffed congas. I felt as if scant privacy was being offered me here. Next thing I knew a *Time* reporter would pop in.

I felt awkward. My personal history of providing was marked by nothing so much as guilt-ridden solitude and privacy. Public or even quasi-public providing on demand was unpracticed. Particularly feeling like I was doing it in front of a campfire full of drunken, howling Mexicans.

I'd had various discussions in conference rooms with the other writers at *Under the Law,* where, blocked by a story point, we'd amused ourselves by confessing the most public places each of us had provided. Going by the tollbooth. Into a mailbox among a rack of such receptacles along a back aisle in the Builders Emporium.

But that hadn't been me. My admission of public chicken choking to the other writers—the Pirates of the Caribbean ride at Disneyland—had been a lie.

"Ay que mordado la vando . . . rrrrrrrrapiene de los cuando . . . Eeeee-hah!"

My hands were cold. I looked down. Nothing.

Mr. Hotshot! Mr. Big Fucking Deal! Mr. Hit Show! Mr. Huge Fucking Ratings!

Relax.

I flipped through some of the magazines, which were so shredded they looked as if they had been eaten by goats.

Who, and at the mercy of what malformed palate of depraved sexual appetites, had brought back this selection of stroke books—*Milky Boobs, Mammoth Mams,* and *Wet Nurse?*

Page after page of gals with circus tents billowing from their torsos. Contorted this way and that, as if the photographer had said, 'Okay, dear, now tie them together and play jump rope with them,' before clicking the shutter. Many of the women seemed greatly to enjoy licking their own nipples, stuffing their beanbag chairs so far into their own mouths they appeared to be suffocating.

"Que lo bando lo bravo . . . ooo lo tornado velveeta . . ."

Mr. Awards Ceremony! Mr. Expensive Tuxedo! Mr. Shiny Limousine! Mr. Huge Fucking Audience Share!

And the women didn't come from America. They were from England. Why should the fact that Millicent K. grew up in a town with a hyphen and in a shire and not a county and wound up working in London rather than Cleveland render the pooch between my legs so desultory when I offered to shake hands?

Good question to be trashing your mind with now.

Relax.

"Eeeee-hahh! . . . Yo soy amigo latigo . . . que el vendo machino . . ."

Mr. Ratings! Mr. Executive Producer! Ha!

Relax.

Mr. Big Meeting at the Network! Mr. Good Table at Spago! Mr. Series Commitment!

Relax.

You make the call: Okay, you've got runners on second and third and two out, the pitch is wild and bounces high off the catcher's mask; while the ball's in the air, the batter swings and hits it out of the park. Is it a home run? You make the call . . .

"Estoy mismo el niño . . ."

I was on the verge of admitting defeat—cutting it off and driving out to the end of the Santa Monica Pier and taking a running start and throwing it as far out to sea as I could. Turn my pud into shark food. Chum.

And then I met Cynthia B.

Cindy was what her friends liked to call her.

She was a volunteer nurse.

She liked helpless little things. She cared for six cockatoos.

She liked to play the field, date a lot of "chaps."

She didn't like rough blokes.

She worked for an advertising agency. Obviously a woman with a hell of a mind to her. Not some dumb "bird."

She came from the Cotswolds.

Who knows what it was. Was it the color of her nipples? The large but nonfreakish scale of her breasts as they tilted up and poked through the back of the cane chair she sat on in reverse posture? Was it the quiet, modest smile on her lips? Was it that streak of gold in her shoulder-length hair? Was it the slender, well-managed voluptuousness of her waist, the peek of her belly button?

Or was it the red boots?

The red boots.

The red boots.

The red boots.

The red boots.

The red boots.

BOTTLE FULLY LABELED, CAP SCREWED ON TIGHT, I PRESENTED MYSELF AT THE front desk.

The Latina reached into a drawer and pulled out a white paper bag, the kind you'd take home from a bakery with a kaiser roll in it. She took my plastic cup, placed it in the bag, rolled up the bag top tight with two turns, and replaced it on the countertop between us.

"Now you take this over to the annex. Across the street. Twelve twenty-nine Avenue of the Stars."

"Twelve—?" I was perplexed.

She nodded. And pointed off. "Across the street. Ninth floor. You give this to them."

"I have to take it over there myself?"

She scowled up at me.

"You want me to do it?"

Very funny. Matter of fact, yeah. Better you do it. Me schlepping around my own genetic roux on the street?

It was lunchtime out on the boulevard. I squinted through my sunglasses into the habitual California sunshine as I pushed out of the office building and into the sidewalk scurryings.

Enough workers spilled from these office towers to approximate an unusual–for–Los Angeles sense of bustle and purpose and civilization. Here, at lunch hour, people actually jaywalked, hustled across streets, waited on lines for coffee, mingled in groups, rubbed elbows.

Yet even here, the sun so irradiated the landscape as to bleach from the scene any sense of real human toil. There was no grit. No garbage. No discarded paper. No bums. No stink. No city.

Just (put on your tap shoes and sing along with me now as we stroll) . . . me and my sperm cup . . . walkin' down the a-ve-nue . . . Me and my sperm cup. . . . all alone and feeling blue. . . .

I had trooped a couple hundred yards toward a crosswalk when I suddenly felt the thrum of my portable phone beating in the breast pocket of my jacket. My ever-present tether.

I didn't break stride. I traipsed on, clutching my white bakery bag, trying to hold it as inconspicuously as possible as I passed through the throngs. I took out my lightweight phone—Mr. Important—and unfolded it and hit the button as I went.

"Hello?" I said, manufacturing a harried tone.

"Sounds like I caught you in the middle of something." It was Mona.

"No problem." I continued walking toward the corner. I might be able to make that light, get over to the lab, get this sperm bag outta my hand as quickly as possible.

"Jimmy Boone wanted to talk to you. He said it was important."

"What about?"

"The crane shot that was set for tomorrow?"

"Yeah?"

"They're having some kind of hydraulic trouble with it. They're not sure if it can be fixed by tomorrow."

"Well, can't they get another crane from somewhere?"

"He's trying, but at this point he says he can't be sure."

"Great. Fuck it!"

"He says he'll keep trying to line up another Chapman crane. But he wanted to let you know about it so that you could decide whether we could do without it."

"Well, we can't fucking do without it. I am not doing without it. That shot is essential."

"He said if that's what you want, then he thought we should be prepared with different scenes to shoot tomorrow morning. Like the bar scene."

"I have changes on the goddam bar scene."

"I know. That's why Jimmy said call the Big Cheese. You could just dictate them to me over the phone."

"Uh—I'm busy right now."

"Oh. So what should I tell him?"

I sighed. I'd arrived at the crosswalk. But I'd been slowed down by my conversation, and the light had just turned. A knot of people waited on the sidewalk. I lingered among them.

"As soon as I'm done here, I'll get back and give you the bar scene. Tell Jimmy he'll have revised pages by the end of the day."

"You're the boss."

We rang off. I pushed a button and shoved in the cellular's antenna and waited for the light to change again so I could cross.

"Excuse me," I heard a female voice say, and I was face to face with a blond, middle-aged woman with peach-fuzz hairs springing from her cheeks. She seemed to tippy-toe toward me.

"Can I borrow your phone for just a second? I wouldn't ask, but it's an emergency." Her voice was throaty. She spoke slowly, each word sticking to the others.

My gaze swept side to side as if to say, "Surely there must be a pay phone in the immediate vicinity." But that never quite came from my lips because she'd already snapped open her purse and was shoving dollar bills at me.

"I'll pay you. Just two minutes."

"You know, I really—"

"I'll only be a second, I promise. Please."

I had no usable means other than plain rudeness with which to avail myself against her request. With a little flip of my eyebrows, I handed over the phone as I reelongated the antenna.

"Okay. Here," I said. Nothing so pressing as to consume the last vestiges of my civility, was there? Even with my bag in hand.

"Thank you so much, you're so kind."

She hit some buttons. Meanwhile, I hoped my little me's weren't choking and dying in the plastic cup held at my side.

"Hello, Herb." Her voice suddenly growled to life into my phone. The light changed, and those around us began streaming out into the crosswalk. "Where in heaven's name did you tell me the hospital was?" she demanded. "I had to borrow this very nice man's portable phone. Where am I? I'm in Century City somewhere and I'm illegally parked and I locked myself out of the car and the windows are shut tight and Chekhov is going to suffocate in there. And I'm sure not going to ask this nice man to help me break in and get him out."

I thought I saw her gaze flame brightly my way, as if the thought of my breaking in to save Chekhov seemed just the ticket. Uncanny, the way people instantly picked me out as a soft touch. Well, no dice. I was not following any more bums into Dumpsters to look for their contact lenses, as Dayna always kidded me about. I took a step back.

"Well, what do you expect me to do? It's locked," the woman croaked, again eyeing me. I backed even farther away.

"Billy! Billy-boy!"

The shout hit me like a poison dart in the back of my neck.

I knew instantly who it was. I was trapped. I had no choice but to slowly, stiffly turn.

It was Peter Ostrow. Striding toward me, the small, round buttons of his eyes boring out from the shapeless, Rembrandt-like smudge of his face. Beaming in all his satanic joviality. The hairy red minus sign of his mustache waggled beneath his nose. At Ostrow's shoulder, bent in knotted, hickory-switch meanness, was his sidekick Jarvis. And suddenly floating behind and above them, in all his icy effulgence, none other than Mark Werner.

Ostrow was brimming with bonhomie. He slapped me on the back as if it were nice to see me even as I involuntarily slunk backward searching for a crack in the sidewalk to hide in.

"Billy baby, we were just talking about you! The man who made it big! You bumped us out of the way, you son of a gun!" He inflated with a big wheezy laugh that did the trick of manifesting real pleasure at my success while crowning himself with modesty. At the same time it was the kind of theatrically self-possessed announcement a king makes before calmly slitting the throat of a troublemaker.

I clutched my sperm bag tighter.

Get us out of here!

"Herb! I can't hear you, Herb?"

Scant feet away I could still hear the accursed woman I'd let use my portable phone. When the hell would I get it through my head not to be nice to people? Otherwise I would have crossed the street and not been left standing there, a clay pigeon for the terror trio. They were headed into a restaurant by whose entrance I had unfortunately stopped.

I nodded toward them.

"Gentlemen," I managed.

"He bestrides the known world like a colossus!" Ostrow carnival-barked of me, patting his broad belly grandiosely.

"How's life with Tony Paris?" A knowing grin revealed the cutlery of Jarvis's long teeth.

"Okay," I said.

"That's not what I hear." Mark smirked, glancing at his two compadres.

"Wanna have some lunch?" Ostrow said. "I'm buyin'."

I stood my ground. Voiceless.

"Oh, you've already bought your lunch."

His gaze had stuck on my white bag. "Whatcha got today? What's Billy like? Ham 'n' Swiss? Pastrami? A hundred bucks he's got a baloney sandwich in there."

He thrust his jaw out at Jarvis.

"It's not—" I began.

Ostrow cut me off. "C'mon, you old cunt! If he's got baloney in there, you give me ten bucks. If he don't, I give you a hundred! You in, you cheap fuck?"

I didn't know what to do. I stood there transfixed. Paralyzed. The wager had come about with lightning speed. I clutched my bag, unable to think. Not able to move. Wanting to run.

Jarvis shrugged, and I glanced toward Ostrow, hoping

some words would come from my mouth to head off my impending doom. But in the microsecond it took for me to glance away, Jarvis snatched the bag from my hand. He smelled a hundred bucks.

"You're on," he said. To my horror, he held the bag up and began unfurling the top.

This couldn't happen! I couldn't let this happen!

I sprang at Jarvis. He reeled back, his mouth in wide-open, stunned shock as I butted into his chest, clawing like an animal.

The two of us went sprawling backward, tumbling into a redwood planter containing a six-foot-high shrub, one of a row cordoning off the restaurant's dining patio from the sidewalk.

Jarvis's glasses went bouncing off toward two shocked diners. The corner of the planter apparently caught him in the midsection. He rolled off the shrubbery, kicking spastically and spraying dirt in the air. Then he slid to the pavement.

He clutched at his side, the wind completely knocked out of him.

"Hnnnnnnnnnnnnnnnnnnnn," he moaned, trying to get his diaphragm back in working order, the breath just whistling from him.

Ostrow and Werner stood there in amazement.

My pants legs were covered with mud where I'd landed in the shrub. I didn't care about that—I fumbled madly for my bag of sperm. I shot to my feet. It was nowhere in sight. I saw Jarvis lying there, inert, holding his gut, all glassy-eyed. But I couldn't see my sperm. The impact had sent it flying.

"It's a milk shake," I said breathlessly in the most controlled tones I could muster for Ostrow's and Werner's ears, as if I hadn't suddenly lost my mind and was simply settling the bet. I searched around furiously for my bag.

"Hnnnnnnnnnnnnnnnnnnnn," rattled Jarvis.

I shouldered through stiff hedge branches and onto the

dining patio. There it was, on the ground by a table leg. My bag. My stuff. I snatched it and in a split second popped back onto the sidewalk, where Ostrow and Werner were still agape over their semiconscious friend laid out on the pavement at lunch hour.

"Hnnnnnnnnnnnnnnnnnnn," Jarvis keened. He'd begun clumsily rolling around, twitching his legs, trying to sit up.

Ostrow shot me a dumb, fearful look.

"It's a milk shake."

I turned and fled.

"Herbie, Chekhov will be on your head," the blonde was rasping into my phone, oblivious to the commotion behind her.

I galloped right past her. She looked up at me as I whizzed by.

"Mister—?"

"Keep the phone! It's yours!" I yelled.

I darted out into the street against the light. Cars screeched and swerved. I could feel the sperm bag bumping in my hand. I could feel Ostrow's and Werner's befuddled gazes boring into my back as I dodged cars like a madman.

But I didn't stop and turn around. Not even when I reached the far curb. I slowed to a barely dignified trot, melting into the lunchtime crowd, getting myself—Mr. Wanker—and my sperm out of there, away from Ostrow, Jarvis, and Werner as fast as possible.

I SAT FOR ABOUT TEN MINUTES GETTING BACK MY BREATH IN A SCUFFED PLASTIC chair in a ninth-floor hallway outside the Reproductive Lab. I looked around for something to occupy myself with after they'd taken my sperm and told me to wait. I wanted something to cast my eyes on. But there was only one magazine glaring at me from the low table by my chair—a copy of the latest *People*, proclaiming Tony Paris the sexiest man alive.

After twenty more minutes or so, a technician poked her head out of a doorway and regarded me as if I were some sort of lunatic. Jarvis. Knocked out there on the sidewalk. "Hnnnnnnnnnnnnnnnnn. Hnnnnnnnnnnnnnnnnn." Unconsciously, I'd been chuckling, and mimicking his death wheeze to myself: "Hnnnnnnnnnnnnnnnnn."

"You can come in now," she said, frowning uncertainly at me.

I followed her into a small office where I was introduced to Morley Madden. He wore a lab coat. He was tall and had a gooney air about him, partly the effect of the cheap black rug on his head. It looked like the sort of scraggly rayon fluff you find glued to a dime-store Halloween mask. There were lots of papers and graphs tacked messily to a bulletin board behind him.

"So," he said after he'd bade me take the chair opposite him. He nodded with a kind of thrilled piety. He leaned across his desk and hugged a three-foot plastic sphere, apparently a mock-up of a gonad. He grunted and wrestled with it for a bit, puffing with effort. When it failed to yield, he grabbed a bulky stapler from his desk and gave the gonad's top a sharp smack, and the wrinkly front half of the giant walnut fell away on a hinge toward me and banged my knee.

Madden relished the next five minutes, jabbing with a pencil at the ball works, explaining about veins and the epididysomething and different kinds of sugars and proteins, but I wasn't terribly interested in this orientation tour of his testicle fun house.

"Have you ever heard of Tenzac being used as a male contraceptive?" I said as soon as I could break into his *Masterpiece Theatre* introduction.

"Tenzac?"

He considered for a second and reflexively jerked around toward his bulletin board as if an answer might lie pinned there or in the bookshelf beneath it. But he quickly looked back blankly toward me.

"It's an ulcer medication," I offered. "Some type of antihistamine, I think. I've been taking it."

He shook his head. "I've never read anything about it. But let's see."

He sat down and grabbed a glass slide from his desk.

"Valerie should be done with her workup soon, but this'll give us a rough idea." He hit a few switches and slid down the length of his desk and swiveled around a big television monitor for my viewing.

He hit another switch, and the TV screen lit up.

"This is a normal specimen," he said.

I saw dozens of sperm wriggling and thrashing across the screen, their tails whipping them forward vigorously. Like a squadron of PT boats or something, JFK proudly at the prow. They almost seemed to create wakes behind them, to send rooster tails of spray into the air. Madden pointed at the monitor.

"Move straight ahead. Very little abnormally developed. Well-shaped heads. High motility."

He hit another button, and the screen went dark as I heard the sound of a videocassette being ejected.

"Let's take a look at yours," Madden said. Valerie had just entered and placed a glass slide on his desk before exiting.

He grasped it, wheeled his chair up to a high-tech microscope, and carefully laid the glass slide down, centering it beneath an eyepiece. He clicked a switch, filling the television screen with light. He fumbled with some focus wheels. Suddenly, coming sharply into view, there me were.

There wasn't a whole lot of movement. Not exactly a PT boat attack—more like a sailing flotilla.

"God," I said. "Jesus!"

"A little sluggish," Madden said.

A little sluggish! Panicking, I leaned forward to get a closer look.

Some of the cells showed movement, but others seemed to drift aimlessly. Fat, flat bubbles.

I searched for signs of effervescence. Of champagne. Of whipping tails creating wakes.

There. There were a few. But some were whirling idiotically around and around. One guy chasing his own goddam tail like a cretinized dog. Others doing a weird, dervishlike dance. Some spasmic, spiraling fit.

Now others swam into view. Some doing the hundred-meter freestyle, but others swishing along languorously in a stroke appropriate to a Channel swim.

"What the hell?" I muttered.

A few others glided by. A geek with two heads. Another sideshow freak with two tails!

I bore in on the TV screen. Suddenly, I saw Caddigan and Blue again, those hellish shades of my darkest, tortured imaginings, swimming around in the TV screen with my sperm and laughing at me. Caddigan cast a devilish look back at me as he rode atop one of my weaker swimmers, bouncing it, strangling it, hopping off. Blue blew me raspberries, then turned and aimed a kick that bounced off the head of one of my hapless, dim-witted, twin-tailed weaklings. The poor little guy flubbed over and landed with a cartoonish flourish, a reverberating bass drum. Splat.

Caddigan and Blue ran over to a small circle of my twirling, aimless seed. The two bullies looked back at me in unison, derisive sneers on their faces. And then, sarcastically, they mimicked the sperm, clapping, spinning, and doing the kazatsky. Hey, hey, hey, hey . . . hey, hey, hey, hey, they spun about stupidly. . . .

Madden flicked off the light. "Not optimal. What can I tell you?" He looked sympathetically at me.

"You think it's the Tenzac?"

"I don't know," he said. "Let's see." He slid a weighty *Physicians' Desk Reference* from his shelf and began flipping through it.

I took a deep breath and tried to steady myself.

Just then Valerie came in and handed Madden a piece of paper. He scanned it. He shook his head.

"The count—not great. And the motility's below where we like it. More abnormal forms than we want."

"I know this sample is not optimal," I said. "But tell me, is it possible that a specimen like mine could get a woman pregnant?"

"We can't say for sure about those things. All it takes is one, as they say."

"But you don't seem very optimistic about it," I said.

"Optimistic? No," he said.

He returned to the *PDR*. His finger traced down a page and stopped. He read to himself. His eyebrows rose in surprise.

"Hm. Tenzac does have spermicidal properties," he said, looking up. "I wasn't aware of that. This is an ulcer pill? Hm. Fascinating."

"Uh-huh," I said. "Look, what I want to know is, could I still get someone pregnant?"

He slapped the book shut. "Some would tell you that as long as sperm are present and moving, pregnancy is possible. Are these the absolute worst readings I've ever seen that led to a pregnancy? No. So, is it literally impossible? No. But in my expert opinion, these readings don't look so good."

"So you're saying it would take a miracle, huh?"

" 'Miracle' is your word."

He must have seen how ashen I'd gone.

"But this is a good-news situation," he said. "We have here a problem that can be addressed. We've got to get you off that medication. You need some other way to rid yourself of that ulcer, to relieve the stress that's causing it."

"I guess that's true," I said. "I'll have to work on that."

"ALL IT TAKES IS ONE."

That simple phrase uttered by the toupee-topped sperm wrangler kept swimming through my head.

All it takes is one.

Oh, how I wanted to believe in that miracle!

But how to fasten onto that when my heart was so choked with rage and woe and doubt? And when simple reason itself rose in tart demurral to dismiss such a miracle.

The bill had come due, had it not, I mused in all my black despair. The bill for my Faustian bargain. Show everyone I could cut it! Give me success and recognition, I had demanded. Give me fame and fortune! Give it all to me! And, in return, what had Hollywood money and glory begat but nothing of mine?

No emptier man ever trod the earth than I as I left Madden's office.

No more tortured wraith ever sleepwalked about his business. Yes, I watched edited reels of the show, but I was in fact some blinded Greek bumping into Corinthian ruins.

No more hollow soul affixed a cummerbund about his person than I did as Dayna and I prepared for an evening out at some dinner to toast my (ha! the curse of that possessory pronoun—never more for me the possessory pronoun!) show.

She'd been bent over her desk in a production trailer out in the desert late one sultry night, clad in that spaghetti-strap top and her short blue skirt with buttons up the front. They'd been working shoulder to shoulder for days on end. He'd eased himself toward her, praising her work, flipping through her drawings and designs. And he'd slowly moved close to her from behind. Over her neck he'd bent, savoring the bouquet of her succulence and the scents of her floral perfume wafting from the small collarbone-ringed bower in her shoulder by her neck. That tender nook where betimes I'd taken my first sips of Dayna's sweetness!

The Fiend had put his hands around her, a palm on the front of either thigh. Startled, aquiver, she'd looked up, straight ahead. He'd bent forward, exhaling his lust-driven breath in foul gusts about her ear while slowly edging his hands upward, more firmly pressing, sculpting her contours until he'd reached her lovely breasts.

And still she'd not protested. Upon her shoulder he'd pressed his mouth as his fingers squeezed on unimpeded, consented to.

She'd arched her back and his lips had played scales along her neck. Then one finger had tunneled between skirt buttons and pressed on silk canopying the spongy, ever-moistening underbrush below.

Had a shadow crossed her face then? A fret creased her brow? A protest passed her lips? Even as his palm swept across her knee and fingered the hem of her skirt and proceeded slowly, one by one, to flip the copper buttons binding it together, apart?

With one liberating rush he'd swept the fabric up over her hips as she'd moaned.

And then down went all restraints. Down they were tugged. Down her silk panties floated to her ankles. And it was there, over her drawing table, from behind, that Tony Paris threw off the last skimpy impediments to injustice and took my wife.

He'd spent a week out in the desert screwing my wife. All proper deportment had been tossed to the winds, thrown aside in sexual piracy. Cast off, layer by layer, until even her

Tufts T-shirt lay abandoned while they licked and lapped, him having her at will, bumping her, pumping her, taking her.

And giving me a child.

I IMAGINED IT MANY DIFFERENT WAYS, OF COURSE, BUT THAT SCENARIO INVARI-ably triumphed in my brain. Wherever I was and whatever I was doing.

And that was the one I reviewed over and over as I sat in my car late one night near Hollywood Boulevard, where I'd parked surreptitiously by the building wherein Tony and Dayna were burning the midnight oil.

Before confronting either of them, or deciding not to and letting my syndication checks flood and soothe me, I still wanted one solid shred of proof to confirm what circumstantial evidence pointed to. I needed something more to go on. One look. One gesture. One sense. One intimation. One undeniable observation of the two of them together and any unguarded intimacy that would close the circle of my suspicion.

And so, knowing they were working late, I invented some excuse and left the editing room. I drove across town into Hollywood, where Tony Paris Productions had been officed.

The parking lot behind the building was empty of all cars save two—Dayna's Honda and Tony's black Mercedes. Just the sight of those vehicles, a few spaces apart yet in adulterous, tandem proximity in the vast, empty lot, set molar grating across molar.

A church bell chimed many times. A streetlamp threw its grainy yellow netting across the gray darkness. I munched on a drive-away window burger. Wax paper lay as crumpled as all my pride on the floor of my car. Me—the executive producer—reduced to this skulking, cringing surveillance.

The boss, head down in hiding. The new crown prince of national uplift become squalid shamus.

O curse of marriage! That we can call these delicate creatures ours, and not their appetites!

Suddenly, out they came. Not arm in arm, but at a discreet distance, I could see. I jammed myself tight against the car door to glean their every movement with all my eyeball-bulging, ocular might.

Maybe I was wrong.

Maybe they weren't lovers.

The driver's door on Tony's Mercedes opened as they walked toward it. Out stepped the taciturn Beans. He opened the back passenger door for Tony while Tony and Dayna drifted some feet over toward her car, where he would see her in.

She opened her door.

And then she turned toward him.

What I could see from across the street in the infernal, bankrupt light was nothing you might call lewd. Nothing even a midwestern parson might call unseemly. Nothing that would echo infamy in the dark, to you.

They didn't kiss.

There was no passionate embrace.

The actor whose life I'd made simply took his forefinger and pressed it to my wife's cheek. And the pad of his forefinger sweetly traced a line down her face, traced it softly, gently, familiarly, from below her left eye to the corner of her mouth.

That was enough proof for me.

Thus branded, she got into her car and drove home.

Ten

INSIDE THE OLD STEEPLECHASE AMUSEMENT PARK IN CONEY ISLAND THERE used to be a titanic slide. I could not have been more than seven or eight years old the first time I was taken there. I remember staring up at it as it loomed above me. It was two stories high, probably, although to my fearful eyes it mounted steeply to the stars.

The top of the ride was reached by trudging up an un-countable number of steps. Old, creaking, dark, walnut-stained slats. The stairs were of such slender width that each planting of the foot demanded precise placement lest you trip and topple off to the distant floor below.

I'd been unnerved at the prospect of ascending that ride. I hadn't been exposed to amusements on such grand scale. There had been a few highly tolerable merry-go-rounds and whips in the small street-corner carnivals I'd visited, where

I'd been tightly belted into my seat by the strong hands of my mother. But nothing so daunting as that mile-high slide at a place so grown-up and legendary as Coney Island. Nothing so harrowing, nothing that turned my hands so cold and clammy and set my heart jackhammering in my throat. Nothing that was such a test of courage.

We called them "sliding ponds" in New York, a corruption of the phrase "slide upon." And like all those smaller versions down which I'd previously skidded in schoolyard playgrounds, this slide was made of sheet metal.

Only it was much bigger. A smooth, broad, shiny lick of glimmering metal this Coney Island slide was—twenty feet or more across. At its foot, shrieking patrons were deposited, whirling to a stop in a large, smooth wooden bowl.

As I stood teetering on the top of the slide, my turn approaching, the bowl below appeared no bigger than a Dixie cup. Goose bumps sprouted over my arms, which were bare below the short sleeves of the wide-collared white shirt in which my mother had outfitted me for my excursion.

A grown-up at the top of the ride finally beckoned with a kind of perfunctory, automatic jerk of the arm that admitted no tarrying. Heart pounding, I seated myself, legs over the edge at the pinnacle of the descent.

"Keep your arms folded in front of you" was the instruction, although I could barely hear anything over the blood pounding in my ears.

There was no turning around. I had to go. My friends had gone. I had to go.

And off I slid.

My stomach rushed upward as I whooshed downward in eye-blurring speed, the giddy likes of which I'd never before felt.

And then, midway down, I lost my balance. At that speed, I remember thinking, who wouldn't have lost control of their balance even a little? I tipped over on one side, then, righting myself, flopped over on the other as I sped down the metal mountain.

My arm skidded against the glittering surface, and I recoiled from a gruesome, searing heat, furiously thinking to myself, "I've got to straighten up . . . I've got to straighten up!"

And then I was at the bottom of the ride, tumbling to a stop in the gentle wooden bowl. Triumphant, exultant, I only then saw along the exposed outside lengths of both forearms the smear of red-and-purpled sanded skin. The first fine brown hairs that had only so lately sprouted in their kempt, manly squiggles had been burned off in large patches. My arms had been rubbed raw.

At a first-aid station, a nurse oozed cool, ugly ointment over my burns and taped large cotton patches to either arm. I was brave. Onward the afternoon went, hot, painful puffs surging, throbbing in my blistering skin, the popping notes of the calliope bursting about me. I held my thin arms out in the cooling air, away from my body, painfully self-conscious of my bandages, those of a diminished child and not a fear-defying man. All the while that fun afternoon—and to this day—I carried the memory of that scorching penalty paid for a moment's unavoidable imbalance.

THE HEADLONG RUSH. THE TRIUMPH. THE INEVITABLE TILT. THE MUTILATION.

Coney Island. Network television.

I had to get off the ride.

But there were five, ten, untold millions of dollars awaiting me if I would just tough it out until we sold the series into syndication. Don't let anything get in the way of that, an ever-more-insistent voice kept admonishing me. Stay the course, focused and above it all, churning away at the job of an executive producer—making your star look good. Coddle Tony Paris. Submit to Tony Paris. And get rich in the process.

Yet Dr. Madden's glum assessment still rang in my ears and demanded action. Paternity! I ricocheted from despair to fleeting hope. And in much the same way that one man on the firing squad is always issued a blank, I knew I needed my ray of hope kept alive or I would go crazy. Call it the equivalent of sucking in your stomach when taking that last look at the mirror.

To have it out with Dayna or not? It wasn't my relationship with her I thought to spare from a showdown. I wanted to spare my relationship with my unborn child, my belief in the long shot that the baby wasn't Tony's but my flesh and blood. Sustaining that belief I feared could not survive an assault that yielded an outright admission of infidelity from Dayna. If I confronted her about Tony, there would follow the sort of words, the base figurings and awful truths, that eat away at a miracle like acids. No. I would try not to confront Dayna. I had nothing to gain by it.

I'd beaten Dayna home by minutes and affected as much as possible an image of newspaper-reading nonchalance as she opened the back door and came in from the garage.

"How'd it go tonight?" I asked, looking up from something I was not reading.

"Oh . . . you know," she said. She shrugged and kissed me and removed her coat. She planted both hands above her buttocks and arched. "The brake pedal is getting really low. I have to pump it two or three times before the car begins to stop. I'm going to take it in tomorrow."

She crossed the kitchen and took a glass down from the cabinet and stood by the sink. I watched her do this small, simple thing, watched her move through the drab kitchen of our house, and I almost cried out under the blow her merely getting a glass of water delivered. The thrill of her rounded new silhouette anointing each molecule of air it touched—

that thrill had been scraped at, as if by some jagged metal, and pain shot through me instead, pain at the loss of something precious, so very precious its loss rendered everything left behind not worthwhile.

She dug around in the refrigerator, asking me if I wanted anything to eat. She took out a plastic container of some health salad with brown rice and vegetables.

"I already had dinner," I said, picturing those crumpled wrappers in the car and the smell from them wafting up and making me want to vomit while I'd peered at her and Tony.

"Editing going well?" she asked.

I nodded. "Only a couple more to lock and put in the can. What'd Henry Kissinger say? 'Peace is at hand'?"

"Congratulations."

"Yup. Hard to believe. I made some big success out of myself. Ready to go off to Mexico or Hawaii and veg out?"

I rose to my feet, dimly aware that I was perhaps a bit too grandly twirling the opera cape of melodrama around me. At any rate, I shuffled toward her as she pulled a fork from the drawer. I tried to appear normal. But I had been drinking. The tall tumbler in my hand held the remains of my dessert —five fingers' worth of bourbon.

"Tony's got this zydeco sort of tune he's working on," Dayna said, picking at the salad and not quite looking at me. "All this electric blues accordion. And he wants to make a video for it over hiatus. He's thinking he wants some sort of a roadhouse look. I told him, if he wants high cotton he's going to have to go down to New Orleans."

"New Orleans."

"Somewhere around bayou country for a practical location. If he wants the Cajun look. That marshy green, the cyprus swamp. Two-lane blacktop. Because I can't achieve the same thing for him here."

I opened the dishwasher and put my tumbler inside, saying

"Yeah?" in an unenthusiastic attitude she could not have missed.

"I wish you wouldn't do that," Dayna said.

I hipped the door closed. "Do what?"

"Put your glass in there like that."

"Like what?"

She reopened the door. She shoved what I'd just put in onto one of the blue plastic spikes along the outside of the rack. "The tall glasses go on the outer ledge."

"Oh. Thanks. Now I know how to put my fucking glass in the fucking right place in the fucking dishwasher."

I grabbed the dishwasher door and slammed it shut with all my might. There was the sound of glass shattering from within. Dayna drew back slowly.

"Are you okay?"

"Nothing wrong. You got any more criticisms? Any more rules I broke?"

"I'm not criticizing you, Billy—I'm just asking for a favor when you put a glass in the dishwasher."

"Your life must be awful, stuck with a depressed fuckup."

"Your life's the one sounding awful right now."

"Yeah, maybe it is. What did you tell me a few months ago—you were going to have to do something about it? Well, maybe now it's my turn to do something about it."

"What's going on, Billy?"

I stood there staring at her, about to charge stupidly down a dangerous alley I knew better than to enter. And I would have. I'm certain of it. But in the next moment Dayna's mouth gaped wide open. Her hand shot to her stomach.

"I think I felt something, Billy," she said, breathlessly. "I think I felt it kick."

The focus in her gaze was all inward now. Then she gasped. Her eyes skipped back and forth.

"Come here," she said, not looking at anything, a tentative, amazed smile washing everything else off her face. But at first I didn't move. I couldn't move.

"It's probably your uterus expanding," I said.

"I swear I felt something. Come here." She glanced at me. "Do you think it could start this soon?"

But I stood there frozen.

"Come here. Don't you want to feel your baby?"

"It's probably just gas."

She lifted her skirt and put my hand to her lower abdomen just above the waistband of her pink panties and pulled me toward her.

"Feel anything?" she asked.

"No."

"There. Just keep your hand there." She pressed my palm into her belly and began moving it around, searching for the right place. "It's a flutter. Very light. Shhh."

"I can't feel it."

She slid my hand around some more, trying to get me to feel the baby. But I wanted to remove my hand, to wrench it from her. Yet I didn't. She had both her hands clamped hard over mine, drawing it into her, making me feel for something until I didn't want to take my hand away anymore. And then I kept my palm pressed to her flesh, as if were I to remove it, I would fall off the world.

"Come on, baby, say hello to your daddy," she whispered downward. Then she looked up. Her face was just below mine. And she smiled at me as she huddled into my body. And I felt like I was going to cry. I pushed my face past hers because I didn't want her to see anything. And I could not keep from leaning over to rest my head upon her hair. It smelled of strawberries. And then I felt something quickly comb across my hand as if from the inside of a drumskin.

"I felt it!" I couldn't help exclaiming with a muffled laugh, suddenly high from that stroke across my hand, the announcement of some new desire, slight yet as fearsome as the mass adulation that had swept us away in the parking lot outside Rose's many, many nights before.

"That's your daddy," Dayna said, whispering down at her belly. Her voice was just about exploding with delight.

"You think that was the baby? You sure it wasn't just gas?"

"That's your baby saying hello."

She looked up at me, now all wet-eyed, and moaned with relief and satisfaction. And we stayed like that for minutes. Balancing against each other, her crushing into my chest, my hand deep beyond view along her warm belly, sliding around, cupping her flesh. And then Dayna started kissing my neck and we swayed harder against each other, never looking up, my face buried in her hair, Dayna nuzzling at me, unbuttoning my shirt, brushing her hand across my chest and then lower. I felt her tug my zipper down, and I didn't stop her when she reached for me, and I didn't want to. And all the while, even afterward for a long time, we continued to stand there, balancing against each other in the kitchen, not looking at each other except to peck or nibble each other's neck. All there was then was the hum of the refrigerator. I wasn't looking at her, only at the tumblers in their glass-front cabinets and the yellow-and-white tile backsplash framing the window over the sink when I said, calmly, barely above a whisper, "I don't want you working for Tony Paris anymore. I don't like the guy. I don't care if you like the guy. I don't want me having one relationship with him and you having another. I don't want you having anything to do with him at all."

And she wasn't looking at me when she said what she said, so I didn't see her face. I only know she quickly responded and in a way that made me believe her. "You know," Dayna said, her face still buried in my neck, "I've been thinking the same thing myself. He really is a jerk. Anyway, that's what I was starting to tell you. That I told Tony he'd have to shoot in Louisiana, but I wasn't going. I told him I was quitting tonight."

Then she pulled from our embrace and looked at me. "I want to get ready for our baby."

We kissed, and I watched my wife go off to bed. Her and her pregnant belly. Let us both keep our secrets for now, I thought. Let me nourish mine. Leave me to believe somehow that it was my blood quickening in her womb. Leave me the chance to hope and somehow believe that. Give me a place to fall.

I forswore rage at Dayna at that moment. Once she had voluntarily disconnected herself from Tony Paris. Once she'd told me that whatever their relationship was, it was over and done with. Not that there mightn't be thunderclaps at some point, but right then my attention turned, and the person I was most angry at was the monster loose and rampant in my life who without question had been sired by me.

He would have to be undone. And it was my responsibility.

The sharp tip of my resolve that night I aimed at the bosom of Tony Paris.

How would I do it? Innumerable methods for mischief swarmed to the forefront of my mind. A series of 3:00 A.M. phone calls to awaken him from his beauty sleep was far too impish. Better yet, how about a series of ski-mask-and-sock-full-of-nickles-type, jump-out-of-the-bushes, cold-cock stuff? Thrash the rake. Fracture his leg. Blacken those onion orbs. Loosen a couple teeth. Get that jaw wired shut. Or maybe just break every window in his brand-new house. Or feed a water hose into his basement. Maybe steal his beloved Mercedes and play demolition derby with it in some parking structure.

But my hand—no other—rightly had to grip the sword. It was my quest.

I had created him, this monster; him I had to destroy.

And whatever the cost to me, well, with a chivalric acceptance, I would proudly account it the price of justice in the dick-swinging wasteland called Hollywood.

I set upon my revenge with Senecan composure. The question was merely what would be the most sublime way of meting out justice.

Resolve was not hard to maintain.

Not least because Tony had become such an unendurable shit at work. It was impossible not to want to throttle him almost every second. "Tony had a notion" meant "Get this done without delay"; "Tony was wondering" meant "Change this ASAP or there'll be trouble"; all of it now flowing through the new producer he'd wanted, a cousin of Lloyd Wells named Gene Gladwynne, who had line-producing credits that qualified him for the job. I never treated him as more than a spy and plant of Tony's. However outwardly constructive and helpful he attempted to be with me, from the day of his installation I'd felt only more deeply cut out of my own show.

Tony intruded into nearly all facets of the enterprise by season's end. Technically, he had license, since he was now a "producer." He would change little things on the set without telling me. Or I would get word of impromptu meetings he'd have, meddling with writers on individual scripts, leaving them to storm up to me, waving pages and babbling protests I was, ultimately, unable to redress. Utterly bad form. He was perpetually involved in the casting choices through his proxy Gladwynne.

The final submission demanded of me was allowing Tony to direct our last episode of the year. From my first meeting with the tentative, modest actor, the change in Tony was now complete. He no longer cast about that one diffident eye by which most of us check our actions. He was big, swaggering strides now and loud, stomping steps. His tone was carelessly strident. He insisted on squinting through the camera to line up each shot. He was a shoulder knifing for primacy in every group discussion he entered. He was looking past you now even when speaking to you and was seemingly stone-deaf to whatever anybody else said, including me pretty much. In short, Tony Paris had become someone who "knows what he wants," the show-business parlance that too often robes rude, egomaniacal pricks in the mystique of idiosyncratic genius.

For the final episode of the year I felt I had written a worthy script. An obstetrics nurse, selflessly devoted to helping crack babies, was dying of Lou Gehrig's disease. She was confined to a wheelchair. You know about this one. I don't care who or where you are—maybe your face was melted off in a schoolhouse fire; or maybe you're just plain dead and you've spent the last couple years not breathing, with your eyes shut, decomposing and belching maggots in a sealed mahogany box six feet underground—you still know all about this one. Tony had seemed to like the script when I gave it to him, gussied up and garnished as it was with my most heartfelt assurances that I knew he was the one to direct the hell out of it (the fucking asshole), the only one (the fucking asshole) who could do it justice.

One morning soon after we'd begun filming—it was just after I'd hatched my plan, if I recall correctly—I'd rushed down to the set to read the list of categories in which we'd been nominated for the prestigious North American Golden Armchair Awards. Each name, each category—photography, set dressing, props, wardrobe, lighting—drew cheers from the crew. It seemed like everyone in our company got nominated for one of those awards, including the absent Ralph, who, of course, got the biggest ovation. The nominations were a windfall of recognition for our new, smash hit. Whatever goodwill and camaraderie survived at that point welled up in the company. It's one of my fondest memories.

Tony also got caught up in the reverberating good spirits.

Later that night he met me at the ADR stage with all sorts of appreciative words. His directorial debut was progressing famously.

"What'd we get, thirteen nominations, Billy?" he said with a huge grin, his forehead wrinkling with delight. "Imagine me with one of them little golden armchairs on my mantel. Ain't that a kick? You're a great big genius, you motherfucker, you. Hey, we oughta celebrate this. Really celebrate. The circus is in town, y'know? I'm gonna rent it for one night—the whole circus. Maybe just for you 'n' me. Huh? The whole goddam circus just for us."

"Sounds great," I said, laboring to reflect his good humor as best I could. Stuck in a tent next to the Fiend while inhaling airborne elephant shit for three hours? On the other hand, maybe I could surreptitiously saw through some cage bars. I wondered how Tony Matinee Idol would look wriggling around in the sawdust beneath a lion's mane.

The ADR stage was a sound studio, a quiet-as-a-pin room containing a mike and a podium and a technician behind a glass partition. ADR is additional dialogue. No matter how well a script works in telling a story, there may be times on the film when an additional line or two will help the finished picture and is required of an actor. Say, for example, while he's still off-camera but approaching the frame you might want to hear a character's voice drawing near. Or, perhaps, back to the camera while his mouth isn't seen, you might want to hear an actor's vague phone conversation. Stuff to fill in dead aural spots.

But occasionally you could make whole worlds and plots turn with the sly insertion of a word or sentence.

Additional dialogue work, not to mention the more time-consuming job of looping lines that might not have been distinctly recorded or delivered correctly in a take, had become a tiresome chore for Tony, a request lately, invariably, met with an irritated groan and an attempt to beg off.

That night, though, as I said, the Fiend seemed in a good mood. He entered the stage and moved to the podium all smiles. He was enjoying himself in his new role as director and coproducer. He was over the hump in this shoot, with only a few days left to go.

The Fiend was wearing his jeans and his two-hundred-buck sneakers, laces fashionably untied, and a baseball cap turned backwards and his Bopulator Brothers T-shirt. The sleeves were rolled up high, revealing the impressive handiwork wrought by his recent workouts with a personal trainer. I commented on how well-built he was looking and, gee, how he certainly didn't seem any the worse for wear following an exhausting season, whereas the rest of us appeared to be falling-down, concentration-camp-like skeletons. Something obsequious like that, something that left splinters from the floorboards in my chin.

"Gotta look buffed for the movie," he said.

"You look like an Adonis, kid," I said in my best fawning, boxing-manager's voice. I shook my head with admiration. The Fiend was set for his first starring movie role during our hiatus between production seasons over the summer. It was to be that bust-out, big-budget action picture directed by Sky Van Dyke the script for which I'd seen on the couch in Tony's trailer. About a gunslinger-type human transported out of the past to rid a weird planet of cyborgs of a virulent invading life-form in the year 2567, or something like that. A movie that was designed above all else not as a piece of cinematic art but to look just right on a large soft-drink mug that would be given away free with a special cheeseburger-and-fries combo at a chain of fast-food restaurants. That was true art in America. Tony was slated to shoot in Spain. A big salary—a couple mil. And the aforementioned Big Soda Cup push. A whole vehicle for Tony, just nine months ago Mr. Bit Part. The career was gangbusters, right on track: If this

picture was a hit, next time out whatever the action pic was
—and who really could tell one from the other?—he could
demand a piece of the Big Soda Cup take and, like all the
other finest actors of his generation, become part owner of a
wildly overpriced restaurant better known for the T-shirts it
sold than for the cuisine.

"Whatdowe got here?" he said, focusing for the first time
on the paper before him containing the lines he was supposed
to say. He stroked his perfectly stubbled chin. " 'No one
touch her'?"

"Yeah," I said, "that's the line. Simple. Ready for a take?"

"Sure," he said. "Let's knock this off fast."

The Fiend cleared his throat. The technician readied the
sound levels and the mike.

"Rolling," came the voice from the booth.

" 'No one touch her,' " Tony said.

"Cut," I said. "Can we just get another for protection?"

"Sure. Just keep rolling," Tony announced into the mike.

"I hope you'll be in town for our wrap party before your
tour starts," I said. "You gotta be there."

"Wouldn't miss it for the world," he said. "The star's
gotta be there."

"I'm not sure if Dayna can come," I said. I paused. "With
child."

"With child?" He looked puzzled for a moment.

I gestured toward my stomach.

"Oh . . . pregnant." He nodded, considering. "Anyway,
let's do this . . . one, two, three, 'No one touch her.' "

"Cut," I said. I stood up and smiled and walked over to
him.

"That is fucking perfect," I said. I clapped the Fiend heartily on the back. "That's just what we need. Sorry I had to
bother you with it."

"Anything you need," the Fiend said.

OF ALL THE PLACES YOU GROW MOST ATTACHED TO WHEN WORKING ON A SHOW, the one that gets deepest into your bones is the editorial building. Not the office where you write. Not the conference room where you have meetings. Not where you eat. Not even the stage.

You spend most of your time in the editing rooms. That's your late-night home, where you fix and fuss, and curl up beneath your jacket on an old, stuffing-spilling sofa to catch fifteen minutes of sleep between viewing new cuts. That's where you jiggle and tune, frame by frame, holding the guts of the work in your hands.

Many, if not most, shows nowadays are edited on elaborate computerized systems, such as AVID, where the cutting block has evolved into a Macintosh mouse. But Ralph had wanted to stick to doing it the way he always had—on film. And I grew to love cutting the old-fashioned way too. From editing bays up and down narrow hallways painted in industrial hues, the disembodied voices of actors abruptly squeal as snippets of scenes are wound and rewound through the old Moviola machines. They screech to life and stop and then screech once more, this time startling the ear with an incomprehensible, Slovakian-sounding eruption of dialect as the sounds stumble out backward from their tinny speakers.

The odd squeals howling like winds from the editing bays. The dark hallways with their sickly light. The cruel, sewing-machine-stitching-like sound of editors' pumping feet as they play negative through their gears. The whine of speedily winding reels as picture and sound are synced up. The flashing, plastic shiver of negatives (the sound of light!) hung over a bin, clattering together like the trains of some exotic beaded curtain as an editor's hand unhooks a new take, or replaces one, from the strip of coat-hanger holders above the canvas basin into which the strips of film pool. The chop of the cutting block. The smell of fresh, new negative. It all combined to make the surroundings seem perpetually midnightlike and haunted.

Charged with piecing together the same simulative perfection as any mortician, the cutters approached their art with a sardonic, autopsical humor. Every grotesque tic, yawn, and cockeyed mug an actor might make, every dumb goof and misstep and garbled pronunciation, every second of life captured by the camera passed through their hands for examination and assessment.

Here, in the chemically scented, morguelike dissection room, away from the rest of the company and its requisite courtesies, each artless shot of a bald spot or wide ass or horselike pace or moronic elocution would be inspected, judged, held up to general laughter and ridicule.

And at two in the morning, at the peak of exhaustion, pictures of stumblebum actors could provoke helpless hilarity. Or merciless criticism. The editors worked their magic nonstop, stoked on endless amounts of delivered Chinese food, deli, and pizza. Putting the show together. Saving it. Making it as good as it could be and sending the once-dismembered horror out into the world all patched up and pretty as a sixteen-year-old coming down the stairs in her prom dress. These were the exhausted medics, the mordant black wits. It seemed that some of the editors never saw the light of day from the time in midsummer when the camera began rolling until the late spring evening a week after the final episode had wrapped shooting.

I'd spent so much time in those warrens. There is almost nothing you can't do in editing. It was ultimately where, thanks to Ralph's help, we had found the look and feel that stamped our series. Week by week, night by night, reel after reel, every frame of each episode had lovingly been crafted into place.

Unfortunately, here, too, Tony Paris now intruded as

first-time director of his very own episode—the thirty-day wonder looking to lunch with the grunts in the boiler room. The platoon of cutters threw up a grudging decorum and tight-lipped politesse in response to orders from auteur Tony —formerly just the celluloid stiff whose gruff, inept ad-libs and difficulty in matching his own movements from take to take they'd mocked and cursed the week before.

They'd run them for each other to derisive hoots before snipping them from the reels and dropping them into the garbage. Now, though, Tony insisted on going through take after take. Pure vanity! How did his biceps look in this take as compared with take seven? We didn't print take seven? I swear I remember my biceps looking very bulgy in take seven. Why don't you print up take seven so I can have a look? My vein looked just the way I like it in that take, I have a photographic memory.

As to any artistic concerns other than the definition of his torso, Tony was less demanding. He had no objectivity about his performance, not a shit to give about that of anybody else except to make sure it didn't crowd his own, and zero understanding of the story he was supposed to be telling. He had no sense of the entirety of the meal he was supposed to be preparing.

Instinctively, he lumped too much ham on the plate. It was next to impossible to convince him that his "biggest" performances weren't his best. That an assortment of facial twitches and lip contortions he thought profoundly moving might better have been found in an instructional film on Tourette's syndrome. Precise, understated, controlled, subtle —these were concepts beyond Tony's ken.

So it was slow going for a while. The one stricture which imposed a deadline on our work, and therefore probably saved Tony from assassination at the hands of mutinous editors, was that the season was just about over. We were running so far behind in postproduction that we had no more than a few days to muck around with the reels before they'd have to be delivered for broadcast. There was no time for exhaustive cutting. The network even had to dispense with its own usual screenings of rough cuts because there was just no time for us to respond to whatever notes they might have.

I backed away from the process as Tony pulled his chair front and center, so to speak, before the machine where he'd be shown successive cuts. It was okay with me that his interference now made it clear to every last gofer of the company that this was becoming more and more Tony's show.

"I'll just take care of some niggling little problems on reel four" was the attitude I adopted those final days before we had to turn over the film.

You want to run the show, go ahead, dickbrain.

You want the say-so, bite down on it hard, you prick.

Oh, it was all just peachy with Tony. He sat there and approved or "locked" reel after reel.

The Fiend!

The Unsuspecting Fiend!

And so, very late one night, I sat by myself, just me and a pile of empty pizza cartons, in an editing bay down the hall from where Tony Paris held forth doing final editing on our last show of the season.

Just me and a sly smile.

Just me and my plan.

Just me and a simple little optical effect I'd ordered.

A simple little fade-out. Three seconds. Seventy-two darkening frames of film. The noose into which I put the Fiend's neck.

From one reel I calmly unspooled across the cutting block a scene between Tony and the forlorn, dying nurse. This scene took place late at night in her apartment. In it, she'd finally cracked, weeping and bemoaning her impending demise and solitary, unloved state.

"I feel so lonely, Father," she said. "Doesn't anybody want to love me? Why isn't there anyone to hold me in his arms?"

And there, at the end of the scene, I calmly snipped off the footage of O'Dell's commiserating dialogue in response: "The good Lord loves you, sweetheart, you must put your trust in God." Ended without those words, the scene left an altogether different moment on the film—a wordless, very tender look between the two while O'Dell reached for her before he spoke.

I withdrew from my jacket and spliced in the seventy-two frames of fade-out. What was now suggested was something potentially carnal about to transpire between priest and woman that was deliberately left to the viewer's imagination as we went to commercial.

On the next reel, a similarly small nip was the final nail to be hammered. The stake through the heart!

Suffer, you Fiend!

Suffer and die!

There is a telephone call from the dying nurse to Father O'Dell some weeks later. She ends the call by telling him she's decided to take her own life, and the camera pans off him, across his back, and holds on the window.

Snip! Remove the "suicide" part of her conversation.

Snip! As the camera locks, looking out his apartment window into the nighttime city skyline, I fished from my pocket my second instrument of destruction, my coup de grace: the excess lines Tony had unwittingly recorded days earlier with me at the additional dialogue studio.

Snip, snip. Tape, tape.

And so, while he was answering the call from the distraught woman he'd apparently slept with weeks before, we would hear the Reverend Joey O'Dell say in nonplussed puzzlement: "With child? Oh . . . pregnant." As if that's what she'd just informed him she was.

Snip, snip. Tape, tape. Go to commercial.

My web was woven.

You want balls, motherfucker, you got 'em.

You want to fuck some babes? Done.

"How's it going?" I said innocently, scant minutes later, looking in, briefcase in hand, at Tony, sitting in front of the KEM machine down the hall.

He swiveled around.

"I love it," he said. "This is gonna be a killer episode. I did a great job, if I do say so myself."

"Well, I'm leaving it in your hands. Can I trust you to play producer? We've got to rush this over to the video transfer by tomorrow. Otherwise we miss the airdate."

" 'Ey, don't worry. I got everything under control here. Every frame in this is gonna be perfect. Go get some rest."

Behind Tony's back, a couple of the editors rolled their eyes at me.

"G'night," I said. "Good work."

"G'night."

OUTSIDE THIS LATE, THE STUDIO WAS DESERTED. THE BUNCHED OFFICE STRUC-tures and humped soundstages, the parked honey wagons in their lanes, were all emptied of the day's commotion.

The air had misted and moved in upon the enervated silence, washing everything in a dull gray. The honeycomb of buildings, so abruptly voided of their coursing humans, stood mute and mummified now as the sound of my footfall echoed off their sides.

Overhead, shardlike stratus clouds clung and tore from each other's grasp and trailed fog in from the coast.

I felt released as I walked across the lot to my car. A season done. A show built. The last episode locked. My work over.

The only life stirring around me in this slumbering dream factory were the cats.

Every lot has strays. Dozens of them crawled across the grounds at night, picking at the garbage, nosing among the bins of unused film, slinking behind the shrubs.

The directors, the writers, the producers, the executives, the Tony Parises of this world, would fade away. The best they might hope for, ironically enough, was one day to be enshrined in a sidewalk whose wet cement had received their names or palm prints. The highest honor in this business fittingly still meant getting walked over by anybody. The pinnacle was a repository for dog shit. People throng here looking to claim immortality, but at the dream factory only the scavengers endure.

I was racked by no remorse after that night. Odd, one might say, given my high jinks. But there was no second-guessing. And the more I probed my psyche for self-doubt and found none, the better I felt. The calmer I felt. I was suffused with a languid, unshakable satisfaction that carried me majestically through our wrap party just a few nights later.

And a great wrap party it was. I'd made sure we spared no expense. We held it at a chic club on the Sunset Strip, one of those exclusive bars you want to bomb but will die to get into. We had live music and sumptuous catering. The place was jammed. Not just with the entire company and their spouses. But with all the actors who'd worked on the show. And with all the network honchos. And stippled with young, beautifully blooming women who ached to be seen by Tony or discovered by anyone.

"Thank you, man, you're beautiful, man, I love you, man" was the mantra that evening as Dayna and I squeezed through the crowd.

It was one of those raucous affairs, combining the three elements of a good party—flowing spirits, cramped space, music so loud you have to yell to be heard.

I don't remember all the particulars very well now. Maybe

because I was a little tipsy myself. Maybe because I attended the revelry with a certain seigneurial remove, arriving late and leaving earlier than most, affecting the pose of a benign parent tolerating his naughty youngsters.

I remember crawling up on a table and commanding as much silence as could be mustered and thanking everyone in the place for his or her participation on the show that season. Some gracious words of caring and admiration tossed with a couple self-deprecating jokes.

"And to the man who really carried us," I said, raising my glass at the conclusion of my remarks, "our own wonderful Father."

A circle parted around the corner table at which Tony sat. And everyone applauded him as he lurched to his feet and climbed onto his table, kicking drinks across his guests' laps in the process.

"I'm fuckin' bombed!" he greeted the crowd, swaying uneasily. He concluded by raising his arm and making the sign of the cross over the room: " 'Ey! Dominus Vo-fuckin-biscum, muthafuckas!"

He collapsed into his booth after that.

And the party raged on. It was volcanic. And, as I say, I remember little. Just the shifting of the packed torsos and the almost stroboscopic glimpsing of riding skirts and sweating flesh. Moist mouths in alcoholic abandon. Ungainly bear hugs and evaporating reserve. A prim male from our accounting office prone on the dance floor, sport jacket shrugged off and writhing like an epileptic iguana. One of the writers, Gina Spiller, walking around with a bunch of grapes on her head and saying to anyone, "Eat me, I'm sixty-nine cents a pound." The writing team, Ray Cappel and Dennis Fink, laughing uproariously and pulling at the pockets on each other's pants and shirts, shredding their clothes as they chased each other through the crowd. The sudden crash across the room where Tony in a peak moment of conviviality had expressed his pleasure by turning a table upside down and was tossing champagne glasses out a window onto unsuspecting passersby on the street.

"We owe you a lot, kiddo, and don't think for a second I'm ever gonna forget it," I remember being told at one point as an arm jerked me into the fondest of embraces. The arm belonged to Carlin Alemo. He delivered a big, wet smooch on my cheek and clasped my shoulders. "You brought this network back. You stuck your finger in the dike. They're predicting a thirty-five share for your last show. You're a major, major talent for us, and I'm telling you here and now the next six months of my life are all about what can we do for Billy. How can we make Billy happy and fulfill his dreams? I mean it. You are priority number one, baby. The door is open—anything you want. I'm picking you up, all twenty-two episodes for next season right here and now. Your next new series, this is me ordering thirteen. I love you."

What the hell, I let Carlin fawn away.

And then they scattered. The writers to cool drinks in tall glasses and snorkeling in Maui and Kauai. The AD's and grips to the decks behind their homes in places named Antelope Valley and Rancho Cucamonga and Flintridge; or to the steering wheels of their trailers, wheeling them out of their backyards and off to Joshua Tree or Yosemite for camping trips and fishing. The wardrobe assistants took to their bathing suits and bicycles and staked out patches of sand on the beaches.

Everyone was pretty much gone within twenty-four hours. The hubbub died. The whirlwind blew out. Silence descended. It was hiatus time.

A few editors stayed behind to clean up and store film before the start of next season, which was a good six weeks away. Gladwynne and I were in and out of the offices, tidying things, answering letters, returning phone calls, heading for the hills.

I had finished restoring some semblance of order in my office by Wednesday night. I boxed up some scripts. I packed some things into my briefcase. I turned off the light by my typewriter. And I bade good-bye to Mona for the evening and the season.

I closed my office door and headed for the exit.

Suddenly the telephone rang.

And then another phone started ringing.

And then another.

In moments all the phones in the office jumped to life.

I looked up at a wall clock.

It was seven o'clock. Our final show wouldn't be on for another two hours.

Ah!—but it was ten o'clock back East! There the show had just gone off the air.

It wasn't even 7:01 yet. The office was clanging with ringing telephones.

"Hello?" I picked up one receiver.

"Is this the *Father Joey* office?"

From the static I could tell immediately the call was long distance. It was a woman's voice, her broad northeast lobster-pot accent pitched with barely controlled dismay.

"Yes," I said.

"Well, I'm calling from Augusta. I just want to tell you how terribly disappointed I am with your show tonight. I have been a fan of whatsisname, Tony Paris, this whole year, and every week my whole family does Bible reading and watches your show together, but after tonight I am just so upset I want to die. How could you do that to your fans? I am just so devastated . . ."

Her voice shook.

"I'm sorry to disappoint you, ma'am," I said.

"Well, I don't know who I'm talking to, but I just had to get this off my chest. I think it's vile. Just vile!"

She slammed the phone down on me.

All around the office the telephones were hollering as if they were in some sort of mechanical seizure. Mona scrambled to answer them. So did Gene Gladwynne. By the looks on their faces, I could tell they were not getting pleasant feedback.

"What the hell are you people trying to do?" another voice, a man's, boomed at me when I picked up. "Half of Ocala down here watches your show. I had twelve people over here for a party tonight to watch the last episode of the season. And we're just outraged! I want to strangle you folks. Don't you goddam people have any respect for this country to have a priest who we look up to go ahead and get a woman pregnant? You've lost yourselves a lot of fans down here . . ."

"I'm sorry you didn't like the show, sir."

"Hello, I'm from Paducah, Kentucky, and I never thought I'd be calling up a television series, but I am just so angry at your show tonight . . . I mean, having a holy man father a baby . . ."

"I'm sorry, ma'am."

From Myrtle Beach: "I just do not see how Tony Paris can have the nerve to get some woman pregnant like that . . ."

"Gee, sir . . ."

From Lafayette, Alabama: "Your show was nothing but blasphemy! I'm disgusted! I don't know what kinds of things you all believe in out there in Hollywood, but lemme tell you something about the rest of God-fearing, Christian America, mister—"

From Hagerstown, Maryland: "Anyone associated with your show better not set foot in Maryland ever . . ."

"We never set out to intentionally offend anybody, sir . . ."

From Memphis: "I would personally like to punch Mr. Tony Paris in the nose . . ."

"I'm sorry, ma'am, he's not here."

"Well, you just tell him I am absolutely brokenhearted that he could do such a thing to that poor woman. I send my kids to Sunday school, and they have just been sitting here and crying since your show went off the air. What am I supposed to tell them? I am never watching your show again."

"I don't know, ma'am."

"I'm a priest here in Dover, and I intend to make your show the subject of my sermon this Sunday, and it will not be a very kindly one. You will all rot in hell!"

All evening the calls rained in. Nonstop. We were deluged. I've never experienced anything like that response. So immediate. So urgent. So distraught. Mournful, staticky voices in extremis with disappointment.

America was angry.

They were pissed off in Paramus. Aggrieved in Asheville. Burned in Brattleboro. Tearful in Tallahassee. From every corner of the country, moving westward through the time zones, the calls swamped us as the show went off the air.

Some great and remarkable communal response deluged the wires. A resounding consensus blanketing the country from hill to hill and house to house hurled an imprecation at us. We had come into their lives and destroyed something good. We had taken something decent and beloved, something admired and prized, and we had trashed a cherished trust. At dinner tables. In bars. By convenience store checkout counters where clerks whiled away their time glancing at the TV screen. In lonely hotel rooms where wet shower towels lay draped on dressers by the monitors. In paneled dens with French doors giving onto tranquil gardens. In teenagers' bedrooms. In gas stations. In rest homes. We had been invited into all those places and had insulted our hosts. They felt violated.

Our priest had broken his vow of celibacy.

And he'd gotten a helpless, dying woman pregnant.

We had no respect.

We'd scorned America.

America would never watch our show again.

I stopped answering after a few hours. I just stood there, letting the phones ring like crazy, listening to the sound of America vomiting.

Finally, I smiled to myself and left.

Eleven

$\mathbf{A}$T HOME THAT NIGHT I LUXURIATED IN A DEEP, PEACEFUL SLUMBER BESIDE my pregnant wife. When I awoke the next morning, the whole world had changed.

I need not describe here each stab wound sustained by *Father Joey* following our season-ending broadcast. Besides, you already have read or heard most of them.

The show was censured on the floor of the U.S. Senate.

The Pope himself felt compelled to denounce our "licentious propaganda."

American pulpits thundered against a television series so popular for its uplifting tone that had plunged into such immorality.

Numerous religious and educational groups announced boycotts of the series' sponsors.

Plenty in that to trouble the network brain trust. But what seemed to addle the suit mind most was that in the last half hour of the show the ratings dropped from a 34.5 to a 7.6, meaning that after hearing that Reverend O'Dell had impregnated the woman, over twenty million American households had angrily turned off the show.

Egad! It conjured up pictures of moms and dads hurling tots off their laps and into walls in a headlong rush to switch the set off. One newspaper story reported that around the country over one hundred sets had actually been destroyed in anger. Nobody at Network Research could recall anything approaching such a viewership hemorrhage.

The network switchboard was overloaded for three straight days from all the protest calls.

I had to admit to myself that I might have used a tad too much explosive in my demolition job. But as with any hit— and I use that word not in its entertainment industry sense but in its pejorative, Sicilian meaning—I had to make sure the job got done. As a showbiz legend once put it: *"Sic semper tyrannis."*

My keelhauling was not unexpected. True to the revenge pact I'd made with myself, I didn't absorb the denunciations with bitterness, even in the face of the vehemence with which they were delivered. Actually—I don't like to admit this, but I'm being scrupulously honest here—the more hurtful the blows, the greater was my serenity.

Go-Go phoned and went into a shrieking fit after she saw the show. This was unusual because she had many subtler means of rattling her clients than screaming at them. But a spontaneous, countrywide sinkhole this size was unprecedented in her experience. When that back-page ad in the *Times* appeared—signed by two presidential candidates; three former cabinet secretaries; the cardinals of New York, Boston, Chicago, Los Angeles, Philadelphia, and Houston; the head of the Academy of Television Arts and Sciences; and Paul Newman—Go-Go scrambled into damage control to save my head. My head meant her wallet. Unaware, of course, that I was the psycho who'd steered right into the iceberg, she tried painting me around town as the daring artist, the shake-up-the-rules sort who was merely attempting to push the show to an even greater crescendo. I, admittedly still a bit unseasoned in the commercial vicissitudes of high art, had misjudged the depth of viewer repugnance at this new story tack. In effect, So he made a little mistake.

Go-Go assured all that I had a Nixonian "secret plan" in my back pocket for resolving the series' stunning cliffhanger. Accuse me of trying too hard, of daring too much, of being a trifle headstrong. But don't ask a genius to rein himself in. My secret plan would amaze and astound the world.

I sort of enjoyed that spin. Me as the intrepid Captain Ziff, dagger in my teeth, hair blowing in the breeze as I swooped down from the yardarm onto a deck full of grimy pirates at the network.

"You have a way out of this story, don't you?" Go-Go finally said to me after holding America at bay for a day. She regarded me warily. Her naturally confident voice sank with uncertainty. We had met somewhere in the North Valley, beyond the trawling limits of even the lowliest industry wags. She definitely didn't want to be seen at any high-profile haunt in town with the likes of me.

"Actually, I don't have that figured out."

"You don't."

"No. I just kind of thought I would come up with something over the summer. Y'know, just wing it for now," I said. What cheek!

She eyed me coldly, calculating just how disingenuous a remark I'd made.

"Wing it?" Then she laughed. "A twenty-million-dollar pot of gold waiting for you, a hundred million a year for the network, you're gonna wing it? I mean, really, forget what I stood to make here, this is not wing time, doll, I have to tell you. Tra-la-la this is not."

It was totally beyond her belief. "You better have a story line out of this mess, that's all I can say. Come up with something, doll. Carlin's going to want to hear something, I can promise you."

I watched her slide out of the booth and disappear. If there had been two workmen passing, lugging a big piece of plywood, she would have walked out using it as a shield. Slinking off, it's called, with her head tucked to avoid the rotogravure boys. She didn't want to be seen hatching plans with Hitler.

The townsfolk lit their torches and ran en hell-bent fren-zied masse to set my laboratory on fire. Yet I blithely sipped my sherry and read my first-edition hardcover on the settee in ascot and smoking jacket.

This sounds irresponsible of me, I know. Cavalier. Repre-hensible would be a better word. Actually, it's not my word. It was Carlin Alemo's word. One of them anyway.

"This is fucking idiotic," he said to me seventy-two hours after the episode ran and he had been helicoptered off a white-water rafting trip in Zimbabwe to fly back and tend the catastrophe. No more what-can-the-network-do-for-Billy-my-man attitude. Hardly. That morning the spittle spurted out of his mouth as the tidy little gent called me on the carpet.

"Do you understand that against all odds, against all odds, we—you and the network—us, took this thing, this scene in a script of some other show, this little poor, fucking orphan hangnail, and invested and trusted and sweated and labored and humped and sold and prayed and watered and researched and created one big, blooming hit out of it? Do you know the odds on that?" The hooding muscles around his small, shiny blue eyes flexed and twitched as he thundered at me in his office. His lips pursed and unpursed. "Do you have any idea of how much trust we put in you? I feel personally betrayed."

"I'm sorry, Carlin. I slipped up. I went to sleep for one second on the watch. I'm sorry. I don't know what else I can say."

"Slipped up? You didn't just slip up. You fucked America, pal. You slid it right in Uncle Sam's heinie! Cyanide in Tylenol was nothing compared to this! You buggered the whole goddam country from sea to shining fucking sea! And you raped this entire corporation and its three quarters of a million faithful stockholders and their families and dependents and I am very, very hurt. I am personally offended."

"I'm sorry, Carlin."

There were no good explanations for how I'd sodomized the United States of America. Under the gun. Rushed and tired. Somehow a couple errant cuts, a flub by the sound editor. But none of that was important. And never did I intimate that there was any blame owed anyone other than myself.

I didn't have to affect contrition in his office, please understand. I'd done what I had to do, but I felt bad about the rest of it. I did feel bad. Not that bad, but bad.

"We had a Wednesday night here . . . whoa, baby!" Carlin lifted his eyes heavenward, bringing his palms together and waggling the steeple in helpless woe. "I got two half hours whose hearts are beating only because they're sucking on the oxygen from your show. I got two new hours ready to slot in one at a time after your show, use you as the incubator, so then we take a Wednesday night and now we make a switch and all of a sudden boom, now we got a Monday night along with it. And then a Friday night maybe on top. I am building an entire fucking sonofabitching week from your one hour, mister! A whole week! From your show I can build an entire fucking network making money. Which means we pay for a decent fucking news division! We get affiliates running to sign up! We get a late-night franchise! We beef up our in-house production arm! We open a cable channel! We get advertisers drooling! Then you go and take down Uncle Sam's pants! Do you understand this company was about to float a new half-a-billion-dollar bond issue next week? Do you realize that Moody's just lowered our fucking bond rating thanks to your little slipup? Do you have even the slightest idea of the extra cost to this company of having to float Single motherfucking A bonds now instead of Triple A's! That's at least a quarter of a point, maybe more. You're talking twenty-five, thirty-five, fifty million bucks. So we may not get that money. Our plans are out the window. That's a lotta people who're gonna be out of a paycheck!

"I don't know what we do, maybe it was a dream, maybe the fucking priest was drunk and he imagined the whole goddam thing. Maybe they put some goddam fucking LSD in the communion wafer or someone blew it into his ear—y'know, using a straw—through the screen in the confessional. Yeah, maybe that's it. But I'll tell you one fucking thing: We are not going to ask America to love a goddam fucking priest who goes out and violates his fucking vows and gets some fucking dying woman knocked up! I am not dealing with some fucking motherless kid O'Dell fathered! And I'm not dealing with abortion, I'll tell you that! No fucking way are we dealing with abortion! This network is not going to deal with fucking abortion!"

He was uncontrollable. He stalked around the room as if looking for someone to strangle.

"Y'know, there doesn't have to be a kid or an abortion, Carlin," I said evenly after a moment, "if the woman dies before the fetus is viable."

He stopped and looked at me. I went on. "I mean, it does happen to be a basic rule of dramaturgy to get your characters in trouble."

"Fuck goddam fucking dramaturgy," Carlin erupted again.

"You can have a goddam priest fathering a three-toed fucking sloth, do it at the Neighborhood Fucking Playhouse, not on my goddam national network! Get your own fucking network and do it! Fuck dramaturgy! He's a fucking drunk, and that's trouble enough for me!" Carlin hollered. "We got an entire country that hates our star! Now you want to kill a fucking baby!"

I thought it best to talk no further.

He took some deep, restorative breaths as he stomped about, pursing his lips and twitching his cranium. It was what seemed like minutes before he had regained any control of himself.

"We're issuing a statement this afternoon apologizing for any slight given in this matter," Carlin finally said coldly. "Now, whatever happens, this kind of slipup as you call it will never take place again with this network while I'm here or while you're here. I would appreciate it if any press statements you make you clear with my office first. Now, finally, I have to tell you that your further involvement with the show is under consideration. No final decision has been reached. Call your lawyers, if you want, call that bitch who represents you, call the goddam Writers Guild or the ACLU or Amnesty International or Helsinki fucking Watch, tell 'em to check Paragraph 24 of your contract, tell 'em it is our carefully considered legal opinion that you just wiped your hindquarters with it. That's it. I gotta get back to damage control."

And I was dismissed from his office.

Well, that was as rough as it got from the network. Pretty rough, I have to admit.

But however loud the shouting, even while Carlin seethed and splurted and threatened me across his Berber carpeting, I remained in my fortress, warmed by the sweet contents I sipped from the snifter in my hand.

Two-hundred-proof revenge.

During all the yelling and screaming, my mind's eye had never left Tony Paris. Tony of the onion eyes and mischievous smile. Tony of the bullying ways and wagging dick. Tony of the monster ego and Hollywood Walk-of-Fame future.

I had turned cover boy Tony into box-office poison.

The guy was commercial curare. A goddam leper. He didn't know what hit him.

He called me from location in Majorca. He'd gotten off the chartered Learjet with his personal trainer, expecting a bevy of adulatory press, popping flashbulbs, a red carpet, and a shower of silk panties tossed in his face. Instead, he'd been handed a message to call Lloyd Wells. And when he heard what Lloyd Wells had to tell him, he maybe sensed why shooting on his Big Soda Cup picture had been pushed back until the studio executives and their legal leg breakers could find a way out of the pay-or-play mess they had on their hands—about to make a fifty-million-dollar picture starring Mr. Bubonic Plague.

"What the hell is going on back there?" Tony asked pitifully when he got me on the phone at home. I was pouring myself a glass of beer, tearing open a bag of corn chips, watching a baseball game. Alcohol hadn't seemed to hurt my gut so much as of a week or so ago. And I'd stopped taking the Tenzac. I had, amidst all this insanity, what the shrinks call *la belle indifférence*.

"Some people didn't like the last show," I said, munching real loud in his ear. "Hey, the Dodgers are on. You get the Dodgers over there? Piazza—can this stud swing the lumber or what?"

"My directing was good," he wailed. His voice vibrated with panic. "I stand by my directing and my creative vision."

"I know you do, Tone. I'm behind you totally. Your direction was terrific. Skillful. Deft. Sensitive. Truly the arrival of a major new talent."

"Thank you, man, thank you."

"You have a huge future there, if that's the way you want to go. But I'm not sure this is about that. Some people may think so, but I for one don't."

"What, the girl thing? That's why everyone's got a hard-on for me?"

"That they think you knocked her up, what can I tell you? Go know. Look, I'm not going to say that it isn't my responsibility, bro'," I said. "I wouldn't say that to you. I'm not going to remind you I asked if it was okay to leave the episode in your hands that night. That would be a cop-out. I'd never do that. That's not where I live."

I couldn't resist a little fun. His ego was bleeding out, dribbling down his inseam and collecting in little puddles around his untied Nikes. He complained to me that according to Lloyd some of the network and movie projects executives had been crawling over each other to get him to do were suddenly not exactly top priority. They were backing away. They were looking for the door now. Actually, picture the Triangle Shirtwaist fire.

"Everyone's getting cold feet," Tony whined through the phone. "I just don't get it! All of a sudden, in this film I'm here for, Sky wants me to play the part in a blond goddam wig. They're tellin' me to grow a mustache and wear an eye patch and get some cockamamie injections to make my lips bigger. And they want me to wear some mouth appliance to make me look like Mr. Moto or some shit. The picture stars me, right, but suddenly they don't want me to look like me, for Chrissake."

"Hey, Tony . . . Tony? . . . Tony!" I suddenly shouted into the phone, pretending like I couldn't hear him because the long-distance connection had gone bad. He was still jabbering when I hung up.

The flight from Tony Paris had begun. In earnest. Perfect. You wanted a babe for Joey O'Dell?

Fine, you got one.

We'd all gotten what we wanted.

So that's what really happened to the show. No matter what you read in the magazines or heard on those tabloid TV shows, what I just gave you is the truth. About Tony Paris. About *Father Joey*. About everything.

I'm not utterly blissful with the way it all turned out—I mean, some of the glibness with which I've related this tale is, admittedly, rascal's bluster. I do not lightly dismiss being hated by a nation. Nor (even less lightly) throwing down the incinerator chute millions of dollars that would have come to me had I not sailed my show into the middle of Montevideo Harbor and blown it to bits. That money would have made me rich. It would have secured creative independence for me as a writer and a stable future for my family—both withering issues in any writer's life. It was a momentous decision, a turning point, one whose ultimate ramifications I do not yet know. One thing I've learned, though, is that sometimes the most momentous decisions don't turn out to be the hardest.

Anyway, considering the uproar and fallout, I'm all right. And by now I can say I've never been better. I got what I wanted with Tony Paris. With a cherry on top. True, I now possess a reputation as something of a loose cannon. Watch out, I might roll across the deck and crush your leg. Work with me and get gangrene.

But don't think the fact that I dented up a hit series and cost a large American corporation somewhere, according to *The Wall Street Journal's* figuring, in the neighborhood of a quarter of a billion dollars has disqualified me from the business. Not so. Before she told me that she'd rather not represent me anymore, that I was something of a bad reflection on her reputation, Go-Go fielded a few inquiries and passed

them on. The suits view me with a weird, respectful fascina-
tion, as if I were a platypus who could write.

But who wants to go into that now? I'm not big on my
career at the moment. Far from it. I sit down and write all
the time when I get the chance. But go out to Hollywood
and pitch episodic ideas? I muse more often about taking
the civil service exam in Montpelier or getting my teaching
credentials here, where there's a mud season and where the
sap flows and where sometimes you'll get stuck for miles
behind a slow-moving tractor on the road and where, when
autumn bursts forth, it looks to Sophie like someone's stuck
Trix cereal all over the hillsides.

Not that I don't still follow things in Hollywood. I might
be the only person in sight of Mt. Mansfield who gets *Daily
Variety*. I know what new shows are on the networks' sched-
ules this year. And I know just what the people working on
them are doing. They're in the thick of things now, getting ready for the next ratings "sweeps" period. They're crack-
ing stories, threatening everybody with not renewing
contracts, drawing sketches of their *Architectural Digest*
"media centers" in the margins of the notebooks in which
they write the pilots that become the latest hit shows, the
new computer codes for your VCRs.

They're strutting along as usual in their nonstop orgy of
self-congratulations, the way Monsignor Connolly does
every year at the Humana Prizes.

I actually got an invitation to this year's luncheon. From
my old pal Peter Ostrow, extending his brilliantly perverse
hand, the back sculpted by Rodin, the palm one of Dante's
apes. He and Jarvis and Werner had gotten their usual nomi-
nation this past year. Not for their show—for mine.

Carlin had called them in after I'd been canned and begged
them to save the *Father Joey* franchise. They had pulled off a
TV miracle and built back its ratings some. But I don't mind.
I don't care that Carlin gave them huge contracts and series

commitments to clean up where I'd dropped the ball. I don't care if what I created is to all intents and purposes dead. I don't care if they're cackling about me, thinking me the world's biggest fool, thinking they're getting some sweet-as-butterscotch revenge by taking over for me and getting a Humana Prize in the process. Mainly I don't care because to do their salvage job they had to write Tony out of the show. I went down past the common to the town library last week —the *Readers' Guide to Periodical Literature* has no mention of Tony Paris in the last nine months.

Not that I think his career is terminated. In show business, everybody bobs back to the surface, however bloated and unrecognizable they've become. There's an infomercial somewhere in Tony's future, a gig as a beauty-pageant judge or a gameshow host, and a comeback story in *People* about all he had to endure. But at least he served hard time in the one place he never wanted to see again—square one. I'm fine with that.

I can stand here in this moldy old farmhouse room—the one we don't even bother heating, with the cheap molding coming away from the walls and the ugly lime green wallpaper with its bubbles and splitting seams and the sticky red Armstrong linoleum floor that's rolling up at the edges and the spiderweb-crossed window casements with hills of beetle carcasses piled in their sills facing out at the Green Mountains in the gloomy light—and I can easily picture that glittering Humana ballroom and everything Monsignor Connolly had to say. His puffy pink head bobbed around like a balloon as he described a Hollywood that was more like ancient Athens than the bums' paradise it really is. He handed out his prestigious awards for brotherhood, but what's the prize? Money. And I guarantee nobody admitted that the ballroom was really jammed because the money you get when you win a Humana Prize is tax free.

Dayna, it turned out, misses that phoniness about as little as I do. We feel as if we have both been gathered up in a giant palm and placed down out of harm's way. As we bend over our baby or our work—me at the typewriter, she at her drafting table or easel—you might easily think us bowed in prayer and giving thanks.

There were never any broken dishes or overturned chairs or lawyers' phone numbers for Dayna and me. It never got to that. Slowly, very gingerly, we let a little peace and quiet work on us. We recoiled from Hollywood. And whatever had happened blew over. Not very dramatic, I know. But maybe that's the whole point, at least for us. There wasn't really an epiphany or a magic solution. We simply dwelled.

We applied ourselves to each other, directed our attention, which in our case required a lot of directing, because we had to get ready for a newborn and a new town. And things got better.

Maybe one evening you see it in how you and she are working together in quick coordination, setting out the staples on a picnic blanket at an outdoor concert. She brought this. You brought that. You busy yourselves, hand things back and forth. Then you recline on the grass. From the horizon comes music. Your fingers find each other along the ridge raised by a root twisting above the lawn. It's a balmy L.A. evening, the summer night like a bubble bath. You walk home chatting in the dark. The leaves from the trees swoop overhead and dust you in whispers of a world without end.

"You know, I can't wait to take the kid to Hershey," I said to my pregnant wife one such night before we'd moved as we strolled home from getting ice cream.

She looked over at me with an odd expression and laughed. "Hershey? Pennsylvania? What's there?"

"The best place in the world," I said, and that was true.

As things had developed, my most fervent desire in life had nothing to do with scripts or deals anymore, it had to do with making a car trip with my kid. My kid in the backseat squealing at different license plates as we drove. My kid praying we'd find a motel with a swimming pool that had a water slide. I lay in bed night after night thinking it all over. Where we'd drive, where we'd stop, but mainly where we'd get to: Hershey. How broad and blue the Susquehanna would look as we motored across it under the summer sunshine. The elms and maples swaying and bunching, beckoning in eastern abundance.

"You can smell the chocolate for miles," I said to Dayna. "Miles! I mean the whole world—the entire everything—smells like a Hershey bar. I was there once. My dad took us. I can remember the streetlamps are shaped like Hershey's Kisses in their silvery wrappers. And you can eat all the chocolate bars and Reese's peanut butter cups and Kisses and syrup you want. They've got these huge vats of the best-smelling chocolate on the tour of the factory. Hershey, Pennsylvania—it's called 'the sweetest place on earth.' "

"Uh-huh," she said, amused and cutting me kind of a cagey smile. That was when I knew things would be okay between us.

The way I look at it, no way was that baby in her belly not mine. I created Tony Paris. And if—*if*—who I'd given birth to had in turn sired my child, well, then there was a bond there somehow—crazy as it might sound—as strong as blood and maybe even deeper. Call it a rationalization, or maybe me giving myself a place to fall, but there was actually something weirdly immaculate and unique about it all, if that was the case, the child having been created by something out of my imagination. My demiurge. So what might that make me? Grandpop? Godfather? Author? All of those could be boiled down into one word.

I can hear that word now, coming to me from the yard,

where the falling flakes are whiting out everything—tree limbs, the meadow, history too. As tight as the windows are sealed against the winter, it penetrates. From down the hill, Sophie is calling: Daddy. It's time to take my camcorder outside and tape over my fiery self being kicked apart. It's time for another ride in the snow.

ABOUT THE AUTHOR

ROGER DIRECTOR was born in New York City and graduated from Haverford College. Formerly an award-winning journalist with the New York *Daily News,* he has also written for *Vanity Fair, The New Yorker, Esquire,* and *Los Angeles* magazine. Now a screenwriter and producer, he lives in Santa Monica, California, with his wife, Jan Cherubin, and their daughter.